© Brad Roaman

About the Author

PHILIP GALANES is a corporate and entertainment lawyer in private practice. He is also an award-winning interior designer of commercial and residential spaces. His first novel, *Father's Day,* was published in 2004. He lives in New York City and East Hampton, New York.

Emma's Table

A Novel

PHILIP GALANES

HARPER

NEW YORK . LONDON . TORONTO . SYDNEY

HARPER

This is a work of fiction. The characters, incidents, and dialogues are products of the author's imagination and are not to be construed as real.

A hardcover edition of this book was published in 2008 by Harper-Collins Publishers.

HarperCollins books may be purchased for educational, business, or sales promotional use. For information please write: Special Markets Department, HarperCollins Publishers, 10 East 53rd Street, New York, NY 10022.

FIRST HARPER PAPERBACK PUBLISHED 2009.

Designed by Emily Cavett Taff

The Library of Congress has catalogued the hardcover edition as follows:

Galanes, Philip, 1963–
Emma's table : a novel / Philip Galanes. — 1st ed.
p. cm.
ISBN 978-0-06-155383-7
1. Women ex-convicts—Fiction. 2. Businesswomen—Fiction. 3. Interior decorators—Fiction. 4. Social workers—Fiction. 5. Overweight children—Fiction. 6. Life change events—Fiction. I. Title.
PS3607. A38E46 2008
813′.6—dc22

2007041944

ISBN 978-0-06-155407-0 (pbk.)

09 10 11 12 13 OV/RRD 10 9 8 7 6 5 4 3 2 1

For Lil' Kim and her perjured testimony,
And Richard Nixon at the Watergate;
For Don Imus and his besmirched coeds,
But mostly, of course, for me.

Emma's Table

Chapter 1

SATURDAY MORNING: *Black Coffee and a Pinch of Brown Sugar*

EMMA SUTTON CLICKED AND CLACKED ALL AROUND the auction house, her sharp heels tapping just as quietly as she could manage. She was a regal brunette of sixty-odd, who'd parlayed a small career as an interior decorator into an enormous one as media darling; Emma was a household name, in fact. And she had been for fifteen years—thanks to her regular appearances on *Oprah*—with a sea of magazine spreads and a mountain of books, an endless stream of television segments on the best daytime shows, and a petrified forest of Emma-branded furniture, all dedicated to the stylish American home. Her allure had always been easy to see: she was just like you, only better—which was somewhat at odds with the latest feather in her cap, a conviction for tax evasion and lying under oath, complete with a stay in the federal pen.

Yes, she sighed, with a huff of breath—having spied an old woman with her jaw hanging down—*the* Emma Sutton, she thought, coveting the attention and feeling pestered by it both. She couldn't go *anywhere* without being recognized; she wouldn't have had it any other way.

Emma glared down at her shoes.

She hated making noise when she walked.

"So unladylike," her father always told her—like whistling out on the street. "Men don't marry girls who whistle, Emmy." That's what her father said, whether she was whistling or not. He'd never made any secret of his hopes for the girl: an early marriage and a life lived on somebody else's nickel.

Of course, her father was long dead by now, and she herself the mother of a grown-up girl, and there wasn't much to be done for the tapping at FitzCoopers in any event: miles and miles of taupy concrete, all polished smooth, with swirls of darker brown and rusty red mixed in, and not a carpet in sight. Emma knew they'd spent a fortune making the floors like that, but she had no earthly idea why anyone would. It's like a two-car garage in here, she thought—her long back as straight as a mile, and those perilous heels tapping just a little louder than she would have liked.

The people at FitzCoopers had arranged the more important pieces from that morning's auction into a large circle all around the exhibition room. *Treasures of French Modernism*, it was called—like a racetrack made of furniture, every treasure propelling her one step closer to the finish line. The exhibit took up the lion's share of the huge loft space; a stubby little partition on wheels was all that separated the circular display from the tidy grid of gilt chairs that lay beyond it—just lying in wait for the auction to begin, a sturdy oak podium for the auctioneer up front.

Emma looked hard at every piece of furniture she passed on her circular route. She furrowed her brow before each one, focusing her eyes like the lens of a camera; then she'd blink—closing the shutter, opening it fast—as if she were obliged to memorialize each piece in turn. She would have set up little groupings of furniture, she thought—not at all sure just then, only trying the notion on for size.

Something has to give, she decided—shaking her head at the ugly loop and setting to work on a nicer composition. She pictured the curvy sofa from the corner paired up with the coffee table in front of her; then she tossed in the velvet chairs by the window. Emma nodded her head in approval, floating little arrangements like that all around the room.

From the time she was a girl, Emma had known you couldn't just *expect* people to see the value of a thing. No, she thought, you have to *work* until they see it, and keep working, even then.

She wasn't quite finished with the exhibition space either. She'd add some nice rugs too, she decided. She pictured them soft and worn, old Persians like the kind she used to find at tag sales for a song—back when she didn't have much more than a song to spend. She saw rugs like grassy green lawns over hard-packed earth, rugs like tender skin over skeletons of bone.

She was almost pleased, but tired too.

Emma never stopped working—like a scullery maid practically, even in somebody else's auction house. She was always trying to make things nice, to raise herself up in the world's esteem—only to watch people cheer at her every setback, just like her father had done a million years before.

They used wall-to-wall carpeting before me, she thought, her well-groomed head lifted high.

Emma wasn't overestimating her impact on interior design:

what she said went—whether it was covering a wall in elaborately flocked paper, or assembling a crazy quilt of rugs on the floor. When Emma Sutton spoke, America listened.

She tried her best not to hear the soft clickings of her shoes—the very way she'd tried shrugging off the sting of her father's low regard: without much success, it turned out.

It was only half a year since her "difficulties" had passed. That was how she thought of them: the bruising trial and the prison stretch, those humiliating months of home confinement, and a waterfall of wretched press—all for some stupid little tax return that shouldn't have made a jot of difference in the world. And even after her confinement, Emma still wasn't entitled to take back the reins of her company. That was part of her punishment too. Emma Sutton couldn't run Emma Sutton, not for the time being anyway. Her lawyers didn't think she'd be able to for five more years, at least. She just worked there now, like any other employee—assuming any other employee could make everyone in the building tremble in their boots.

Emma looked up—a little warily—as a fat young woman in a flower-printed coat jumped out from behind a Prouvé cabinet, walking straight up to her. "I love your dining table for Target," the woman sang, clasping chubby hands before an outsized bosom, like an old-time soprano on an opera stage.

So I see, Emma thought to herself.

She smiled at the young woman and thanked her, waiting just a beat longer before she walked quickly off. Emma needed her fans—especially lately—but she liked them better at a distance.

In truth, she wasn't entirely sure she wanted the reins of her company back again. She'd never admit it, of course, not under sodium pentothal even, but it was true. The company she'd slaved over for twenty-five years—birthing it first, then raising it right, her very lifeblood in former days—didn't seem *enough* to her anymore, not the way it used to. It spun like a top now, even without her—throwing off more cash than she could spend in ten lifetimes. It crossed her mind that that might be the problem. The only thing they really needed her for these days were the "photo opportunities": Emma posing on one of her freshly minted sofas, Emma splashing her hands in one of her new stainless sinks, not a drop of water on her silken blouse. She only smiled for the cameras now, for the magazine covers and the more important inside spreads, those endless television segments on the best daytime shows.

She'd reclaimed her regular spot on *Oprah*.

Still, Emma thought it might be time for a change. She knew it was, in fact, but only in flashes—the way that sun dappled leaves in the country, shooting gold straight through the green, but only when everything came together just right, the sun and the branch and the pale green leaves.

There's more to me than this.

It had come to her first in her awful prison bed, that scratchy gray blanket up around her ears. At the time, she'd put it down to stress. But the feeling echoed for her still, and more and more often, lately. It had that morning even, as she was gadding down Park Avenue in a chauffeur-driven Town Car, all the colored stop-and-go lights flashing. There may well have been "something more," but Emma hadn't a clue in the world what it was. Still, she'd reinvented herself more than once, and she had every faith that she could do it again—or if not faith, then no alternative, which Emma knew was often better.

"You can't keep a good girl down, Emmy," that's what her father always said—though it seemed to her, frankly, he spent a great deal of time trying.

She walked by the Nakashima table then, the piece that had drawn her all the way downtown that morning. Two long slabs of honeyed English walnut, with fluid edges—not all squared off—and a swirling grain pattern, like so many drops of motor oil on a rain puddle, a whirling taffeta made of wood. The planks were joined together with three small butterflies of much darker hue—rosewood probably, she thought—the grain of the butterflies running perpendicular to the longer planks.

It looked like a ten-foot gentleman to her.

The table seemed to stand back almost—disappear—letting the wood itself take center stage. Emma bent down low, as if to inspect its trestle base, but her objectivity was long gone by then. She was already in love.

It was perfect for the dining room.

She'd passed it twice already that morning. She stopped before it once again, but not for a second longer than she'd paused in front of the old Hermès desk, just before it on her circular route. Emma was careful not to spend much time looking at the pieces she was actually interested in.

She didn't like to tip the competition off.

This walking in careful circles was something she'd always done, like turning up at the auction houses in person. She'd continue to do it too, for good reason: it worked. Emma knew the flighty girls who were drawn to employment at places like these—little scraps of paper in a brisk wind. She'd employed more than a few of them in her day, watching them forget to execute bids that were sent in absentia, or neglecting to call people who'd arranged to bid over the phone until it was too late. Those girls were already fully engaged, scouting the room for eligible men—like buzzards in Fair Isle sweaters. Emma was far too efficient to depend on girls like those for her success. She'd bid in person, thank you very much, but she had a new plan up her sleeve this morning.

If Benjamin ever gets here, she thought, walking to the complimentary coffee buffet. She'd seen enough of the Nakashima table. She didn't need to look at it again, wouldn't.

Her assistant wasn't even late yet, but Emma was already mildly annoyed with him. She tried shaking it off. She picked up one of those ugly brown undercups from the long table—plastic and reusable—and slipped a papery white cone inside it. He's probably lazing around with that hippie girlfriend of his, she imagined, pouring herself a coffee. She skipped the iced bowl of single-serving half-and-halfs and the artificial sweeteners. She took a sip from the cup and put it right back down on the table.

It was terrible.

She didn't dwell on it though. She felt her attention turning to a nicely tailored suit on the far side of the room. It's not *that* nice, she thought, slightly annoyed at her own keen interest. Then she noticed the man who wore it, a tiny Asian with salt-and-pepper hair—like a full-grown adult who'd been photo-reduced to just seventy-five percent of full-grown adulthood.

He was studying the Nakashima table, *her* Nakashima table.

Emma felt a terrible seizing in her chest—giving the lie, she knew, to so much of her bluster. She was as prone to fear as anyone else in the world. Maybe more so, she hated to admit. She refused to give in to it, wouldn't dream of letting it show. Emma picked up that plastic cup again and straightened her back. She took another gruesome sip of coffee.

It's not fatal, she thought. He might just be looking.

But she didn't believe that, not for a second.

She studied the man breathlessly, fluttering with nerves like a hummingbird at the end of a leafy branch. She felt her composure deserting her entirely, and all for some silly table she didn't even need. She couldn't shake the feeling either.

The tiny man was engrossed in the table, circling it slowly and peering from every angle.

Oh, yes, she thought, he's definitely a bidder.

Emma could picture them in mortal combat—bidding paddles lifted high, like dueling pistols made of wood. She abandoned her coffee for good and consulted her wristwatch one more time. She forced herself to admit that Benjamin had four minutes still before he'd be late.

She tried to forgive him.

BENJAMIN BLACKMAN MOONLIGHTED FOR EMMA on the weekends. He was her Saturday/Sunday assistant. He came on duty Fridays at five and stayed the course with her until Monday morning. He'd never heard of such a thing before he came to New York. Back home—on the Cape—people took the weekends off; but here, apparently, all the moguls had their Sunday help.

He was walking in front of the big discount store on Astor Place.

He paused on the sidewalk, and gazed in through the dusty plate glass that ran the length of the block. He craved a shot of its swarming life, but all he saw that morning was a jumbly mountain of cheap white socks, and a tower of suitcases that looked like flimsy cardboard boxes painted black.

Where is everyone, he wondered?

He let his eye follow a narrow passage deep into the store, like a footpath through the forest. He saw merchandise looming tall as silver birches, their cellophane leaves glistening in the air-conditioned wind. Benjamin realized the store was closed. It was before nine still, all that screaming fluorescence notwithstanding.

Good thing too, he thought. He didn't want to be late for Emma.

He'd been working for her for nearly two years now—from before she went away to prison—and his tenure in the organization made him something of a veteran there. Emma tended to swat people away like flies. It wasn't so complicated for Benjamin though. He simply reached back into his boyhood—toward that fly-swatting mother of his own. He only needed to remember who came first—*always*: his mother, back then, and now, Emma.

Benjamin needed the money too.

He had to supplement his tiny salary as a social worker at Public School 431 in Forest Hills, and the only person, he'd found, who was terribly interested in a thirty-three-year-old English major from Williams College with a long string of brief job experiences under his belt, and a quick master's in social work, was she: Emma Sutton, the she-devil of home design.

He smiled to himself, secretly proud of his celebrity attachment.

He pictured his lady boss, smiling out falsely from every

television set and glossy magazine in the land. Emma paid him twenty-five dollars an hour—nearly twice what he earned at PS 431.

I'd better get going, he thought, or I'll be late.

Benjamin didn't move a muscle though. He just exhaled deeply and watched his breath curl away off into the sky, like a wisp of smoke from a chilly cigarette. When he turned away from the window, his reflection flashed back at him in the glass—quick as lightning, then it was gone. He twirled back again to find it, but without much luck. So he took a small step forward, and turned the whole damned window into a mirror—a full story high and a city block long. Benjamin studied his face in earnest then: the deep green eyes and wavy brown hair, the long sharp nose that looked best from straight on—not beaky at all.

Benjamin's fingers were nearly frozen by then—even inside his thick suede gloves, they felt as if they might snap off. So he walked on, past all that plate glass, only sneaking oblique glances at himself in profile, just like everyone else in the world. He went so far as placing a tentative foot on the black rubber pad that sent the store's automatic doors swinging inward—as if it might read his heart through the sole of his shoe—but those doors stayed closed to him this morning.

Still not opening time, he guessed—which made it easier for him to keep walking, straight down to Lafayette Street and to Emma Sutton, his difficult part-time employer.

She'd arranged to meet him at the fancy new auction house there.

In truth, Benjamin was quite fond of Emma. She surprised him too, from time to time anyway. She actually seemed to take account of him, which was more than his own mother ever had; and the so-called work she asked him to do was a joke compared with his day job. He made dinner reservations and called people on the phone; supervised the workmen and her ever-changing travel arrangements; kept her stocked in shiny black Town Cars and steaming cups of coffee, no matter where she might be. And as silly as it was, Benjamin took pride in his work. He liked to get things right; he wanted to please her.

Occasionally, she seemed to appreciate the effort.

But she'd never asked him to an auction before. He worried about what she'd need him to do there.

Benjamin was walking quickly then, and not just for fear of antagonizing Emma. Lafayette Street was a bitter wind tunnel that morning. It was just two more blocks, but he knew they were long ones; and neither the tall buildings on either side of him nor the clear, sunny sky was doing a thing to cut the frigid wind at his back. He heard a sort of clattering behind him—not quite footsteps, but persistent—and right on his tail. He turned to find an empty coffee cup swirling in the wind, following him almost. He kept walking, and somehow the little cup kept pace, bouncing along the sidewalk in the wind. He tried going faster even—just to see—rooting for that cup every second. When the scraping sound grew faint, in fact, he slowed down a little, let the thing catch up with him again.

Benjamin checked his watch, and felt nearly confident for a change. It was before nine still. He might even make it to the auction house first. He let the pleasure of beating Emma to the punch wash over him like a blast of steam from a subway grate. He closed his eyes for just a second. When he opened them again, he saw the little blue cup swirling out into the street.

He felt an icy slap at the side of his face when he stepped into the intersection, his overcoat flapping in the opposite direction. He watched the cup blowing wildly in the wind, sure to be run over in a matter of seconds.

Benjamin opened the auction house door.

JUST ABOUT THEN, A LITTLE GIRL ACROSS THE river—Gracie Santiago—wedged herself tightly into the crook of a tweedy brown sofa. She spread her work onto the coffee table in front of her: ten sheets of red construction paper and a pair of safety scissors, a booklet of silver-foiled stickers and golden stars, a tub of white paste. Off to the side—sequestered safely from the rest—lay a baby blue envelope, stuffed to the gills and closed up tight, its metallic bunny ears bent back against the flap.

Gracie was making Valentine cards. The holiday was just a week away.

Her mother had suggested a box of cards from the grocery store, but Gracie dismissed that idea out of hand. She knew she had to do better than that. So she begged her grandfather for art supplies instead. He was a much softer touch than her mother ever was, especially when he picked her up from school. There was practically nothing he'd refuse her then, not if she asked him right, anyway. Gracie smiled down at the proof in front of her—all the supplies she'd ever need.

Back when she was a first-grader, two years before, Valentine's Day had been easy as pie. She'd given store-bought cards to every kid in class, and she'd received nearly as many in return—one from every girl and most of the boys. She'd followed the same approach the very next year, copying out all her classmates' names, even the ones who weren't so nice, and the ones who hadn't given her a card the year before. The results had come as a terrible surprise, like falling off a cliff. Gracie received just a handful of cards in return, and not a single one from the Skinny Girls—the pretty ones who sat together at lunch, ruling the roost at PS 431.

People seemed to be growing meaner by the second.

Maybe if I was skinny too? she thought.

Gracie looked down at her pajamas—a riot of creamy ponies on a pink flannel field. She couldn't help but see how her body pulled those horses tight, the rolls of fat that strained at the seams. She'd heard of third-graders who hadn't received a single Valentine, their handmade bins, folded from sheets of white notebook paper, hanging empty from the sides of their desks.

Gracie was sick with worry.

She looked vaguely in the direction of the television set. How she'd love to turn it on. Forget all about Valentine's Day and her stupid red cards; just watch a Saturday-morning show instead. But Gracie wasn't allowed to touch the television until her mother woke up, so she only stared at the glassy black screen, as if a very dull program were on just then, her little mouth falling open.

She'd nearly forgotten her plan.

She picked up a sheet of construction paper and folded it neatly in half. Gracie was going to make beautiful Valentines for every single third-grader—even the mean ones, and those few who were less popular than she was herself. She'd hand them out the day *before* Valentine's Day. Maybe when her classmates saw how nice she was, when they realized all the trouble she'd gone to—making them all such pretty cards—maybe then they'd see that she deserved one too?

It could happen, she thought.

Her grandfather thought it could.

Gracie picked up the scissors and cut five half hearts, guiding the safety blades around the tidy red fold. Then she opened them up—those mirror-image hearts—glittering them liberally and jeweling them with foil, until they twinkled beneath the overhead lights. She opened up the baby blue envelope next, pulling out photos of the same pretty blonde: Paris Hilton, a hundred times. Gracie was wild about the girl, her straight blond hair and toothpick frame. She cut out every picture she could find—some of them smudgy on cheap newsprint and others shining back at her from magazine stock. She pasted a picture onto every red heart, right at the center, its absolute place of honor; and at the moment of pressing her fat thumb down, gluing Paris Hilton onto Valentine cards, Gracie couldn't imagine that her plan might fail.

She thought of Missy Hendricks, with her pretty pink face and long blond hair—the third grade's answer to Paris Hilton, a classroom of girls kowtowing to her all day long. Missy reigned over PS 431 with an iron fist, heading up the posse of Skinny Girls, deciding everybody's fate.

Missy ignored her mostly, and her minions followed suit.

But not always, Gracie thought.

Missy had approached her at recess one day, not long before—just after Christmas, a month or so back. "Come with me," she whispered.

Gracie could picture that blond hair still, like the wispy fluff inside corn on the cob, fluttering in the very smallest of breezes. Missy leaned into Gracie as she spoke that day, and her long hair leaned along with her, in a perfect, swinging plane.

I should have known better, Gracie thought.

She could remember the way Missy smelled—of apples and cinnamon, like the dark red candle her mother kept on the kitchen counter.

Gracie popped up from the sofa and began fiddling with the elastic at her waist. It dug into her round tummy.

The thought of Missy Hendricks made her nervous.

She began smoothing the ponies on her flannel thighs, petting them. Gracie walked into the kitchen—lifting her feet high with every step, a little like a pony herself. She didn't want her mother to hear. She wasn't allowed to eat anything before breakfast. She opened the refrigerator and basked in its chilly white light—just looking at what there was to eat.

Gracie thought back to the playground in spite of herself.

She'd been wearing her brand-new parka that day at recess when Missy singled her out. It was a Christmas present from her mother, her favorite one—that puffy coat in fire-engine red. She'd thought it was odd, even at the time: What would Missy want with me? But Gracie brushed her doubts aside. It was Missy Hendricks, after all, the truest of queen bees. She was only too happy to trail in the pretty girl's wake, following her to that corner of the playground where the gym jutted out. It was private back there, where the popular kids played.

Gracie discovered a gang of kids on the other side. They began laughing and snickering as soon as she appeared.

"Ladies and gentlemen," Missy announced—talking into her clenched fist as if it were a handheld mike, "may I present Gracie Santi-HOG-o."

Everyone laughed.

Gracie turned to leave. She should have known better. But Missy grabbed the sleeve of her coat, and the other kids—about a dozen or so—joined in the fun.

"Santi-HOG-o," they cheered, "Santi-HOG-o."

Gracie pulled away from Missy, but an older boy pushed her down onto the pavement before she could escape. She was afraid her downy coat might rip.

"Santi-HOG-o," the boys screamed. "Go back to the barn!"

Things got worse by the second. They all began rushing then—laughing and screaming and oinking like pigs. The boys made a ring around her, and Gracie was trapped on the ground beneath them. She tried to stand, but it was no use: there was always another boy to push her back down. So she closed her eyes, and kept them shut. Gracie prayed that she could wait them out—all their shouting and cursing too.

And then they went silent in the blink of an eye.

Perfectly quiet, Gracie remembered.

She knew they were there still, but something had happened to shut them up. Gracie opened her eyes slowly. It was Miss Watson, her teacher, looking as angry as she'd ever seen her.

"What's going on here?" she barked.

Gracie thought her heart might break.

She loved Miss Watson with all her might. The last thing she wanted was for her to see her like this, to know—for certain—how unpopular she was. Gracie felt terribly ashamed.

"Get out of here," Miss Watson said in a furious voice, yelling at the boys who were circled around her, the gang of Skinny Girls hanging off to the side. "I'll deal with you later," she promised.

The children scattered to the winds.

Miss Watson helped Gracie to her feet. "Are you all right?" she asked, in her kindest voice. Gracie nodded, brushing the dust from the sleeves of her bright red parka. She kept her eyes averted, afraid she might cry—and not because of the kids on the playground. Gracie didn't care about them.

Well, that's not true, she thought.

She cared about them plenty, just not as much as she cared about Miss Watson. "I'm fine," Gracie said.

She didn't want her teacher to think she was a loser.

"What happened here, Gracie?" Miss Watson asked.

"Nothing," she replied. "I just fell down."

"Gracie?" Miss Watson said to her—her voice filled up with disbelief.

"I'm fine," she said. "Really."

She'd rather have Miss Watson think she was a liar than know the truth about her. And no matter how many times she asked, Gracie would never change her tune. She'd never tell on Missy Hendricks, or those fifth-grade boys who pushed her onto the ground. She'd be as silent as a jungle gym, keeping her shameful playground secret until the day she died.

Gracie closed the refrigerator door.

There was nothing good to eat. There never was.

So she sneaked a pinch of oatmeal from the canister on the counter—all dry and flaky—and a clump of brown sugar from the cabinet by the sink. Then she ground them together in the palm of her hand, running a chubby finger over the sticky granules and sharp flakes. Gracie popped the concoction straight into her mouth. It tasted like heaven to her—so hard and sweet, like an oatmeal cookie almost.

And her mother would never suspect a thing.

WHEN BENJAMIN WALKED THROUGH THE FRONT door of FitzCoopers, Emma was the first thing to catch his eye. She *is* Emma Sutton, he thought. There was no getting around that. She also happened to be the only one in furs. A long, silvery chinchilla hung down from her shoulders—its wide sleeves empty, as if she were a double amputee. He could make out a tweedy gray pantsuit beneath it. He knew there was an outsized handbag dangling from the crook of her arm. He knew it just as well as he knew his own name. It was simply hidden from view at the moment, beneath a drapery of fur, like an expensive leather secret.

At least it's cold outside, he thought.

He'd seen her turn up in chinchilla as late as May.

Emma began to click across the room, heading straight for him. Her shoes looked brand-new to him. Benjamin looked down guiltily at his own, brown leather like an ugly tiger cat—scuffed-up patches of brown and beige, mysterious patches of black. He was beyond a shine.

Benjamin felt a little warm. He began unbuttoning his winter coat. She always made him nervous at the start.

"Morning, Benjamin," Emma called, smiling when she reached him, just inside the front door still. She was always friendly and nice—until she wasn't.

He checked his wristwatch right away, afraid he'd heard a curt note in her voice. "Am I late?" he asked. He knew he was on time, a little early even, but he felt jittery all the same. He liked to get off on the right foot.

"Not at all," she said, smiling still, but there was no warmth in it at all.

He felt a flash of annoyance then—first at her, then back

at himself. He knew he wasn't late. And he knew even better that he'd been foolish to think he might beat her here. Emma's idea of nine o'clock was eight thirty to the rest of the world. Or quarter to nine, he thought, at the very latest.

She reached out and touched the sleeve of his coat. "You're right on time," she said, squeezing his forearm a little. Benjamin felt the silver fur against the back of his hand, softer than human hair by far, softer almost than skin. He felt some of the heat that was gathering inside him begin to dissipate. Emma readjusted the fur around her shoulders, lifting it up and drawing it in close, as if she'd grown chilly, standing so close to the door.

A black leather bag peeked out from beneath the fur.

I knew it, he thought. He took pleasure in how well he'd come to know her.

An old woman walked up to them then. "You're Emma Sutton," she said loudly, an unmistakable thrill in her voice, "aren't you?" She sounded as if she were speaking to the Virgin Mary—or to Katie Couric, he thought, at the very least.

Emma nodded.

"You're much prettier in person," the woman said, smiling sweetly.

Emma looked back at her through squinted eyes. "Thank you," she said, smiling tightly. She looked straight past the mixed message, but turned her back on the old woman as quickly as she could.

Benjamin loved moments like these.

"So what's the concept?" he asked, surveying the circle of old furniture; it looked a little battered to him. "Are we buying something?" he asked, slipping an arm from the sleeve of his coat, just making conversation.

He watched her face contract in a flash, all her handsome features squeezing shut—eyes and mouth and brow in a fist—and just when he'd thought it was safe too. Benjamin felt a catch in his throat; he knew he was in trouble. Emma glared at him—in the general direction of his chest, it seemed. He thought it might be his sweater, at first, looking down at the offending wool.

"Come with me," she said, refreshing his memory of what her curt voice sounded like. She led him off to a private room.

He felt sorry for upsetting her and frightened for himself.

But as he trailed behind her, crossing the room, he began to cast off those crumbs of fear—like Hansel in the forest. She's just being ridiculous, he thought. Anyone who heard me is going to see her bidding in five minutes anyway. He noticed the complimentary coffee table in the corner of the room. He longed for a cup, but thought better of mentioning it at the moment.

Another flash of annoyance coursed through him: he decided he was entitled. "Do you mind if I get a coffee?" he asked, feeling defiant.

"In a minute," she said.

He supposed he could wait.

Emma led him to a deserted office in the back—just a few makeshift desks with wooden tops and filing cabinets underneath for legs, those ergonomic chairs that promised no more backaches, and an old fax machine. It was a marked contrast to all the fancy brass and glowing wood in the exhibition room.

It was a relief to him.

She extended a bidding paddle toward him once they

were safely inside: a white rectangle the size of two Visa bills laid one on top of the other, and just about as thin. There was a small white handle protruding from the bottom, and three red numbers—one, six, eight—painted on both sides. It felt like a challenge to him, the way she handed it over, as if she were offering him a gleaming saber from a velvet-lined case. He knew he was supposed to take it from her, but he didn't.

"I want you to bid on a Nakashima table for me," she said.

He didn't know what a Nakashima table was.

"Are you leaving?" he asked, his insides mixed up like a complicated cocktail: one part dread, another part hope.

"Not at all," she said. "But you'll draw less attention than I will."

Benjamin was confused.

"We won't be sitting together," she told him, in a tone of voice that suggested that *this* was the piece of information—the not-sitting-together part—that was supposed to help him make sense of the story. It didn't. He felt prickly heat at the nape of his neck, the beginnings of moisture at the peaks of his brow. It made him nervous not to follow her precisely.

"We'll get a better deal this way," she said, sounding impatient.

It doesn't take her long, he thought.

Benjamin took the paddle from her outstretched hand. It was lighter than he expected, made of balsa wood maybe, or even lighter still—the kind of wood he used to make model airplanes when he was a boy. He couldn't begin to account for how burdensome the thing felt in his hands.

"You'll do fine," she said, smiling warmly. She always smiled once she'd gotten her way. He must have looked nervous still. "Honestly, Benjamin," she said, "I've seen half-wits do it."

Twenty-five dollars an hour began to seem like chicken feed.

Emma told him the lot number of the table: "Twelve thirty-three," she said, as if it were the departure time of some commercial airplane. She insisted that he write it down. His heart dropped as he comprehended it—when he realized he'd have to sit through twelve hundred pieces of furniture. He was only slightly relieved when she informed him that the auction began with Lot 1000. Two hundred and thirty-three pieces of furniture still sounded like an awful lot of furniture to him.

She showed him a picture of the table in the catalog—"To avoid any confusion," she said. He feigned nonchalance, but looked very closely. He studied the lots that came before it too, hoping he'd remember them later, like warning bells chiming in advance.

Maybe I *can* do this, he thought, a silky ribbon of confidence swirling through the fear. He was going to make her proud.

"It all moves very quickly," she warned.

He really did need that coffee though.

Then she told him how high he was entitled to bid: "Up to seventy-eight thousand dollars," she said.

"What?" he cried. He had absolutely no idea.

Emma grabbed him roughly by the arm.

He didn't make another peep.

That's twice my salary, Benjamin thought—on an annual basis, as if he needed to clarify. He knew that Emma was rich. Everyone knew that. She was Emma Sutton, for Christ's sake. But she'd always seemed so sensible to him, especially where money was concerned—not at all the kind of person to fritter it away. Of course, everything has to be perfect too, he thought, balancing out his understanding of her as if he were sitting on a seesaw: wanting to please her, on the one hand, and disapproving of such terrible waste, on the other.

Benjamin looked up.

She was waiting for him to compose himself again. She looked as if she wanted to stare the silliness right out of him.

"Ready?" she asked, a little smugly.

He felt as exposed as a little boy fresh from his soapy bath. He nodded silently, and looked straight into her eyes—just the way she liked. He hoped nothing too terrible had shown.

She explained a few more things to him: described the bidding increments—in hundreds, then five hundreds, then thousands. She stressed that he wasn't *required* to spend seventy-eight thousand dollars—as if I were an idiot, he thought—only *entitled* to, if the bidding ran that high.

Benjamin kept nodding.

But he couldn't get those seventy-eight thousand dollars out of his head. He laid them down side by side with his own prospective earnings for the day—two hundred dollars, cash. And he'd thought he was doing well too.

"I need to take care of something now," she said, disengaging from him and walking away. He heard her heels tapping lightly against the concrete floor. She stopped and looked back at him, over her shoulder. "You'll sit on the left side of the room," she said. "Understood?"

Then she took a few steps more, and turned back again. "Facing the auctioneer," she told him, "of course."

Of course, he thought.

Benjamin nodded one last time, and watched Emma walk away for good. He followed her to the doorway of the little office. She was heading straight for the table where people were picking up their bidding paddles. He watched her move to the front of the line.

Of course, he thought. She was taking out an insurance policy on him then, getting herself another paddle, in case he screwed up. Benjamin felt as disposable as the painted balsa wood in his hands—as flimsy as a model airplane and just as worthless to the woman who was walking away.

Chapter 2

A MID-MORNING SNACK:
Eight Slim Carrot Sticks

GRACIE'S MOTHER—TINA SANTIAGO—SNEAKED OUT of her bedroom and crept down the hall, a lithe jungle cat making its way through a grassy clearing. She was an elegant young woman of twenty-seven, small and thin, with long dark hair and black Latin eyes. She navigated those floorboards expertly too, avoiding all the regular creaks, placing her feet so quietly down.

She made it to the kitchen, undetected.

She wanted one strong coffee, at least, before she had to face the day. Saturdays were for cleaning house and paying bills—worrying over which checks to write and which to leave for later. She had to make sure she'd have enough to cover the rent when it came due.

Tina had been up for a long time that morning—lying in bed and listening to her daughter plod down the narrow hall, get to work on her Valentine cards.

It was a small apartment, and the walls were thin.

But it was more than that: Tina was like a radio tower where her daughter was concerned, searching out signals of any kind. She was afraid she lacked the normal quotient of motherly instinct. She'd had the girl when she was so young, after all—only a girl herself. She rarely just *knew* what Gracie was feeling—at least not to the extent she thought other mothers did. So she watched her like a hawk instead, trying to ferret out what she could, imagining how her daughter really was.

She heard her playing in her bedroom then.

Tina was grateful for these few extra minutes of peace and quiet. She'd slept so poorly the night before, tossing and turning for stretches at a time—dozing for a minute, then waking with a start. She'd met with Benjamin Blackman after work, the social worker from Gracie's school, and she'd relived the meeting for most of the night, turning it over and over in her worried mind, her stomach growing spikier and sour. Blackman covered the same old ground, his agenda nearly identical to their first meeting. He called it a "progress report," but Tina was hard-pressed to see the progress: Gracie was just as withdrawn as before, just as fat too, and the playground bullies who made her life so rough weren't being any nicer.

"I hope we can avoid drastic measures," Blackman told her, looking down into his notebook as he spoke. He was always on the verge of writing something down, his shiny black pen forever hovering above the page.

He never looks at me, she thought—not anymore.

Tina had no idea what a "drastic measure" might be. Her daughter was only nine years old, after all, and her tormenters weren't much older. Still, she'd been afraid to ask him, sitting at Blackman's beat-up desk, in his tiny office right next to the gym. They couldn't be good, she supposed, whatever they were—and what was worse, Tina suspected that Blackman would move heaven and earth to make sure they rained down on her, drastic measures like pellets of hail. He'd made it perfectly clear—in his look and his voice—that he blamed her for all of Gracie's troubles.

But I'm not to blame, she thought, fussing with her old coffeemaker, heaping spoons of coffee in. Am I?

Benjamin had behaved much differently toward her at the start, and Tina couldn't help but think their relationship might have taken a friendlier turn. It was just after Christmas, and she'd been called down to the school: some older boys had been caught teasing Gracie on the playground. Tina took an hour off from work. She remembered sitting on the long wooden bench outside the principal's office, waiting for Mr. Spooner to finish with another parent inside.

"So what did you do?" she heard.

It was a man's voice, speaking to her. He was sitting on the bench too, just a few feet away. Handsome, she thought—thirty or so, with dark brown hair and a clean white shirt.

Tina didn't know who he was, or what he meant by his question either.

"To get sent down here?" he added. "To the principal's office?"

He smiled at her then. His teeth were white, and his eyes as green as her father's old Buick.

"Spitballs," she answered, smiling back.

Tina watched the man's eyes lingering on her, his book lying open in his lap. Not leering, she thought—not at all. It was more appreciative than that. It had been a long time since

Tina crossed paths with a good-looking man. She hoped he'd keep looking at her.

"How about you?" she asked him, in return.

"Smoking in the boys' room," he said, with a smirk.

But Tina knew already that he wasn't a bad boy at all.

The two of them chatted for a few minutes more—all bubbly and crisp. She thought he might ask for her number—hoped he would, in fact—but the principal interrupted them, opening his door before they got that far.

"Mrs. Santiago?" the principal said, looking straight at her.

"Yes," she answered, standing up.

She turned to the younger man to say good-bye.

"You're Gracie's mother?" he asked, from his seated place on the wooden bench. He looked barely able to contain his surprise.

"This is Benjamin Blackman," the principal told her, "the school's social worker. I've asked him to join us." Tina was pleased to shake his hand. She'd be only too happy to continue their conversation inside, but Benjamin seemed to change on a dime. In a matter of seconds, he turned chilly and cold. He'd met with Gracie several times already, it turned out, and it was obvious—to Tina anyway—that he liked her a lot. He praised Gracie's intelligence and her sly sense of humor. Tina liked him even better then. She felt doubly confused by his sharp change toward her. It was as if he stopped liking her the moment he found out she was Gracie's mother.

She had experience enough with men to know that plenty of them shied away from women with children, but that didn't make sense to her—not where Benjamin was concerned.

He works in an elementary school, she thought, for Christ's sake.

Tina sat down at her kitchen table, sipping at the large mug of coffee, then putting it down. She folded her arms across her chest—as if she were chilly, or needed protection. She rubbed her hands against her soft flannel sleeves, her flesh and blood like a chafing dish beneath, keeping the cotton warm.

She wondered about Benjamin Blackman—for the ten thousandth time—but Tina couldn't work it out.

EMMA SMILED IN APPROVAL AS SHE WATCHED THE Asian man take his seat—on the right side of the room, of course—facing the auctioneer. Everything was falling into place that morning. She made her way back to the row of chairs where he was sitting, toward the back of the tidy grid. It wasn't far from where she would have sat on her own, even if there'd been no tiny Asian to contend with. Emma took a seat exactly three chairs to his right.

Close, she thought, but not too close.

She liked to keep her competition in view.

Emma knew with certainty that the man was watching her then, as she crossed her long legs and feigned ignorance of him. She *was* Emma Sutton, after all, and a trimmer, prettier Emma Sutton at that. She'd lost fifteen pounds in that federal lockup—what with all the time in the world for exercise and the hideous prison food. It was a hell of a way to lose it, she thought, but she was glad of the outcome all the same. She'd managed to keep the weight off too, those terrible middle-aged pounds that no high-end spa or personal trainer had ever come close to eradicating. She'd assumed they were hers for life, and the mere thought of them, shed as neatly as a snake's scaly skin, gave her something like hope for the future.

Emma looked at her neighbor, who seemed a little startled by her still. There was hardly a man or a woman alive who didn't know who she was, who wouldn't be a little rattled by her appearance in the flesh. But there are more than enough bidders for me to sit here, she decided, and not so many that anyone would take either of the empty chairs between them.

It was all working out fine.

She slipped the chinchilla from her shoulders and settled it on the nearer of the empty chairs between them. She placed her large handbag on top of the fur and reached in for her copy of the auction catalog and the extra bidding paddle—just in case.

She only needed to wait for her moment, but Emma was too impatient for that. As soon as the man looked back at her, she smiled at him sweetly, then turned away fast, before he had the chance to do much of anything in reply.

"No one likes a girl who comes on strong," her father always said.

Just then, a young man—about Benjamin's age—began to make his way to the dark-stained podium at the front of the room. He was wearing a bright green shirt with fat candy stripes and a loudly patterned tie. Emma took a moment to imagine precisely what an auctioneer *ought* to be wearing.

He's too young to be the auctioneer anyway, she thought. He must be a technician, for the microphone perhaps.

But when a tepid smattering of applause broke out for the boy in the fat candy stripes, Emma was forced to admit that he was the auctioneer after all. Probably some kind of auctioneer-in-training, she feared. She pictured them slogging through the lots, one by one—like a pair of green rubber boots inching through thick garden mud.

Emma liked an auction to move like the wind.

The young auctioneer introduced himself, his amplified voice booming all around the room. Then he announced the first lots, with just a whistling hint of the microphone complaining. It was a suite of bedroom furniture by Jean Royère: a bed and a dresser and a nice easy chair, all made of quarter-sawn oak and decorated with iron circles that were painted brick red.

They were nice enough. The paint looked original, at least.

The bidding began.

Emma watched closely as the lots went out high, all three of them—well above the estimates printed in the catalog, but not so high as to suggest auction-room insanity, or to bode ill for her Nakashima table. The young auctioneer moved briskly to a set of four wooden stools by Charlotte Perriand.

Emma checked her watch.

We might be out of here by lunch, she thought, with something like affection for the auctioneer taking hold just beneath the nubbly tweed of her suit jacket.

She looked over to the other side of the room and spotted Benjamin right away—the back of his head anyway, his dark wavy hair. He was sitting all the way up at the front, in the second row, on the aisle. She could just make out his profile: the strong nose and deep green eyes. He was a good-looking boy, she decided, as if he were just a stranger in the crowd.

She made a note to tell him about sitting farther back the next time, about trying to be invisible in these rooms. She hoped no one made too much of her speaking with him before the auction began. It would be awfully lucky if he liked this, she thought. He could be an asset to her at the auction houses—with that thrift-shop coat and those worn-out shoes.

It surprised Emma sometimes how warmly she felt toward Benjamin. He was dependable enough, she supposed, and trustworthy—nothing like those terrible young men who'd gotten her into all that trouble, the lousy accountant and that phalanx of lawyers.

She turned the bidding paddle over in her hands, raising it slowly toward her face, as if she were looking into a handheld mirror. But it was more than that, she thought: Benjamin was always looking out for her. That's what clinched it. As helpless as he was—like a baby bird practically, blind and broke and squirming in the nest—he acted as if the only thing he cared about was taking care of her. Like a little man, she decided, smiling as she shook her head at the very idea of making so much of a part-time assistant in shabby clothes.

Emma watched idly as the four wooden stools gave way to a low wooden daybed—also Perriand, according to the catalog anyway.

She doubted it. These days, if it was white oak, they called it Perriand.

She turned back to Benjamin again.

She'd decided what to do. She was going to take him on as her full-time assistant. Teach him the ropes and move him up through the ranks. She was determined to do it.

He's smart enough, she thought.

But Emma didn't complete her thought; she didn't need to. Smart, she meant, but not brilliant. Not half as talented as her own daughter, Cassy, with all the promise in the world, but none of the desire—floating from one useless job in her organization to the next, and wanting more money every time she turned around.

Oh, well, she thought—life is long.

It was an uncharacteristically mellow view for Emma. She hoped her daughter might come around, but in the meantime, she'd get Benjamin the hell out of that elementary school. It was a waste of his talent.

"The prices are strong this morning." The voice came from somewhere close by. It took her that long to realize that the Asian man had spoken to her, unbidden—interrupting her succession plans at Emma Sutton Everywhere.

"Excuse me?" she said, though she'd heard him perfectly the first time. She looked back at him, smiling indifferently—it was one of her trademarked looks. He repeated himself—"prices," "strong"—with just the smallest trace of an accent, wrapped loosely around his vowels. He sounded as if he were attacking an overstuffed sandwich, using his teeth to cut through the stringy roast beef.

His blue suit was immaculate.

"Yes," she said. "But you don't often see such unusual pieces."

They were as common as dirt, in fact. Emma could name three shops, right off the top of her head, where you could find that same bedroom suite, and several more that stocked the alleged Perriand daybed—and all at much better prices. She'd only said it to see what the tiny man would make of it.

"I see," he said, sounding sincere.

She nodded back.

"I don't know much about antiques," he whispered, as if it were a crime.

"Oh," she sang. "I just assumed you were in the trade." Emma smiled at him coyly then, as if she'd offered him a compliment—or a delicious hors d'oeuvre on a pretty lacquered tray.

"Oh, no," he replied, a little bashful: compliment taken. "I work at the United Nations," he said. "At the Japanese delegation."

"Really?" she said, dragging it out, as if it were the most fascinating thing she'd heard all year. "Are you a collector then?" she asked, getting straight to the point. "We don't often see civilians here."

"Not really," he said. "I've come for a table, I hope."

Emma's stomach fell like a riverbed stone, splashing into a pool of chilly water.

"My wife loves Nakashima," he said.

Coming from him, the name sounded awfully Japanese—so fast and sharp. Emma felt her fear spreading like a virus, as if his native pronunciation gave him some sort of edge.

"I want to surprise her with it," he said.

Things were getting worse by the second.

She held the man tightly in her gaze. She needed to steady herself, and size him up too.

"There's a Nakashima table in the auction today," he said, as if she were staring out of confusion.

"That's right," she said, returning to her senses. She corrected her wilting posture. Sat bolt upright and composed her slack face, clenching her jaw muscles tight.

"Have you seen it?" he asked.

"Yes," she said, trying to calculate her next move. "It's beautiful," she told him. There was no point denying it. A blind man could see that much.

"What's the estimate on it?" she asked, as innocent as a child.

"Thirty to forty thousand," he told her, turning quickly to its picture in the dog-eared catalog. He handed it to Emma.

"It's stunning," she said. She meant it too. It really was, even in the hands of their mediocre photographer. She gazed at the picture for a moment longer, and not just for her neighbor's benefit either. "You've checked the dimensions?" she asked, looking back up at him, hoping for a flicker.

"Yes," he said, sounding pleased with himself. "It fits perfectly."

"Good," she said, nodding. "It's a big table."

Emma turned back to the auction for a moment. She felt tired, needed a little rest. She looked at the television screen at the front of the room. "Lot 1032," it read, in thick black type, "Desk by Jacques Adnet." Beneath it, a photograph of a pretty writing desk, very simple—every inch of it wrapped in saddle-stitched leather, even its thin, thin legs, with their elegant bamboo design.

All that leather, she marveled, and still it looks light as air. Emma had one just like it at her office. She watched happily as the price flew to nearly three times what she'd paid for hers.

"This auctioneer is good," she said, turning back to the Japanese man.

She knew what to do.

"He's moving so quickly," she added.

"What do you think of it?" he asked.

"The Adnet?" she replied—as if she were confused.

"No," he said. "The Nakashima table." He pointed to his catalog, sitting open in her lap.

"Well, it's beautiful," she said, halting a little at the end, holding that last syllable in her mouth like a lozenge. Emma closed the catalog and handed it back to him, hoping that she'd planted a seed of doubt.

"Is there something wrong with it?" he asked.

Emma smiled. He'd heard.

"Well, the estimate's a little high," she whispered, nearly mouthing the words instead of speaking them—as if she were reluctant to pronounce the truth out loud. "I wouldn't pay a penny more than forty for it," she whispered.

"Thank you very much," he said, looking back at her, as earnest as a Boy Scout. He nodded his head in quick little strokes. "You're very kind," he said, looking down into his tiny lap, suddenly bashful. "My wife will be sorry to have missed you," he continued. "She's a big fan of yours."

"Don't be silly," Emma told him. "It's my pleasure."

She tried relaxing into the backrest of her little gilt chair. To her credit, she felt terrible about what she'd just done. In fact, she almost wished there were a second Nakashima table in the auction that morning—a perfect clone of the first—so she could let her neighbor have it. But there isn't, she thought, a little sadly, and so she'd done what she had to do.

Emma knew that wasn't the case. She didn't *have* to do anything.

Still she racked her brain for something more, something that might help this man, and something that might hurt him too. Like a consolation prize maybe, or some scrap of additional insurance she might lay on. Emma felt torn, and that was new. The ends still justified the means, but she felt bad about it, at least—feeling bad in lieu of doing good.

That has to count for something, she thought.

"Let me give you my card," she said, reaching deep into the alligator bag between them. This was virgin territory for Emma. She wanted to make it up to the man, even as she assured her immediate success.

"You know," she said, in a lively voice, "I can think of two or three lovely Nakashima tables around town."

The man stared back at her.

She looked at his tiny shirt collar, pressed up against his little neck.

"At reasonable prices," she added, lowering her voice again. She'd already decided to negotiate an excellent deal for him on one of the other tables—like a silent kind of apology maybe. "Just in case this one doesn't work out," she said.

Emma wasn't lying either: she *could* think of a few perfectly nice Nakashima tables for him—just not this one.

This one, you see, was already spoken for.

A LITTLE LATER THAT MORNING, TINA SANTIAGO stood at her kitchen sink, scrubbing a fat carrot beneath a stream of cool water. She'd pulled her hair away from her face, and looked down into the sink as she worked, the carrot popping bright against the white enamel, all glistening wet.

"Shit," she hissed.

Just as she reached for the tap, ready to twist it shut, she spotted a familiar cluster of stains—a trio of them—right above the silver drain. She'd nearly missed them too: those three rusty marks, vaguely circular in shape, like drops of coffee on a white tablecloth, the biggest one smaller than a dime.

She hated them with all her heart.

They reminded her of work, of the little discs of chocolate they made down at the plant, each one wrapped in golden foil and dropped by the handful into cheap black netting. "Davy Jones' Locker," they were called, for most of the year, shipped out to candy stores by the carton—except for that one brief stretch in autumn, when they pasted a Star of David on and called them "Hanukkah Gelt"—Davy Jones' locker turned Jewish for Christmas.

Tina was the bookkeeper there. She'd started as a secretary several years before, and she was nearly proud of the way her quick wits and organizational skills had moved her up the ranks. She practically ran Accounts Payable these days.

Now that she'd seen those stains, it was too late to turn back. They were all she could see.

She gave the carrot a brisk little shake—sent droplets raining all around—then she laid it on the draining board and searched for the Comet beneath the sink. She had a go at those stains then, really put some muscle into it too. It was her four millionth attempt at rust removal since they'd moved into the place. She rarely used that sink, in fact, without taking a crack at them.

Is it me, she wondered when she was finished, gazing down at the stains like a lousy housewarming gift from some careless tenant who'd come before, or are they fading a little?

She dried her hands on the side of her jeans, sitting low on her slim, slim hips. Tina knew those bastard stains would outlast them here—just like the golden coins that Davy Jones had spilled across the ocean floor, lying there undiscovered a hundred years later, if you believed the candy packaging anyway.

She picked up the carrot and looked it over.

She knew carrots weren't as good as celery or cucumbers. According to the nurse at the Free Clinic, they had twice the calories.

Tina hunted for the good knife in the cutlery drawer.

But Gracie wouldn't eat celery or cucumbers. She'd tried them before, plenty of times, but the girl wouldn't budge. And carrots had to be better than cookies, she thought—or cupcakes. She spotted the paring knife and removed it carefully from the cutlery drawer, began carving away at the few remaining blemishes. The carrot looked even brighter, all nude like that.

Gracie skipped into the kitchen, a little heavy on her feet, while Tina chopped the carrot into thin little slivers, the way her daughter liked it. It was her morning snack.

The girl began singing as she skipped, just as softly as she could: "*From this valley they say you are going.*"

Tina thought she recognized the song.

Gracie sang the line again, a little louder that time: "*From this valley they say you are going.*"

Tina looked at her daughter's face when she skipped into view; she saw the strain there—her brow furrowed, eyes squinting—as if she might pluck the next line from the air around her head, a musical mosquito buzzing all around her face.

Red River Valley, Tina thought, with a spark of pleasure at naming the tune.

"*From this valley they say you are going,*" Gracie sang for the third time, a little faster now, as if she were rushing to arrive at the elusive second line—which appeared, as if by magic, on her mother's lips. Tina sang it softly, so that Gracie could hear it if she wanted to, but not so loudly as to intrude on the little girl's skipping and singing.

"*I will miss your bright eyes and sweet smile,*" Tina sang.

She remembered "Red River Valley" from her own grade school days, singing in unison with the pretty young music teacher. She remembered taking her turn, strumming the tense metal strings of an autoharp, the music teacher taking her hand so gently in her own and turning it over—as if she were going to read Tina's future—but showing her how to brush the metal strings instead, with just the nail of her index finger.

Gracie sang the first line again, and then the second.

"You have such a pretty singing voice," Tina said, smiling at her. Neither of them remembered the third line, but it hardly mattered: her daughter beamed back when she skipped into view.

Tina couldn't help but see that Gracie barely navigated the narrow passage between the countertop and the small linoleum table at the center of the room. She couldn't help wincing as she heard her daughter's feet come thudding down. Gracie was only in third grade—just nine years old—but already she weighed one hundred and ten pounds, twenty pounds more than any other kid in class.

Of course, she's taller too, Tina thought—a little desperately. But only by an inch or two, she was forced to admit. There was no way around it really: her daughter was obese—to borrow from Blackman's harsh vocabulary.

Gracie's weight was a constant worry to her.

It had been for years—since the little girl turned four or five. She'd been normal weight before that, toward the high end of those percentiles the doctors always gave her at the end of her annual physicals, but normal-looking anyway. Then for no reason, or none that Tina could work out, Gracie began puffing up like a helium balloon, right before her very eyes. She'd watched her daughter's face change utterly—her sweet little features stretched out wide, a neck as thick as her own.

It started a few years after Tommy left, so that wasn't it. And Gracie's medical tests were normal, according to the nurse at the Free Clinic anyway. She had a "slow metabolism," they told her, which would make it hard for her to lose weight, but it didn't explain the magnitude of Gracie's problem.

The little girl just didn't eat that much, it seemed to her.

Tina was sure there must be more tests they could run.

And so she circled around and around, driving in endless loops on this mysterious cul de sac—fat, she thought, very fat—without the slightest idea why, only growing more frustrated as she drove. That circle never opened onto any kind of road, and Tina never came closer to anything like a sensible explanation. Meanwhile, her little girl's arms and legs grew fatter and fatter—there was no denying that—like a knight in fleshy armor, as if her true limbs were hidden away, someplace deep inside.

Tina felt her head begin to pound.

Sometimes she thought she should pack it all in, and take her father up on his offer to come live with him. She knew it would be easier, but Tina was too independent for that. She wasn't ready to give up on herself just yet—or Gracie either, for that matter.

She fixed on the horrible pants her daughter was wearing, denim nearly as wide as it was long—small pink kittens embroidered on the back pockets, mocking them both. She couldn't see anything else. Tina hated herself for starting down this road—the dominoes of unvarnished truth clicking lightly, one into the next, the first tile knocking its neighbor down, which toppled the next, in turn.

She felt her cheeks heat up with guilt. *What kind of mother?*

She felt her stomach roiling, and the cruel observations flowering as fast as popcorn popping in a bath of boiling oil. She felt powerless to stop them.

I've done what I could, she thought, haven't I?

She'd been to the school nurse half a dozen times, and brought Gracie to the Free Clinic every year. She'd shared her worries with the chilly nurses there, while Gracie played in the waiting room—towering over the other children like a full-grown dog with a litter of puppies.

Stop it, she thought.

Diet and exercise, diet and exercise—that was all they ever told her. But what about the twenty pounds of extra blubber, she wanted to scream? What about that?

Tina was sure they blamed her for it.

The last nurse she'd seen had given her a more reasonable program, at least, one that acknowledged the facts of life. That a little girl needed a snack, for instance, if all the other kids in class were having one; that Tina couldn't afford to buy those specially packaged diet meals. She'd been following the new diet religiously: baking chicken instead of frying it, serving applesauce for dessert, and never a portion bigger than the little girl's clenched fist.

"Will you have a snack with me?" Tina asked, carrying the bright blue bowl of carrot sticks to the table.

Gracie clapped her hands, skipping in one last circle all around the room.

Tina had lost plenty of weight since they'd started the new diet. Her clothes hung loose all around her, and she hadn't needed to lose an ounce to begin with. It made her look even lovelier, though, a little haunted around the eyes—so large and liquid brown—her cheeks all hollowed out.

Gracie frisked over to the table, like an unwieldy baby animal from some nature program on TV.

She hadn't seemed to lose a pound.

Tina watched the girl's face fall when she saw the bowl of carrot sticks. She watched her pull it right back together again too—the way she always did. Sometimes she wished that Gracie would just ask for a cookie. That would make this so much easier. She'd have a right to be angry then. But the little girl never breathed a word of complaint. She just sat down at the table, looking vaguely ashamed of herself.

Tina felt another pang.

"Go ahead, sweetie," she said, smiling at the girl.

Gracie reached for a handful of carrot sticks—just a little greedy—her chubby fingers twice as fat as any carrot in the bowl. Tina took a handful herself. She bit into one, ever hopeful, but they tasted of nothing, just like always. Still she chewed and chewed, smiling at her daughter all the while.

The little girl smiled right back.

"They're tasty," she said. "Aren't they, Mommy?"

"LOT TWELVE THIRTY-TWO," BENJAMIN WHISPERED, pronouncing it just like Emma taught him to, as two smaller numbers. "Exceptional Desk by Jean Prouvé." He'd been murmuring the lot numbers since the auction began, the titles too. He read them off the large television screen at the front of the room—like a good-luck habit he was afraid to break.

He hoped no one heard him.

"We'll start the bidding at seventy-five hundred dollars," the auctioneer boomed, leaning into his microphone.

Just a plain wooden top, Benjamin thought, and a pair of

black legs. It didn't look so "exceptional" to him. Seventy-five hundred dollars was a great deal of money as far as he was concerned.

He'd begun to grow nervous again, after a brief spell of relative calm. The Nakashima table was up next. His fingertips felt clammy against the fleshy heel of his hand; he squeezed the paddle tight—as if he might need to hoist it high at any second.

It's not even my turn, he thought, so annoyed with himself.

He willed his fingers to loosen their grip, felt grateful to them when they did—on command even. He wiped his sweaty palm against a corduroy thigh.

Happily for Benjamin, there was a great deal of spirited bidding on the Exceptional Prouvé Desk—a small reprieve. He dreaded the arrival of Lot 1233.

He looked back at Emma, sitting on the other side of the room. She was chatting amiably with an Asian man. Cool as a cucumber, he thought—not nervous at all. He hoped she'd be happy with his performance.

Benjamin flinched when the gavel crashed down.

Curtains, he thought—the pounding gavel like a death knell to him, the desk an oaken corpse with thin black legs, ready to be carted off to the morgue.

"Sold for nineteen thousand dollars," the auctioneer cried. "To bidder number . . . ," and then he paused, waiting for the winner to hoist his paddle one last time. "Two hundred and forty-five," the auctioneer called, closing the book on the Prouvé desk.

Benjamin gripped his paddle tight. It was his turn now.

He felt his shoulders locking into place, somewhere up

around his ears. He willed them downward—tried mightily to relax—but he was well beyond that sort of control by now.

"Lot twelve thirty-three," he whispered, as soon as the numbers appeared on the television screen, "Nakashima Table in English Walnut." Benjamin heard the auctioneer speaking the same words, nearly in unison.

"We'll start the bidding at fifteen thousand dollars," the auctioneer said, leaning back into his curvy microphone, as if he were going to take a sniff—a fragrant black lily sprouting up from the oak. "Do I hear fifteen?" he asked.

Benjamin hesitated for just a second.

Emma had told him to jump in early. "And stay in too," she'd said.

He felt a flash of heat inside his sweater, and the beginning of moisture beneath his arms. He forced himself to raise the paddle up, but he knew he'd been too slow. The auctioneer confirmed as much, nodding his head at someone behind him. "Fifteen thousand from the lady in blue," he called, his voice a pleasant singsong. "Looking for sixteen now."

Benjamin jerked his paddle high, nodding his head when the auctioneer looked at him. He liked the way it felt. Sixteen thousand dollars was a lot of money to him; he was proud of amassing such a sum.

"Do I hear seventeen?" the auctioneer called.

There was a brief pause.

Could it be so simple, he wondered?

"Seventeen thousand from the lady in blue," he heard, "and eighteen from the gentleman at the back."

He supposed not.

Benjamin raised his paddle up again, a little more smoothly that time. He was getting the hang of it. The fear that made his movements all jerky at first seemed to have been washed away by liquid of another stripe: a sharp adrenaline flooded his system, lubricating all his joints. He wanted to win—and not just for Emma anymore.

"Nineteen thousand from the young man."

He basked in the attention.

"And twenty from the lady."

Then the auctioneer looked off to his left. "Twenty-one from the bidder on the phone," he said, pointing to a young woman sitting off by herself. She had three beige telephones on the table in front of her—like birds sitting on a fence—one of the receivers up at her ear.

Emma was right: it *did* go fast.

Benjamin lifted his paddle again, unbidden this time.

"Twenty-two thousand from the young man," the auctioneer cried quickly, squeezing the air from every syllable, from the gaps between words too. He moved right on to the lady in blue, then on to the gentleman sitting at the back. Benjamin wheeled around in his chair to take a peek at the competition—the lady in blue, who was much older than the sort of lady he expected, and the gentleman at the back: the Asian man who was sitting next to Emma.

That's a coincidence, he thought.

At thirty-four thousand, the lady dropped out. She was replaced quickly by a middle-aged man with an overtanned brow, his thin gray hair scraped into a weaselly ponytail. The auctioneer called him "Man in Vest."

Benjamin admired the auctioneer's tact. That vest was about the last thing he would have noticed.

"Looking for thirty-six," the auctioneer called.

Benjamin raised his paddle, but he was feeling tired—

running this race of no determined length. He didn't know whether to sprint or settle in for the long haul.

Is it me, he wondered, or is the pace slowing down?

He felt almost certain they were going to take a breather at forty-two thousand. The girl with the phone pushed up against her ear was trying to coax another increment from her bidder on the line. She was talking a great deal into the tan mouthpiece, but Benjamin couldn't make out what she was saying. Whatever it was though, it wasn't enough. He watched her shaking her head at the auctioneer, pressing her lips into a thin little line. She hung up the receiver.

Ponytail Man brought the bidding to forty-three.

Benjamin sailed past him.

Then the man with the ponytail dropped out too.

It was just him then, and the Asian man sitting next to Emma.

"Forty-five."

"Forty-six."

"Forty-seven."

"Forty-eight."

"Forty-nine."

"The young man at fifty," the auctioneer cried, like the title of a painting or an impressionistic poem. "Fifty-one at the back."

Benjamin nodded.

"And fifty-two thousand from the young man," the auctioneer called.

There was a long pause—an unnatural quiet, as if everyone in the room had decided to stop breathing.

"Any more?" the auctioneer asked, his eyes roving all around.

Benjamin turned in time to see the Asian man shaking his head. He looked defeated. Sayonara, he thought—immediately begrudging his choice of words. He tried to forgive himself. It wasn't the worst thing in the world, he thought: just the competition of the auction room leaching out—like air hissing from a punctured tire.

"Fair warning," the auctioneer called, like a conductor on a train—his vowels starting small, then opening wide. He was looking all around for some kind of last-ditch effort.

Why won't he let me win? Benjamin wondered.

The auctioneer's vigilance hurt his feelings.

But the Asian man had made up his mind, and the girl on the phone was sitting back—all her lines vacant. The old lady in blue was at the coffee bar, pouring herself a glass of water. Benjamin couldn't find the man with the wormy ponytail anymore. Poor Loser in Vest, he thought.

It seemed a little late for someone new to be jumping in.

And still he worried.

The pounding gavel made him flinch.

"Sold," the auctioneer cried, "for fifty-two thousand dollars, to bidder number . . ."

Benjamin lifted his paddle one last time.

"One hundred and sixty-eight."

He turned around in his seat, a little-boy smile plastered on his face—as if he'd won a game of German dodgeball, or a blue ribbon at the science fair. Benjamin looked for Emma. He hoped he'd find her smiling back, clasping her hands in pleasure as she did on TV. So pleased to have won, and grateful to him for winning it. He found her in profile, a benign expression on her face. The fur was hanging off her shoulders again as she gathered up her things.

She's leaving? he thought.

Benjamin tried to catch her eye when she turned back around. He watched her ignore him. The adrenaline that had been racing through him like a car chase not five seconds earlier came to a screeching halt then. He felt his stomach lurching forward, as if some careless foot had been heavy on the brakes, his body slammed back hard against the vinyl upholstery. He hadn't understood that separate seating would extend beyond the four corners of the Nakashima table.

He watched Emma leaving, with the Asian man in tow.

Benjamin felt himself deflating, losing pressure with every second.

I guess it makes a *kind* of sense, he thought, our finishing out this charade. He'd been hoping for a little company though, to relive the thrill of the chase, and the crash of the gavel pounding down.

He turned back to the front of the room.

"Lot twelve thirty-five," he whispered, in perfect unison with the auctioneer, "Magnificent Hanging Light by Serge Mouille."

Chapter 3

SUNDAY AFTERNOON:

A Gingersnap—or Twelve

EMMA'S DAUGHTER, CASSY, ROLLED OVER IN BED.

Even with her eyes pasted shut, she knew this wasn't her room. The mattress was too soft, for starters, and the sheets too grainy. The pillowcase felt rough against her cheek.

Where in hell *am* I? she wondered.

There was an awful smell: dead cologne, she decided—a winter blanket of sickly sweet laid on top of stale air. She wiped the sleep from her eyes and let her squinting vision confirm what she already knew: not hers.

I've really got to knock this off, she thought—for about the hundredth time in as many weekends. Cassy suspected she might be the very last thirty-four-year-old on earth who was still trying to "find her way"—as her shrink so kindly put it—like this.

Whoring around's more like it, she thought.

She turned to the outsized lump on her left, staring and staring with all her might, trying to untangle the knot of blankets and sheets and limbs. She could scarcely make them out in the blackness of the room. There were two of them, she saw, with a smirk of disgust. A man and a woman, tangled up like a pair of earthworms in a pot of dirt, each one indistinguishable from the other, and both of them mixed up with the soil itself.

"What's your *problem*?" she asked herself, the very way her mother had a million times before. She was careful to reproduce her mother's tone—judgment masquerading as concern.

Cassy was deeply ashamed of herself, and frightened that she was doomed to repeat this scenario forever, marching ad infinitum with the ranks of the unloving and unloved.

"What's your problem?" she wondered again.

She knew already what her mother thought. Emma was prepared to blame the girl's father for the endless string of disappointments her daughter dished out. His walking out on the family when Cassy was thirteen explained just about everything in her mother's book: the lack of a stable male figure, the poor example of throwing in the towel.

"Quitters never win," her mother told her often enough.

A drug-fueled sexcapade with a couple of perfect strangers was almost to be expected.

Cassy leaned back against the flimsy wooden headboard.

"What's the first thing you remember?" Dr. Winters asked her, years before. It had taken them months to get to this place.

"Today?" she asked, looking back at him in confusion.

Dr. Winters had been her mother's idea. He was much younger than the sort of shrink Emma normally turned up for her—not much older than Cassy was now.

"No," he said, smiling back at her. "When you were a girl."

"That's easy," she said, without a moment's doubt. "I was sitting on my mother's lap." She couldn't have been much older than four or five, but she remembered it as vividly as if it were yesterday. She'd been wearing short pants, she supposed, or some kind of skirt. Her legs were bare, at any rate, and Cassy felt the rough wool of her mother's slacks against the soft skin at the back of her legs. She remembered the scratchy feeling to this day, the warmth of her mother's flesh beneath: that padded perch of two long thighs, and the pillowy backrest of her mother's breasts.

Cassy exhaled softly.

"What were you just thinking?" Dr. Winters asked.

He must have seen her thoughts go roaming off. He seemed more interested in that than in the memory itself.

"She didn't like it," Cassy told him. That's what she'd been thinking.

"How so?" he asked.

Cassy shook her head. She wasn't sure exactly.

"Did she push you away?"

"No," she said. That wasn't it. Her mother let her stay where she was—she *tolerated* the girl sitting there—but Cassy knew she didn't like it. "You're awfully warm," her mother might say, or "Don't squirm, sweetie."

But Cassy never squirmed.

She'd never do a thing to jeopardize that fleeting prize—the warmth and safety of her mother's lap. The fault lay somewhere else inside her.

It's all ancient history now, she thought.

And as to her present predicament—waking up in that

mysterious bed—Cassy had no one to blame but herself. She was too ridiculous for words, running around on a Saturday night and picking up strangers in a crowded bar, dancing on a cloud of disco drugs. She couldn't pin that on anyone—not her father or her mother either.

Cassy stared hard at the knot of flesh beside her, until she was certain she'd counted every arm and every leg, until she was sure there wasn't another. She felt nearly vanquished by her gluey eyes and thick, parched tongue; by her shame at her behavior the night before; and now by this, her most vexing challenge of all: how to extricate herself from this crowded bed without one more second of contact with these two strangers.

The more she woke, the harder her head pounded.

It's time to step up, she thought—assume a little responsibility for herself.

Cassy swung her legs off the side of the bed, then twisted back to the couple behind her, afraid that the waves of motion might have roused them. She was safe still. They looked just as dead as before. She stood up from the mattress and aimed for the door, staggering a little with her first steps.

She found her balance soon enough.

Of course she did. Everything's going to be fine, she thought, taking the doorknob firmly in hand, its brass as cool in her sleep-warmed palm as a tumbler of ice water on a shimmering hot day. She didn't turn it, and she wouldn't let it go.

No, Cassy just held on tight.

To the casual observer, Cassy Sutton was every inch her mother's daughter: tall and brunette, exacting as hell. They were like topiary practically, mother and daughter—two stands of privet pruned smooth, and not a single trace of plant life left. They were too perfect really, having locked their messy, human selves away.

Cassy went to Smith College, just like Emma had, and she'd tried her hand at decorating even—in Emma's very shop—but that hadn't worked at all. It turned out that Cassy wasn't suited to a service business: she'd already exhausted her desire to please. Still, she ended up working in her mother's organization—floating around on the business side—most recently as president of the Emma Sutton Charitable Foundation, doling out precisely as much money as her mother's new accountants told her it was tax-advantageous to do.

But that's where the resemblance between them ended.

Like mothers and daughters from the beginning of time, Emma's appetites had affected her daughter's profoundly. Cassy had watched—firsthand, after all—as her mother slaved for money and power, the admiring acknowledgment of the whole wide world; and as Emma grew in fame and prestige, her daughter couldn't help but notice how lonely it was standing off to the side.

The girl yearned for a tender touch.

So it shouldn't have come as a huge surprise that she chose a different path for herself: dialing her focus all the way down, and shrinking the world to a table for two. It was as if she were looking out through the wrong end of Emma's telescope. Cassy had no use for crowds or fans; she couldn't care less for money or fame. Nothing interested her really—except the prospect of a lover's touch.

She'd made a career of finding it.

Cassy searched for lovers high and low, in nearly every place she went. She hunted straight through her waking life.

She'd be the first to admit she hadn't gotten very far—only tricking herself again and again, confusing heat for the genuine article. Still, she took her job every bit as seriously as Emma had taken her own.

Cassy hoped for the best, and settled for much, much less.

Case in point, she thought, taking one last look around the stuffy bedroom. She shook her head. How could she ever have thought she'd find what she was looking for here? She steeled herself hard and pulled the bedroom door open, marching past the threshold and closing the door behind her.

"There!" she exclaimed, sounding triumphant, but her eyes were squinting near to blindness, her shoulders hunched up around her ears. She walked down a short hallway, past the foyer, and into a perfectly ordinary living room, in what looked to be a smallish one-bedroom apartment—somewhere in the city of New York, she hoped.

She had no memory of setting foot in this place.

She picked up a glossy magazine from the low coffee table, a generic beauty smiling up at her. "Do You Really Want Him Back?" the headline blared. She turned it sideways and read the address off the paper mailing label:

> Karen Donaldson
> 22 Leroy Street, Apt. 4F
> New York, NY 10014

Cassy exhaled as if she'd been holding her breath.

Only downtown, she thought—not so far from her own apartment, up near Lincoln Center. It wasn't so good, of course, that she had no idea who this Karen Donaldson was, or the man in bed with her, for that matter, but Cassy was prepared to take things one step at a time. She knew there was no alternative really, practiced as she was in these disconcerting wake-ups, somewhere far from home.

Even so, she never laid her loneliness down for long.

She could convince herself in an instant—he might be the one!—all on the strength of a stranger's glance. But strangers, she found, after a night or two more, were rarely what they seemed to be. And even with the ones who showed a hint of promise, Cassy backtracked just as fast, turning the smallest imperfection into a man's fatal flaw.

What's your problem? she wondered.

Cassy was terrified—and not of the men, who generally turned out to be harmless enough. What she feared were the imperfections beneath her own lovely shell—those ugly marks that would drive anyone away.

Who could ever deal with those?

Time to leave, she thought.

Cassy gazed down to her wristwatch, but it wasn't there. She hoped it wasn't gone for good. She noticed then, as if for the first time, how naked she was—like Eve in the Garden. She didn't try to hide it either—no fig leaf for her. Cassy marched to the mirror that hung above the sofa and took a long, hard look, daring herself to see a picture of debauchery, a haggard face and worn, gray skin—but somehow she looked just as beautiful as ever: long and lean, with shiny brown hair that hung straight to her shoulders and features as crisp as a lemon-lime soda. Not even a smear of dried fluid, all crusty at the top of her thigh, detracted much from the overall effect.

Lubricant, she hoped.

Cassy needed to know what time it was.

She was supposed to be at her mother's apartment by six thirty, and she had to go home still, had to shower yet and change. She walked to the DVD player in the corner: "17:06," it flashed, in a blue fluorescent light—five o'clock in the afternoon.

That can't be right, she thought. But deep in her heart, Cassy was afraid it would be later than that. Five o'clock came as a small relief.

She'd slept through an entire day.

She looked around for her clothes and spotted a funny little gewgaw on the coffee table instead: just two or three inches tall, and shaped vaguely like a pearl onion, or an outsized teardrop in a rainbow of blues. She saw icy blue and navy blue, powder blue and teal, a trace of deep brownish blue at its base. She bent down to pick it up, admiring the smoothness of the thing in the palm of her hand. At first, she thought it was made of stone, but it was too light for that, she decided, too delicate. It was a porcelain teardrop.

She put it right back where she found it.

Cassy spotted her navy sweater, peeking out from beneath an upholstered chair. She knew she'd find her jeans and her bag in the sweater's vicinity, her silver wristwatch stowed away safely in one pocket or another. She began walking toward them, then stopped in her tracks.

She turned back to the coffee table and plucked the teardrop from its rightful place, stashing it safely in the palm of her hand.

It fit there perfectly.

She wrapped her fingers around its little body, hiding the thing completely from view. Just as she was about to spare a thought for poor Karen Donaldson—to wonder what that teardrop might mean to her—Cassy went a different way instead: I know just where I'll put it, she thought, picturing the small table in her living room, its ebonized top and bleached mahogany legs.

Those blues would look even better against the black.

Cassy felt happy for the first time in ages.

BY QUARTER PAST FIVE THAT AFTERNOON, BENJAMIN and his girlfriend, Melora, were sitting on the subway, rattling uptown toward Emma's place. Benjamin gazed across the aisle, through a window that was built into the car's sliding door. There was nothing to see but rushing motion though, all in subway-tunnel black; so he lifted his gaze a little higher, to a row of advertising placards beneath the car's domed roof. He fixed on a familiar image there: a photograph of a middle-aged man with the peachy-smooth skin of a six-year-old girl.

"Acne and blotchy patches," he read, in tall black letters.

He was mesmerized by the man's strange hairline. It looked as if it had been drawn on with a coarse orange marker. "Skin cancers and lesions," he read, in slightly smaller letters, on the next line down.

Emma had told him that Melora's name sounded vaguely cancerous to her, the morning after he'd first introduced them, on the sidewalk in front of her building, about three months before. "That's melanoma," he'd replied, angrily enough, but he knew she was a little right too.

Emma had been after him to bring the girl to dinner ever since, but Benjamin knew from experience—with his own rough mother—that it wasn't out of any Welcome Wagon instinct. Emma wanted to biopsy the girl and put her cells under a microscope. He'd managed to skirt the invitation, on Melora's behalf, up until now anyway—concocting flimsy excuses and prior engagements for his elusive girlfriend—but Emma wasn't one to relent.

"Bring her," she told him, "on Sunday night."

He'd never considered bringing Melora to meet his own mother, ensconced in her pretty Cape on the tip of Cape Cod, and she'd never requested the pleasure either. Still, he wondered at his knack for turning mothers up. He seemed to find them everywhere he went.

Like lice, he thought.

Benjamin gazed at Melora, sitting on the subway bench beside him. She looked back at him, with just the hint of a smile on her beautiful face, a little hopeful maybe. He'd told her that Emma was wild about her, of course—after their chance meeting on the street—but she was no fool. She'd rolled her eyes and shaken her head. "Like I care," she told him.

But how could you not? he wondered.

Benjamin had begun to suspect that his time with Melora was drawing to a close—the pleasant phase of it anyway. They'd been going out for just over six months. He'd met her on a ticket line at the Film Forum, when Emma was finishing up her house arrest. He'd had more time for matinees back then. They were the only two adults waiting to see the three o'clock show of *The Yearling*. He'd chatted her up while they waited in line, and managed to sit near her in the theater. He'd spent almost as much time gazing at her strong profile—entirely suitable for Mount Rushmore—as he had marveling at the ice water that ran through Jane Wyman's veins, refusing to let her son keep that lovely pet deer.

Benjamin asked for her number after the show.

And Melora beguiled him at the start—with her yoga-teacher charm and live-and-let-live air. She didn't seem at all the kind of girl who'd be bossing him around. Benjamin had enough experience in that department; he knew it didn't work for him. He had a real knack for pleasing women—for figuring out what they wanted, and for giving it to them too. It gave him tremendous pleasure to be that man. But Melora needed to take things one step further, always insisting on one thing or another—the restaurant, the movie, the taxi route even. He gave her what she asked for still, but he felt the pleasure of it stripped away. He could feel a strong resentment building up inside him, like dust accumulating on a window ledge.

He didn't complain about it. That would be too hard for him, but he suspected, as he sat there, that if he'd been able to elude Emma's invitation for a little longer, skate by for just a few more weeks, he might have avoided having to bring Melora around for good.

Benjamin looked away from the advertising placard.

He hadn't breathed a word since Twenty-third Street—nearly three stops now. He didn't want to be rude, but he didn't feel like dreaming up conversation-starters either. He flashed a glance in Melora's direction, then looked away fast.

"What's the matter?" she asked.

"Nothing," he said, looking back at her again. "I wish we were on our own tonight," he said. "I'm feeling a little tired."

"It's no wonder," she replied. "With all the caffeine you've had today."

Caffeine was one of Melora's hot buttons. It stunned him how often she could work the subject in. "Your metabolism must be like a roller coaster," she told him.

Benjamin regretted having to bring her along.

He'd informed Emma, over the phone, about her strict vegan diet—no meat, no fish, no poultry, no cheese.

"Eggs?" she'd asked, hopefully—picturing God-knows-what.

"Nope," he replied. "No eggs or dairy either."

He'd wanted to avoid any difficulty at the table. Melora wasn't the type to take things onto her plate politely and push them around. But he heard the long pause on Emma's end of the line. He knew his girlfriend didn't leave her room for much in the way of culinary magic. All she ever seemed to eat was brown rice and some kind of mushy, orange vegetable that he didn't recognize from any visit he'd ever made to a grocery store. Root vegetables, she called them.

Melora was going on about caffeine still.

"You don't say?" he said, in mock fascination. He'd heard it all a million times before.

"But it's true," she insisted, refusing to give in. "You'd be amazed at the improvement in your energy level," she said, "if you could just cut out the caffeine and white sugar."

The subway lurched to a stop at Fiftieth Street, and Benjamin's stomach lurched along with it. He'd forgotten to tell Emma that she wouldn't eat sugar either.

He shook his head and hoped for the best.

His stomach felt a little nervous to him, as if a shot of brown booze—bourbon maybe, or scotch—were swirling around inside him, burning away as the subway barreled over ancient tracks and took its turns too fast.

At the end of every weekend, before Benjamin was finished with his duties, Emma required a status report on all his various projects: tracking down that rare silver orchid in the swamps of Florida, and booking her Christmas holiday with frequent-flier miles alone; supervising the wallpaper hanger in the guest bedrooms, and checking the references of the new housekeeper. He'd be embarrassed to admit it, but it was his favorite part of the job—hands down. He prepared himself for it extravagantly, with beautifully organized lists that he wrote out longhand, each page flowing neatly to the next, all indexed and cross-referenced and updated to the very latest state-of-play.

Benjamin liked his moment in the sun.

Emma might ask a million thoughtful questions, or barely grunt at him in reply. He'd nearly learned to take her moods in stride, and for the most part, he knew that she was pleased with his work. Never more so, he suspected, than when she could cross an item off her list, nearly stabbing the paper through with the sharp nib of her pen, a wild flourish to signify completion. Emma liked to get things done. It was a welcome change for him too—working on jobs that *could* be finished, just by pressing forward and following up. Such a relief, he thought, compared with the intractable problems he wrestled all week in his work at school: the fractured families and financial struggles, the knots of unemployment and abuse, so many people at the breaking point. No amount of list-making ever seemed to improve things down there, and Benjamin rarely got to cross a single child off his list.

He reached for Melora's hand. He found himself wanting to.

Melora was always supportive of his work at school—interested in his cases, and the career he'd chosen for himself. He could tell that she was proud of him, and he didn't take that lightly. In a city of investment bankers, he knew that finding a beautiful woman who approved of social work was something of a coup. He rested the soft knot of their fingers against his churning stomach.

He felt the soothing relief of light pressure right away.

In the past few months, since Emma had come home from prison, Benjamin's Sunday presentations had grown to include dinner. He was slightly mystified by the development. He even had his own place at the table, as if he were a member of the family. He hated those dinners.

Whatever flush of pride he felt, first sitting down to dine, was long gone by now. Emma's strange indifference to him, followed by sudden bursts of interest, had progressed beyond confusing straight to tiresome. Worse, Benjamin was forced to suffer her daughter's fury at his inclusion, and Emma's strange ex-husband too, so jovial and irrelevant all at once. They were as bad as dinners with his own family—except that with Emma, attendance was mandatory.

He felt a flash of worry that Melora might become a regular guest. He didn't see how he could possibly handle Emma and Melora both, not simultaneously anyway.

Benjamin turned to her in his seat. He caught her studying him beneath the glare of the car's fluorescent lights.

"I have an idea," she said, her eyes lighting up as she wrinkled her nose.

Benjamin's heart sank. Melora thought she looked cute this way, with the nose-wrinkling and all. It usually signaled her wanting something.

"Let's go to the Whitney," she said—the art museum in Emma's neighborhood. "It's practically next door," she added. "And I'd love to show you those Sally Mann photographs."

Benjamin checked his watch.

He had plenty of time before his meeting with Emma, so he couldn't say that he was running late. He couldn't tell her that he needed more time to prepare either; he'd already told her he was ready. Still, a museum visit was about the last thing on earth he wanted.

He wondered if he could tell her about his nervous stomach, roiling like a tumbler of poisonous whiskey.

She'd probably want him to be honest.

Then she could go to the Whitney on her own, or they could arrange to visit some other time. But just then, Benjamin noticed that Melora had applied a light coat of pink lipstick in honor of the occasion: dinner with Emma, her boyfriend's boss. It was so faint he really had to look to find it. Melora never wore makeup, and Benjamin thought his heart might break—at her small gesture of support, and all the outsized forces that worked against it. He wanted to tell her that the pretty lipstick wouldn't make a jot of difference where they were going—about as useful as tying a bright red bow on a curly lamb that was already on the truck to the slaughterhouse.

He didn't say anything of the kind.

He just nodded his head and agreed to the museum visit—wanting to please her, on the one hand, and feeling resentful, on the other.

"Great," she said, sitting a little taller on the subway bench beside him.

Look at her, Benjamin thought, with annoyance flaring through him, like ancient newspaper taking fire from a match. Sitting tall as a mountain in that stupid winter coat of hers, trying to intimidate me with perfect posture.

He used to think that she was showing off, sitting ramrod straight like that—the way ballet dancers walked around on the street, with all that phony turnout, their legs swinging high from wide-open hips: look at me, they screamed, look at me. He felt a surge of anger rising up, but he tamped it down fast. He made a quick excuse instead: She is a yoga teacher, after all. He tried to convince himself that her perfectly straight back—her neck and chest lifted high—weren't meant as any criticism of him, or indifference to him either.

It's just the way she sits, he thought.

Benjamin had so much experience with demanding women. They'd been washed and combed into his head since he was a boy—turning to him briefly and bathing him in light, only to turn away again for much longer stretches, leaving him alone in the dark. He might have been better off, he thought, if they never looked at him in the first place.

Benjamin gazed down at the floor, focusing on the hem of Melora's strange winter coat; it came down in front like two toast points. He was sure that Emma would have something to say about that.

"Benny?" she said, a little insistently, the nickname dwarfed by a strict note in her voice.

Benjamin slumped a little lower on the hard orange bench, like a scarecrow in ratty overalls, no spine at all once it's taken down from those tall wooden pilings. He leaned into Melora like a child, taking shelter beneath her flaring shoulders and that strong, straight back, unfurled so wide.

"Sit up," she told him, as curt as a mother. "You'll hurt your back slouching that way."

Benjamin recognized the tone; he knew he'd put it there himself.

Still, he didn't do what he was told for a change. It wasn't easy for him either. He had to will himself to keep slumping down, to disregard the command of a determined woman.

A LITTLE LATER THAT AFTERNOON, EMMA PADDED into her brand-new kitchen, the kidskin soles of her soft Belgian loafers scarcely whispering against the wide planks of the wooden floor.

The room was all done up in navy and white: shiny blue appliances with brushed chrome trim, and matte white cupboards with blue porcelain pulls. Emma didn't begin to notice her pretty view of Central Park, or the winter sun that was fading back. She was much too distracted for that.

All I need is a little white sailor's cap, she thought, wincing as she studied her kitchen, which suddenly looked ridiculously nautical to her.

She grew nearly panicked over the color scheme.

Emma liked to get out in front of criticism, to nail herself hard before anyone else could.

She'd only had the apartment for six months; she bought it when she finished her house arrest. Ready for a change, she supposed, but it turned out that Emma didn't know much about changing course or reversing direction. What she knew was empire-building and muscling through—digging out Grand Canyons with ordinary kitchen spoons. So she shuffled her real estate instead, selling the sprawling place in Cold Spring Harbor. No more grounds or outbuildings for the tarnished queen of interior design, no more chicken coops either. She came to New York City and bought this place instead—a swank twelve-room affair on the corner of Park and Seventy-first, all crisp casement windows and burnished oak paneling.

The blue was definitely a mistake.

Emma looked all around her, as if her immaculate kitchen were filled with toxic waste. She hated errors. She always had, of course—who didn't?—but lately she'd come to fear them too, as if an inferior paint job, or the wrong kitchen tile, would betray some terrible lack inside her. Back in the old days, before her legal woes, Emma had been much better at pushing straight past her worries. She'd choose a tile and move along; she had faith in herself. But she was at sixes and sevens lately, almost herself again, but not—like an egg with a shadowy crack running down its shell, just a little more prone to danger and rough handling of every stripe, from the frontal attacks in the media to the rolling eyes of total strangers. She seemed to have lost her knack for muscling through.

She'd tried it that way, she supposed.

She saw where it led. In her case, to federal prison and an avalanche of nasty press, a warehouse full of canceled contracts and a near-perfect catalog of every tag-sale line she'd ever cut, a virtual roll call of every cherubic assistant she'd ever reduced to tears.

Emma wanted to find a different way—she *needed* to, really—but she hadn't the vaguest idea where to look.

She walked to her fancy Miele oven—a prototype model that wasn't even in production yet, its slippery blue enamel like a fresh coat of paint. She pushed a small silver button that illuminated the inside and peered in at her pork loin, roasting plump on a silvery wire rack, an enamel pan positioned beneath it to catch the fatty drippings.

Emma felt prickly heat at the nape of her neck.

"Old habits," she grumbled, turning quickly from the oven.

She massaged the back of her neck and felt the tingling dissipate like a pat of butter in a warm sauté pan—all wavy edges at first, then spreading out wide.

I'm just being ridiculous now, she thought, knitting her lips together and turning back to her Sunday roast. These oven lights had been around forever, for twenty-five years at least, and turning them on didn't disturb the meat at all. Still, Emma had been down this road often enough to know that rational thinking didn't scratch the surface of the way she really felt.

"Leave the meat alone, Emmy." That's what her mother always said, back in those far-flung days before oven lights, scolding her daughter for opening that heavy door once too often. "Let it cook already, will you?"

But somehow Emma could never leave a roasting pan alone, or a cake pan either, for that matter. Something in her needed to open the oven door wide, to supervise her handiwork in the light of day—on a minute-by-minute basis sometimes.

It wasn't so complicated really: nothing she cooked ever came out the same way twice, no matter how scrupulous she was about repeating the recipe—every step exactly like the last time, that last time precisely like the time before. Her results were phenomenal, of course; anyone would be thrilled to give a dinner like Emma Sutton—except for Emma Sutton, it turned out. She wanted things more dependably perfect than they ever turned out to be: the roast cooked to medium rare after precisely eighteen minutes a pound, the potatoes browned to golden after just so many minutes more. But cooking wasn't like that, she'd found, so she was obliged to look and look and look.

Of course, oven lights should have changed all that—letting her look all she liked without troubling the meat at all.

Well, they didn't, she thought, a little harshly.

She turned away from her roasting pork and took stock of her exquisite kitchen—as if to verify she really was a million miles and thirty years from her mother's little Cape in North Adams, Massachusetts—that squeaky old oven door.

She wasn't satisfied at all.

"That *blue*," she groaned, the failure vibrating deep within her. Nothing she ever made, or built—no matter how wonderful to the rest of the world—ever seemed to satisfy her. She could never seem to make things turn out right.

Emma knew that oven lights weren't the problem.

Still it's all worked out, she thought—or mostly it had. She turned back to the oven again. Emma considered her husband, Bobby—her ex-husband, she reminded herself, for nearly fifteen years at this point. They'd married young, when she was just finishing at Smith College and he was a brand-new lawyer in town. They'd grown up together, really. They were married for twenty years, and no matter how troubled their marriage was—and it was troubled, of course, Emma knew that—she would no more have thought of divorcing him than she would have thought of divorcing her arms and legs, or breaking up her collection of stainless roasting pans—sized small, medium, and large.

They *went* together, and at a certain point, Emma just assumed that her marriage was forever.

But forever comes and goes, she knew now.

She'd been stunned when he walked out on her—all those years before—his clichéd little valise in hand. It hadn't even occurred to her that all their bickering could come to such drastic ends. And how furious she was: she could have pulled every hair straight out of her head, like handfuls of weeds from a messy garden, her lustrous brown hanks in two clenched fists.

Such a long time ago, she thought, trying to settle herself down.

They'd been divorced by now for nearly as long as they'd been married—which made Bobby's recent reappearance even more surprising.

Emma looked back into the oven one more time, bending forward slightly at the waist, her knees straight inside soft flannel trousers. She brought her face down close to the oven door, her nose pressed up against the insulated glass. She felt the oven's heat against her smooth cheeks. She studied the pork loin that was shimmering in the oven's wavy heat—just two frosted lights, mounted onto the back wall, illuminating the scene. She scarcely saw the roast at first. It was all decor that caught her eye: the coarse peppercorns scattered around the meat, glinting like sequins on a black evening dress, the satiny shards of garlic that peeked out from all the tiny slits she'd cut into the roast. She looked practically starstruck in the reflection of the glass, like a teenage girl with a movie magazine in her lap.

"So beautiful," she marveled—only to second-guess herself a moment later: Or does it look a little dry?

Emma pulled the oven door open and slid the roasting pan forward on its silvery wire rack. She looked and looked, for such a long, long time that she seemed to lose her place entirely—that meat may as well have been an ancient artifact under museum glass, or a bumpy rock from the surface of the moon.

Who knows? she admitted, finally. What wouldn't look dry roasting in four hundred degrees of heat?

So she basted the pork with a long-handled spoon, and saw, once it was moistened like that, that it was browning right on schedule, its skin just beginning to bubble up and crisp. Thank God, she thought, so gratefully—the timing of her roast some kind of heavenly mystery.

When they first sent Emma up to Rochester, New York, to the federal prison there, she was stunned when Bobby turned up—that very first week. "Just to visit," he told her. She hadn't seen him in years. And she was suspicious, of course—assumed that he'd only come to gloat.

Emma was powerfully ashamed of herself.

It was an awkward visit—not half an hour long, filled more with pauses than with talk. But he turned up again the very next week, and the week after that too; and little by little, they found a kind of easiness again—the rancor of their terrible split seemed nearly clownish, fighting for so long over quite so little.

It didn't take many more weeks of visiting for Emma to see that Bobby didn't want her brought low.

God knows what he *did* want, she thought—but it wasn't that.

There weren't many other visitors either, she had to admit. But every week brought another visit from Bobby, all through her prison stretch and the home confinement too; and on his very last visit, on the very last day, Bobby asked her to marry him again.

Such a fool, she thought—shaking her head at the memory of it, but not quite keeping a smile from her lips either.

She took the proposal itself as a vindication of sorts: an admission that he'd been wrong to leave her all those years before. Emma felt relieved at her exoneration—on that count at least. She could use the opportunity to rewrite history, and she had to admit, she loved her husband still.

She suggested that he move back in with her instead—which he did, nearly six months before, right into the new apartment on Park and Seventy-first.

Emma gazed down into the roasting pan.

It was then she noticed the vegetables that were scattered around the meat—the carrots and potatoes and leeks—all hapless and thoroughly uncooked. She sighed through slightly parted lips, tamping down the fire of culinary pride. Her vegetables were greasy with olive oil and littered with spices—like sticky skin at a public beach. Not done at all, she saw, excavating deep into the roasting pan with her long-handled spoon, praying for brown edges on the underside: no such luck.

She checked the temperature knob and then her wristwatch: same cooking time, same heat—but definitely not the same. She didn't need her mother to tell her that she wasn't helping matters, keeping the oven door open like that, staring down into the open roaster while the oven's precious heat tumbled all around the room. But she couldn't bear to close the oven door either. Not yet, she thought—not until she'd worked out some kind of salvage plan for her meal.

She stood stock-still for a moment.

"Damn that Melora," she spat.

She felt her body sizzling with heat, as if she were roasting too—hissing like a snake on desert sand. Emma had made her diagnosis. There were too many vegetables. She'd nearly doubled the number she put in the roaster, trying to accommodate Benjamin's girlfriend and her ridiculous vegan diet.

That's got to be it, she thought, gazing down at her failure-in-progress, simmering in the juices of her own annoyance.

Emma pushed the roaster back into the oven. She felt like slamming the door behind it. I suppose I can take the pork out first, she thought—exhaling long—and let the vegetables cook a little longer.

She felt her neck relaxing.

That might work, she thought.

She shook her head at Melora's foolishness, at the strange piety of refusing her lovely pork roast. "Damn hippie," she grumbled, picturing the girl in the long gypsy skirt she'd been wearing when they met on the street—but Emma didn't care about Melora. She barely knew her. She was only savoring the taste of her anger—like a tasty dripping from her succulent roast, falling safely onto the enameled pan beneath.

GRACIE BREEZED INTO HER BEDROOM LIKE A DIMPLY child actress, all sweet and fake, excited at the prospect of "dressing up" later. She swung the door closed behind her, jaunty head lifted high—but the little girl's shirt was inside out, and her gait all stop-and-start, every step another jerky hitch, as if she were losing her nerve midway through. And when the door slammed louder than she'd ever intended, the dam broke wide: her eyes hopping, panicked, from place to place, and her mouth twitching a little, on the verge of tears.

She'd been having such a nice time too.

She'd tiptoed into her mother's room, as careful as an Indian scout, pressing her ear against the bedroom wall. Mommy's sleeping still, she decided—as good a guess as any.

She'd left her mother napping on the living room sofa, not five minutes before.

Gracie made a beeline for her mother's chest of drawers.

Her Valentine project had inspired her. She was looking for finery—a silky scarf or an old piece of lace—something more to cut up and paste to her handmade cards.

To make them extra nice, she thought.

She found a couple of embroidered hankies that she thought would do the trick. From there, it was just a skip and a jump to her mother's closet. She headed for the frilliest dresses, the ones her mother never wore—all frothy skirts and silky fabrics. She pulled them on, right over her head, in front of the mirror on the closet door, twirling and posing and making slinky faces.

Nothing fit, not one single thing, but Gracie didn't care. She just hitched up the skirts with a satiny blue sash and gave them a flick with her chubby wrists.

So pretty, she thought—like a ballroom dancer—that extra little flourish, just for effect.

If she had to do it over again, she might not have tried the pink swimsuit. It was at once too big and ferociously small, with its strappy straps hanging down, and leg holes drooping to the middle of her thighs, yet dangerously tight over her big, round belly. She looked like a sausage link in pretty pink casing.

Gracie studied herself in the mirror—hard.

The suit looked on the verge of ripping.

Just needs a belt, she decided, nodding at her reflection in the full-length mirror. She tied the blue sash around her middle, concealing as much of her tummy as she could. She only wanted some high heels then, fishing through an old box on the closet floor, where her mother had packed the really high ones away. Gracie slipped a pair of white shoes on her feet—like a Miss America with a mistied sash.

She flipped through a photo album she found in the box, studying herself in the mirror as she did, dipping her left shoulder low—just a little kittenish—alternating looks between her reflection and the pictures in the album.

The photographs were arranged chronologically, as if the subject—a little girl—were growing up before her eyes: just a baby, first, and then a little older. She knew it wasn't her, studying the toddler on the next set of pages. She'd seen plenty of photos of herself. She was sturdier than this, and rounder too. There were pictures of the girl at Gracie's age, and then a little older still.

I think it's Mommy, she decided finally.

It didn't take much longer—or many more pages—for Gracie to think that she might die. She ripped off the swimsuit and kicked the heels back into their box, tossing the photo album in right after it.

Her mother had been beautiful, she saw, even as a girl. Slim and pretty, with large brown eyes.

I'm not getting a single Valentine, she thought, tossing the frilly hankies into the back of her mother's closet.

She felt betrayal burning up and down her naked body.

Her mother had always had long, straight hair.

She put her own clothes back on fast.

Gracie had thought her mother was like her when she was little. Fat, she meant, without going so far as actually thinking the word. And the girl had simply assumed that, one day, she'd grow into her mother, as her mother was now—all slim and lovely, stretched out long on the living room sofa.

She walked down the hall with a fluttering in her chest.

Gracie knew she wasn't like her mother at all.

"I get to dress up later," she said out loud, walking into her bedroom—all sitcom happy. She was determined to put that photo album right out of her head, but the image of herself in a tight pink swimsuit, so fat and ugly, as she gazed at pictures of her mother as a pretty little girl, stretched wide as Lycra before her eyes.

"I think I'll wear my yellow dress," she added, sounding la-di-da, but her fear grew sharper with every additional lap she walked around her little room. "You know," she said, "the one with the pretty flowers sewn right on."

She only had the one dress.

Gracie looked all around, searching for something to light on. She was determined to pretend the whole thing never happened. She spotted a lumpy stuffed horse on top of her toy chest, all mismatched eyes and dingy white fur, the eldest of her toy companions, and the only one that could supply an ounce of comfort to her still, on those rare occasions when she thought to look to stuffed animals for comfort at all. She seized on it.

"Oatsy!" she cried, as if she were meeting a long-lost lover on a snowy train platform. She hugged the horsey close, and carried it with her to her perch on the bed.

But one stuffed horse was not going to do the trick.

She knew that as soon as she sat down.

So she frisked back to the toy chest and flung open its hinged top, surveying all her options. Gracie looked down deep, like a fireman to the bottom of a deep, deep well, searching for the little boy trapped at the bottom. She saw them in a jumble then, all the dolls and velvety animals that had meant something to her once, if only for an afternoon. She pulled them out, one by one—three or four of them, and then some more; she arranged them carefully in a semicircle on the floor, a platoon of campfire girls sitting around half of a crackling bright flame: Gracie, herself, its center point, leaning back against the foot of her bed.

She smiled at the warmth of so much attention.

She felt the pleasure of her kindness too—liberating all those forgotten dollies, bringing them back into the light of day—like throwing another log on the campfire, so warm and crackling bright.

"I get to wear my shiny shoes," she said, addressing the assembly. She was careful not to brag, but those shoes did go with her yellow party dress. Gracie saw them as her just deserts, and not merely for her kindness to half a dozen stuffed animals. She knew enough to know that a reward was in order—for soldiering on, marching straight past that photo album and the pretty little girl inside.

She imagined the pleasure of slipping into those shiny shoes—all stiff and black. She closed her eyes and lifted her chin, picturing the silky bows at their toes. Gracie ran to the shoe bin and touched the patent leather with just the tip of her finger. She didn't want to leave a smudge. Then she frisked to the closet and took the yellow party dress down from its place of honor on the far left side, the very first item on her closet rod.

It was the prettiest shade of yellow she could imagine. Like a stick of butter, she thought.

Gracie felt calm again as her fingers brushed against the yellow taffeta skirt—just a little stiff. She marveled at the tiny white flowers and bright green stems that were embroidered all around the dress. She pressed her nose into the fabric, and smelled the sachet she'd made at school. Roses! she thought.

The pretty dress even smelled pretty.

She carried it back to the bed with her, and laid it down as carefully as she could, its neck up by her pillow and the bottom hem stretching down, as if the dress had agreed to a little nap. Her mother had told her they were going to a party that night—at a church, she'd said. And not their regular church either—some different one, for another religion—and even though she hadn't asked specifically, Gracie was pretty sure that a nighttime party at a brand-new church would have to be considered a Special Occasion.

And Special Occasions are what a dress-up dress is for. That's what her mother always said.

She couldn't wait to slip it over her head, waiting patiently while her mother did up all the tiny buttons that ran down the back. Not to mention the pleasure of walking in those shiny black shoes she wished she could wear every day.

"I know!" she said giddily, but natural too—child actress no more. "Who'd like a cookie?" she asked, addressing all the dollies that were laid out on the floor.

She paused a moment, as if to hear.

"Me too!" she said, skipping back to the closet one more time, digging out a brand-new box of gingersnaps that she'd hidden at the bottom of her special box. She'd stolen them from her grandfather's cupboard while he was in another room, stashing them in her pink backpack.

Gracie opened the box carefully, determined not to tear the cardboard tab that fit so neatly into the slit on the other side. She unfolded the waxy paper that lined the orange box and plucked a cookie out. She popped it into her mouth, chewing just enough to make a doughy paste, which she fingered all over her teeth and gums, coating them in brownish black, then she ran her tongue over the sweetness, with its sharp hint of spice just beneath.

Gracie dealt out cookies to every dolly in the circle.

Then she ate another one herself.

She loved feeling so generous and good, including them all—a tasty cookie for every last one of them—even though she knew how this game ended, every single time.

Chapter 4

SUNDAY LUNCH:
A (Secret) Turkey Sandwich

IN A BUILDING ALMOST DIRECTLY ACROSS THE park from Emma's, Bobby Sutton wrestled a key into a tight Yale lock. He pulled the door toward him, then lifted it up; he knew that only when he'd reached the perfect longitude of lifting and latitude of pulling would he be able to turn his key in that miserable lock.

It always took him several tries.

He was interrupted by the groaning machinery of the elevator, its metal doors opening at the end of the long corridor. He looked up fast, a little squirrelly; he was afraid it might be Emma.

Of course it's not, he thought—once he'd seen for himself that it wasn't.

Bobby was relieved, but every bit as guilty, peering down the beige hallway. It was just the girl from across the hall, with the beautiful figure and the homely face.

Bobby went back to his lock.

It was only his comings and goings from this secret place that gave him pause. He felt happy and relaxed when he was safely inside. He smiled at the girl as she approached, nodded—the way he did with their neighbors on Park Avenue. Friendly, he thought, but not too much.

"Howdy," the girl twanged, in a southern-sounding drawl, breezing right past him down the center of the corridor. She was moving fast—like a plane that had just touched down to land, bumpy and barely under control.

Her voice was a little loud for the narrow hallway.

"Well, hello, hello," Bobby replied, all hearty exuberance then, as if he'd always meant to speak to her—trying to mask his unfamiliarity with the local customs. He was such a pleasant man, the last thing he wanted was to give offense. He made a mental note for next time: a smile and a nod won't do over here.

Bobby went back to his lock—to all his useless lifting and pulling.

He heard the girl's keys jangling on the other side of the corridor. He heard her key turn quickly in its lock. He'd forgotten all about her since the last time he'd seen her there—just coming in as he was leaving, or vice versa maybe. She looked fearless in that short red coat that hugged her breasts, those shiny black boots with their pointy heels. There was a wide swath of naked skin where the coat left off and the boots had yet to begin—a sexy white line down the center of a road.

She doesn't let that face slow her down, he thought, not for a second. It was a sound calculation on her part too. There was nothing to be done for it, after all, with her nose so large and her mouth all slack, those beady little eyes set close.

Bobby admired bravery of every stripe. It was one of the things he liked best about Emma.

He went fumbling back to his keys.

"It's a bitch of a lock," she said, "isn't it?"—her southern accent gone with the wind. She crossed the hall and stood right beside him, in front of his metal door. "The guy before you used to leave it unlocked," she told him.

Bobby felt the chill of the outdoors on her tight red coat. He smelled it on her mousy brown hair. "Well, I *thought* I had it figured out," he said, looking down at his useless arms, all encased in navy cashmere. "But I'm having a terrible time with it today," he said, pulling the key back out of the lock and letting his arms fall down to his sides.

The girl plucked the key right out of his hands.

Bobby was less startled than he would have thought.

"Trick is," she said, "you've got to push it as hard as you can."

"The key?" he asked.

"No," she replied, rolling her eyes, as if she were bowled over by his massive stupidity. "The door," she sang, pushing her shoulder hard against it. He watched the fluttering musculature of her thighs as she pressed her weight against the door. He heard his key turning in the lock.

"See?" she said.

"Well done," he told her.

Bobby didn't remember anything about pushing. In fact, he was fairly certain that his pulling-and-lifting method worked here too. He wasn't quite willing to abandon it yet, but it was hard to disagree with success.

He thanked her.

"*De rien*," she said, lifting her voice up high at the end and batting her beady eyes—the southern belle gone straight to France. She went to such lengths, he thought, to make herself larger than life, which put him in mind of Emma all over again. She dropped the keys into the palm of his hand—from a height—so they gathered velocity as they fell, landing hard against his soft skin.

"There you go," she said, with a lilt in her voice.

Bobby wondered if it was some other apartment door that he was meant to lift and pull. There'd been any number of doors like these over the years. He placed the keys, deliberately, in a small compartment of his briefcase. He was careful to zip it shut. He was adamant about avoiding mix-ups, especially now that he'd moved in with Emma. He didn't want these keys turning up in a trouser pocket, in a jumble of American Express receipts, landing on the foyer table along with the mail.

And they won't, he thought, not as long as I'm careful about it.

"Going out?" the girl asked.

"Yes," he said, "I've got some errands to run."

He was heading back to Emma's place. He'd been gone for a couple of hours already. He didn't want to push his luck.

"It's freezing out there," she said, lifting her shoulders up around her ears, as if an arctic gust had just blown through, making her red coat even shorter at her thighs.

Bobby wondered if the girl thought he lived there. He only came around a couple of times a week, but she wouldn't know that.

He wondered if she had any notion of a "secret apartment."

As a young man, practically a newlywed still, Bobby had rented a small apartment—not so different from this one, he thought—in an ordinary building on the Upper West Side: Sixty-sixth Street, he remembered, just off Broadway. He kept it a secret from Emma, of course. He needed to have a place apart, safe from all her meddling, where he wasn't under glass.

Bobby could see that young man still, with a slimmer waist and a jowl-free jaw, not so different from the man who stood in that hallway then: kindly and good-natured, a little weak. He was no match for Emma at all. So he rented a small apartment, which he set up like a newlywed of one—his bride gone missing. He remembered pondering the arrangement of the living room so carefully. Maybe he should try the couch over there?

Emma wouldn't dream of consulting him on such questions.

It hardly matters now, he thought, which was true enough, of course, but he still felt a pang, wondering what life might have been like with a woman who actually listened to his opinion every once in a while.

Eventually, the apartment on Sixty-sixth Street gave way to another, somewhere nearby—the next in a long line of secret apartments. He'd rarely been without one for as long as he'd been married to Emma. He lived in one of them even, after the two of them separated, all those years before. They were always in this neighborhood, and always fairly nondescript, but Bobby took tremendous care in arranging them. They were a comfort to him.

More like home, he thought, than any of the places he'd lived with Emma.

He'd taken this last one just a week or two after moving back in with her. He'd forgotten the level of scrutiny she put him under, after all those years of living out from under her watchful eye.

He'd come over that afternoon for just an hour or two, to stretch out on the sofa and read the Sunday paper. He was leaving in fine fettle—nicely restored, as from a long winter's nap—with a crisp glass of wine under his belt and a roast turkey sandwich from the deli on the corner.

"I haven't seen you around lately," the girl said.

He'd told Emma he was going to the office.

"I've been traveling," he replied. Bobby wondered whether he'd ever known the girl's name. He suspected not.

"For pleasure?" she asked, smiling at him.

He watched her place the toe of her boot a little farther out in front of her. She began to wriggle it as if she were crushing out a cigarette.

"No," he said, shaking his head, "all for work."

Bobby hadn't been out of town since Christmas.

"Well, I've missed seeing you," she told him, a little kittenish.

He recognized, finally, that the girl was flirting with him. He smiled to himself, having assumed—in all his guilt—that she was trying to pin down some inconsistency in his story, or trick an admission out of him, the way that Emma might have. He felt relieved, but not interested at all. He couldn't imagine why such a young girl would be flirting with him in the first place.

She was barely Cassy's age, practically half his own.

The girl kept smiling at him, her eyes locked onto his.

Then again, he thought—a little emboldened by her interest—why shouldn't she flirt? He was a good-looking man, nearly six feet two and solidly built, with the smooth, clear skin of a much younger man, and a full head of salt-and-pepper hair. I'm not so bad, he thought—and he had some money too, which might compensate for a few extra years.

But the girl didn't seem like that to him, not at all. She was just high-spirited.

Bobby had never had much trouble finding women. He found them too easily, in fact, and his spate of secret apartments had come in handy for trysts as well. But at sixty-four, he was old enough to be this girl's father, and he'd never gone in for that sort of thing. What's more, he'd curtailed his romantic high jinks lately. He was after a more mature companionship nowadays—some mutual pampering, not too much heat.

He was hopeful of his reconciliation with Emma.

Bobby looked down at his expensive shoes, willfully breaking contact with the girl's insistent gaze. He transferred his briefcase heavily from one hand to the other.

"Well, don't be a stranger," she said, the arc of flirtation on its downward trajectory.

He was glad to watch her turn away, back to her own door then. Bobby walked down the long hallway, all covered in wall-to-wall carpeting—a mauve ground with a small, insistent pattern printed on it, like a swarm of busy ants. He passed a succession of metal doors, all painted beige, just like his own. Ten of them, he'd bet, every five paces or so, and every one of them exactly the same.

That's twenty apartments a floor, he thought.

They had the landing to themselves at home.

Bobby called for the elevator, its doors opening the very

second he pushed the shiny gold button. It must have been waiting since the girl decamped. He stood inside the elevator cab, waiting for the doors to close again. He heard the fluorescence of the tiny lights that were set into the hallway ceiling, ticking away like impotent time bombs. He'd heard them from the first moment he'd walked into the place—just ticking and ticking—but no explosion yet.

"DAMN BLACKMAN," TINA MUTTERED, ANNOYED with Benjamin and mildly attracted to him both. Even as recently as their meeting on Friday—the two of them gazing at each other through veils of mistrust—Tina had felt strangely drawn to him. She'd gone to special pains to dress that morning, for a meeting with Benjamin at the very end of the day. She might be crazy, but she suspected, from time to time, that he returned her interest. They were like lame tulip bulbs in April—fighting *not* to push their heads above ground.

But why, she wondered? Tina supposed she'd never work it out.

And she couldn't blame Benjamin for her current problem. It was her fault—not his—that Gracie thought they were going to a party that night. Benjamin may have recommended the Diet Club to her, and he was definitely the one who told her that the group that met at the Baptist church on Sunday nights specialized in families and children, but Tina was the one who'd upgraded a support group for fat kids into some kind of party.

Much as she'd like to, she couldn't blame him.

It wouldn't hurt, she thought, if she met a decent guy every once in a while.

Tina steeled herself as she walked down the hall to Gracie's room. Better to get it over with, she decided—moving slower with every step, as if she were crossing the Mojave Desert. The corridor was only ten feet long.

"Sweetie?" she said, from outside the door.

There was no reply. Tina didn't hear the girl inside either.

"Gracie?" she called, opening the door.

The first thing she saw was a yellow dress laid out on the bed, its lacy neckline beneath the pillow. It looked like a body in a coffin.

That's my doing, she thought, wanting to crucify herself on a cross of cheap yellow taffeta.

"What the hell?" she mumbled, taking in the balance of the scene.

She saw Gracie on the floor, leaning up against her bed, half a dozen stuffed animals arranged all around her—a cookie in front of every one of them, and the orange box in Gracie's hands.

Tina walked into the room.

She saw a trail of crumbs running down the front of Gracie's shirt.

"What's going on in here?" she asked, failing to keep her voice as neutral as she'd intended. "Sweetie," she added—in recognition. She watched her daughter stash the box of cookies behind her back, her head hanging down as she salted the evidence away.

"Sweetie?" she said, but much kinder this time. She hated to see her feeling ashamed.

"I'm supposed to say, 'Come in,' " Gracie told her, "before you open the door, Mommy."

"That's true," Tina replied.

No defense like a good offense either, she thought, admiring the girl's pluck. "Next time I will," she told her. She decided not to say anything about the cookies for the moment.

Where the hell did she get them? Tina wondered.

She'd never bought a box of gingersnaps in her life. Every once in a while, Tina caught Gracie with a small stash of secret food—cookies, usually, or those awful little snack cakes. She suspected her father of breaking down, giving in to the girl—when he picked her up from school maybe, or when she visited him at his apartment. He swore he didn't give her junk though, or not much of it anyway, and Tina believed him. What's more, she knew it would take a lot more than an occasional gingersnap or Hostess Twinkie to have gotten the girl to the state she was in—twenty pounds overweight at the age of nine.

Tina gazed back at Gracie's bed, as if to change the subject.

It wasn't just the dress. She saw a pair of bobby socks, all snowy white with lacy yellow edging, and a pair of patent leather shoes, their shiny toes peeking out from under the bed.

You'd think she was going to a wedding, Tina thought.

She began to have misgivings about the Diet Club. She knew that Benjamin wanted them to go. It might be useful for a concerned mother, but Gracie was only a child. What could they possibly do there, she wondered, that would be worth a damn to her? Talk about calories and exercise?

She pictured cautionary filmstrips about the lives of fat children.

Tina saw a long yellow ribbon dangling over the edge of the bed, not quite touching the floor. Gracie liked to wear it in her hair.

Her heart sank deeper.

She wasn't taking her daughter to the Baptist church that night; she knew it in a flash. She wasn't going to sit her in a room brimming with fat kids. Tina might not have a solution to Gracie's problem yet; she might not have a diagnosis even, but that was her problem, not Gracie's. She was going to shield her daughter from places like the Diet Club, and Benjamin Blackman could go straight to hell if he didn't like it.

Gracie didn't need to be told she was fat.

It's not exactly breaking news, Tina thought.

The little girl was already powerfully aware of her body, she was sure of that much—ashamed of the rolls of fat that showed when she sat in the bathtub, the way she towered over her classmates on the playground at school.

How could she not be? Tina wondered.

She wasn't going to rub her nose in it, not any more than she already had.

"Mommy?" the girl asked softly.

Tina looked down at her.

"Can you turn that frown upside down?" she asked, repeating a line from one of her favorite television shows.

Tina was instantly sorry she'd let her concern show.

She looked back at Gracie, as if weighing the request—tapping an index finger against her chin. "You know," Tina said, dragging it out, as if she could go either way, "I think I *can* turn my frown upside down"—all the words coming out in a rush. She made a funny face too: a big, toothy smile, and her eyes as wide as she could manage.

Gracie giggled.

Tina sat down on the floor beside her and wrapped an arm around her daughter's shoulder.

"I'm sorry about the cookies, Mommy."

"That's okay," she said. Tina meant it too: the cookies were perfectly okay. She watched confusion bloom on her daughter's face. She must have thought she'd be in trouble.

"Are they good?" she asked.

Gracie nodded with enthusiasm, a cheerful smile peeking out.

"*That* good?" Tina asked, sounding impressed. "Well, pass them over then," she said, taking the box of cookies from Gracie's outstretched hand. She plucked one out and ate it thoughtfully. "Mmm," she hummed—not bad at all.

She was going to have to talk to her father again about giving the girl sweets.

Gracie burrowed a little deeper into her mother's body.

Tina felt proud of her close escape, grateful that she'd let the awkward moment pass. Why should she be angry? Because the little girl was hungry? Because she wanted a cookie?

Tina decided something else then too, which had been a long time in coming: there had to be something wrong with the girl, physically wrong. Gracie wasn't fat because she sneaked the occasional gingersnap, or a dozen of them—and Blackman and that bitch school nurse should stop blaming and start helping. They'd be hearing from her, she thought, a burst of confidence shining through.

She offered the girl a cookie.

Gracie shook her head warily.

She probably wants it too, Tina thought, relieved that the girl hadn't taken her up on her offer. She closed the box up tight.

"I've got some good news and some bad news," Tina said. "Which would you like first?"

"Bad, please," Gracie announced, without the slightest hesitation, her face composed, ready for the worst.

"I'm afraid the party's canceled," she said. It was the easiest out she could imagine.

Gracie looked unmoved. "Why?" she asked, her voice flat.

"You know," Tina replied, "I'm not exactly sure. I'm sorry though. I know you were looking forward to it."

"Not really," Gracie said.

"Is that true?" Tina asked.

Gracie nodded. "I was looking forward to dressing up," she said.

"I can see that," Tina told her, motioning toward the finery on the bed.

Gracie looked at the dress with a little sigh.

"What's the good news?" she asked.

"Well, I thought we could go down to the Rec Center and have ourselves some fun," Tina said—inventing her good news on the fly, the same way she'd devised the bad. "We could go swimming if you want?"

"Swimming in *winter*?" Gracie cried, giggling at the very idea.

Tina nodded, smiling, squeezing her daughter's arm with pleasure. "So what do you think of that idea?" she asked.

"I think that's very, very, very good news," Gracie said.

Tina stood up and walked toward the bed. She picked up the yellow dress on its sweetly scented hanger and danced it back to the closet, her daughter watching her every step. She twirled the taffeta, flicking it out in front of her—like a bullfighter's cape in canary yellow.

Gracie was transfixed.

Tina prayed that the pool would be open.

EMMA SLID THE ROASTING PAN BACK INTO THE oven, switching off the interior light with a flourish that looked a little like victory. She walked to the dining room to check on the table she'd set earlier that day.

"Oh," she cried, nearly bumping into Bobby when she pushed though the swinging service door—its useless little porthole window about six inches too low for her, or anyone other than a smallish child, ever to see through properly.

"Sorry, dear," he said.

He held his palm flat against the far side of the door. He wouldn't let her push another inch until he'd gotten himself out of its swinging path.

"I didn't mean to startle you," he said.

She hadn't heard him come back in.

Emma watched him gazing at the dining table. It was beautifully set, of course, but she knew Bobby well enough to know that he wouldn't care about that. She watched a mystified look take hold of his handsome face. He wasn't worried about serving pieces, or whether she'd remembered the bread plates. Emma didn't have the faintest idea what Bobby was doing in the dining room then, but she knew with certainty that they were on different errands there.

"Who's coming to dinner?" he asked finally, smiling like a child—her answer the toy surprise waiting for him at the bottom of a cereal box.

"It's *Sunday*," Emma said—to remind him.

But Bobby looked puzzled still. She gazed at his strong features—the deep-set eyes and Roman nose; she watched him worrying his lower lip with his two front teeth. He had no idea.

"Cassy," she told him, only slightly surprised by the chill in her voice. "Your daughter comes to dinner on Sunday nights." Emma's surprise led quickly to hurt, which was just a brief pit stop on the road to anger.

"Honestly!" she huffed.

She didn't want to make too big a fuss about it, but Cassy had been coming to dinner every Sunday night since Bobby moved back in.

Emma needed to change the subject.

She began surveying the table instead, counting the number of settings she'd laid. But she couldn't quite turn the page. Look at him, she thought, taking her husband in—that luxurious mane of curly hair.

Does he even *care*? she wondered.

She hoped he did.

Maybe he was confused? She wanted to give him the benefit of the doubt. Emma checked the napkins then, scouting for wrinkles. She liked a crisp fold. Checking the table always made her feel better.

But how do you forget a thing like that, she wondered—the same dinner, with the same people, every single week? She felt her anger rising up like a tide, its undertow of sadness eddying right beneath the surface.

He probably has to cancel a date with one of his little cupcakes, she thought, her anger seeping out.

Emma had a strong desire to speak again, though she had nothing particular to say, nothing that Bobby wouldn't have heard a thousand times before. She only wanted the feeling of something sharp passing her lips.

Not now, she decided, dragging herself back from the edge of speech, gripping her anger and drawing it close—a silent bride with a fiery bouquet.

Emma felt proud of her tact.

Back in the old days, she used to give way to cyclonic temper tantrums, earth-changing eruptions she hoped might force her husband's hand. Why can't he give me the respect I deserve? That's all Emma wanted to know. It was like the title track of a well-worn record album with her. She knew its flip side just as well: I should have left him first. But Emma didn't want to leave Bobby—not at all. She was delighted to have her husband back, and she knew very well that no material changes in him would be forthcoming.

So what was the use of a temper tantrum?

She didn't even let herself fantasize about them anymore. All they ever did was swing the power over to his side of the ledger. They never got her what she wanted—which was ironic really, because she wanted so little from him.

Emma wasn't one of those wives looking for a soul mate.

God, no, she thought.

The prospect of all that talking made her seriously tired. She could hardly bear to have women friends, in fact, for all the constant *sharing* they required.

No, Emma had always wanted something quite different from her husband, and from their marriage: a thorough immersion in each other's daily lives. It might not sound like much, but it sounded perfect to her. Calendars synched up, and appointments doubly confirmed, whereabouts forever known. That was all she'd ever wanted—for him to know about her auctions on Saturday morning, and the family dinner on Sunday night.

Is that too much to ask, she wondered, for intertwined minutiae, no messiness at all?

Of course, Emma never asked for anything—not outright anyway. For her, expressing need of any stripe, especially one so naked as that, would be worse than whistling out on the street, or letting her shoes clap loud against the pavement when she walked.

She looked up from the dining table.

It was no use. She was too distracted to check the table settings properly. She'd have to come back later. She looked over at Bobby again; he didn't look chastened in the least.

That's the problem, she thought, feeling so defeated, as if she'd waged a ten years' war without speaking a single word. He didn't feel guilty.

Emma knew that wasn't the whole problem. Once upon a time, Bobby had wanted a different kind of marriage with her too: all freewheeling and sexy and close. He wanted to talk about their troubles, and he wanted regular sex. He wanted to be *there* for her—like a cheesy love song come to life. She supposed it was romantic, in a way, but Emma couldn't have a marriage like that; it would be much too much for her. She wouldn't even try, and since the details of her engagement calendar didn't interest him in the least, no one was getting what they wanted in the Sutton household.

And the damned thing still won't die, she thought, nearly smiling as she shook her head.

"You look nice," Bobby told her.

Emma laughed at the ridiculousness of it: missing all her cues, as usual—the scowling face and steely voice, her erect spine, all gone to waste. She looked down at her gray wool slacks and the matching cashmere sweater, all plain and perfect.

And I don't look any nicer than usual, she thought, as a matter of fact.

"Thank you," she replied, smiling back at him.

"I'm going to go in to finish the paper," Bobby said. "Before Cassy gets here," he added, walking out.

Emma didn't believe him for a second. He probably has to cancel whichever chippie he has lined up for tonight, she thought. She knew she was being irrational. They spent their evenings together.

"Damn tarts," she spat, in spite of her strong suspicion that there weren't any.

She felt frustrated and foolish both, but sometimes she just had to vent.

Her gaze landed on a sterling wine coaster at the far end of the table. "The wine!" she cried, clapping her hands and charging like a bull through the swinging service door. She'd forgotten the wine for the table and the backup bottles for the sideboard. She bent down to the wine cooler beneath the counter and brought out three bottles of her favorite red.

It's lucky he made me so mad, she thought.

Otherwise, she might have forgotten the wine.

Emma opened a bottle and poured herself a glass, then sat down at the kitchen island. She knew it was foolish, but she really meant it: she'd rather be angry than forget to decant the wine.

She took a sip, and wrinkled up her nose. Needs to breathe, she thought, standing up again.

Emma opened the second bottle, but not the third. She only wanted that one close by, in case she needed it later. She tasted the wine again. It was better already. She surveyed her immaculate kitchen, wanting to ferret out any problems in advance. But everything was just the way she liked it, gleaming with the shine of religious scrubbing. You'd certainly never know that anyone was cooking, she thought proudly—all the pans and pots and measuring cups cleaned and stowed the moment she was finished with them.

Emma sat down again and took a long sip of wine.

Sometimes she wished she were the type to cry.

"WE DON'T HAVE TO GO," MELORA SAID. "NOT IF you're feeling pressed for time." They were standing in front of the Whitney Museum.

Now she tells me, Benjamin thought.

She must have seen him checking his watch—which he'd only done a thousand times. "We're here now," he said, with a cheerful sort of resignation. "We might as well go inside."

Benjamin rarely held a grudge—or not for long anyway. He was much too busy running toward the next hurdle to carry much baggage from the ones that came before. "And I want to see those pictures you were telling me about," he said, smiling at Melora when he caught her eye.

He just wanted everyone to be happy—with him, mostly.

Benjamin had half an hour still before he needed to be at Emma's place, just a few short blocks away. There was plenty of time to look at the photography exhibit. He could swing through in a jiffy, then hustle over to Emma's apartment to make his weekly status report, and to help with any last-minute dinner preparations.

Or offer his help, at least. She never actually required it.

Melora walked into the museum, and Benjamin followed, close on her heels. They showed their outdated college IDs to the ancient man at the entry desk. Students were exempt from paying for admission, and neither of them could afford the twenty-dollar charge.

That's nearly an hour of work, he thought—before taxes.

The old man waved them past, his eyes too blurry with age or boredom to notice that their cards were ten years out of date. Benjamin looked at his picture before he put it away. The boy on the card didn't look like his son exactly—more like a kid brother, he thought, or some kind of nephew. He and Melora rode the escalator, hand in hand—up one flight, and then another—two grifters floating up to the third floor, to a photo gallery that was off to the back.

It was a long room, thirty feet, at least, and scarcely ten feet wide—like an oversized shoe box, or a roomy grave. Not a window in sight, just twenty-five photographs, hanging cheek by jowl: a straight line of three-foot squares running all around the room, and no one there but them.

I'll be out of here in no time, he thought.

The pictures were all black and white—sepia-tinted and simply framed. Even from a distance, Benjamin could see how nostalgic they were. He felt their soft focus before he made it out with his eyes. They were pictures of children—idealized, beautiful children—all towheaded and sun-kissed and slim. They were naked, for the most part, just one child to a frame, and their long, rangy limbs were captured in halfhearted pursuit: a small boy pulling lightly at a slingshot, a little girl dragging listlessly on a candy cigarette. It may have been the same boy, he thought—the naked back of him anyway—skipping stones on a fuzzy lake; an older girl, with bare buds of breasts, sitting pretty on a smooth velvet couch.

The pictures were meant to be provocative. Benjamin

could see that right away. The photographer—the children's mother—had cast them in a vaguely sexual light, her gaze a little hungrier than a mother's ought to be. A couple of the pictures showed the children mildly injured—a beautiful black eye on one, the graceful arc of a long scratch mark down the arm of another.

Benjamin dismissed the "danger" out of hand. Nothing bad would happen to these lovely children, he knew that, nothing worse than posing for these pictures anyway, and discovering, at some later date, what whopping advantage their mother took.

The children looked forthrightly at the camera.

Why wouldn't they? he wondered. What could these beautiful specimens have to hide?

Benjamin looked at Melora. He wasn't sure what to say. He didn't like the pictures at all. There are dangers enough in the world, he thought, without staging artificial ones. He knew, too, that he didn't like the photographer either—a mother subjecting her children to pictures like this; but what surprised him even more was his suspicion that he didn't like the children themselves—so handsome and perfect and confidently entitled to their mother's gaze.

"Aren't they great?" Melora said.

Benjamin thought of Gracie.

He remembered the first time he'd seen her, standing at his office door—as wide as a penny that had been left out on the train tracks, flattened to twice its normal size by the force of a locomotive roaring through.

He motioned her into his office.

One of the third-grade teachers at Benjamin's school—Alice Watson—had come to him just after Christmas, a month or so before. She had a student, she said, who was terribly fat, and who was being taunted by a wolf pack of fifth-grade boys. She'd seen it happen herself, on the playground at recess the day before, and she'd heard it was happening in the lunchroom too. The boys made squealing animal noises at the girl, and pushed her roughly onto the ground.

He could picture their glittering eyes.

Alice put a stop to it, of course, but when she spoke to the little girl about it, only wanting to comfort her really, Gracie denied that anything had happened. Alice told her she'd *seen* it happening, but the girl wouldn't budge.

It didn't, she insisted.

Benjamin met with Gracie the very next day.

He asked Alice to send her down to him at recess. That was the perfect time, he thought—killing two birds with one stone: taking care of the girl and keeping her off the playground.

She was huge, he saw, when she appeared at the door.

"Hi, Gracie," he said, in a friendly voice—smiling at the girl, but not too much. Benjamin didn't like to come on strong. "My name's Mr. Blackman," he told her.

"I know that," she said softly, checking her impulse to smile back at him. Still, he thought he saw one peeking through.

He asked her into his office and ushered her to a small table he'd set up in the corner, just two or three children's chairs scattered all around it.

They each took one.

"Do you know why Miss Watson wanted me to see you?" he asked.

Gracie shook her head, but Benjamin didn't believe her. He could see the budding shame on her face like small pink blossoms on an apple tree. She knew what he was talking about. She was a wise child, he could see that too.

"She told me that some older boys were mean to you on the playground."

"They weren't," Gracie told him—"not to me." She looked away from him then, casting her eyes down as she lied.

"Really?" he asked, as gently as he could.

"They didn't do anything," she said, sounding determined.

Benjamin watched her fat hands gripping the sides of her backpack, the purple kitten on her T-shirt pulled wider than any kitten ought to be. He knew it would be no use to push. He didn't want to back her into a corner, after all.

He thought carefully about what he ought to say next.

"That's good," he told her, finally.

Gracie looked up at him again. She hadn't expected that. He saw the confusion he'd wrought on her face.

"I'm glad they weren't mean to you," he said.

He watched her confusion turn to relief.

Benjamin was glad for that, at least. He was going to have to take things slowly with her. He stood up from his little chair and walked to the supply closet on the far side of his desk. He found a bin of colored pencils inside—all loose and dull and pointing in every direction. He began humming softly. Then he found a handheld pencil sharpener, and the empty box the colored pencils came in.

He brought them all back to the table with him, certain that Gracie was watching him close. He was careful to keep his eyes off the girl.

He sat down again, smiling lightly as he went about his work. He chose a pencil from the plastic bin—bright apple green. He sharpened it carefully, twisting the pencil in the plastic sharpener, pulling it out slowly to admire his handiwork—all apple green sharpness where the dull tip had been. He laid the newly sharpened pencil in the empty pencil box, placing it in one of the carved-out gullies where the pencils were meant to lie.

Only forty-nine to go, he thought, looking at all the gullies that remained.

Benjamin inhaled deeply and let the breath out slow.

He picked another pencil—this one tomato red—and sharpened it like the one before. He handed it to Gracie when he was finished, without a word. She looked at the pencil for a moment, and then back up at him.

Benjamin was prepared to wait for as long as it took.

Finally, she laid the red pencil into another of the empty gullies, right next to the apple green.

They sharpened a few more pencils, working in silence all the while.

"I don't really care about those boys," he said, picking up another pencil, watching intently as the sharpener did its work—like peeling an apple with a shiny silver blade. He marveled at the long trail of skin that dangled down.

He peeked back at the girl, on a slightly higher alert.

"I don't," he said. It had the benefit of being true. Benjamin really didn't care about the mean boys, not for the moment anyway. "Getting them in trouble is Miss Watson's job."

Gracie extended her hand to him, waiting for Benjamin to give her the pencil, so she could do her job and put it away.

"I only care about you," he said.

He didn't let her take the lavender pencil until his eyes met hers. He hoped she believed him.

Benjamin handed Gracie the pencil sharpener then.

"Which one next?" he asked, pointing to the plastic bin in front of them, letting Gracie choose. She peeked in and picked out a bright pink pencil—the color of Pepto-Bismol. He watched her sharpen it carefully, furrowing her brow as she pushed the pencil in, twirling the sharpener all around it. She pulled it out and examined it with pride, then handed it to Benjamin, who laid it safely away.

"I can help you," he said. "If you want me to."

Gracie looked at him cautiously. She knew he wasn't talking about the pencils anymore; he could see that. The girl was quiet for longer than he would have expected—thirty seconds, at least.

"Maybe," she replied.

Benjamin nodded. He knew it was a start.

"We can talk about that later," he said, sounding cheerful.

He stood up again and walked back to the supply closet. For some reason, he felt determined to give the girl a gift. He knew that he shouldn't, that she might mistake it for a reward—for going along with him just then, agreeing to his help—but he couldn't stop himself. He found a coloring book with a shiny paper cover and elaborate line drawings of horse-drawn sleighs and bundled-up passengers inside, a village of houses with smoke curling off from every cross-hatched chimney. It looked as if it might take an army of Belgian nuns to color those pictures properly.

Benjamin wanted the girl to know he liked her.

"I have a present for you," he said, extending the coloring book to her.

Gracie took it from his hands. She thanked him shyly and unzipped her backpack, slipping the coloring book inside.

He saw a large box of cookies in her pack.

That's not good, he thought—not for a girl who's already obese.

Gracie looked up at him quickly.

"Did your mother give those to you?" he asked.

"No," she said softly, looking straight down into her lap again, just as she had when she lied to him the first time.

So there it is, he thought.

Chapter 5

SUNDAY SUPPER:

Pork Roast and Cardamom Chutney

CASSY LIKED THESE NIGHTS MUCH BETTER BEFORE Benjamin started coming around. She glared across the table at him, sitting at her mother's right hand like a perfect little lap dog. Emma sat at the foot of the table, and Cassy's father at its head; she and Benjamin were placed on either side—just like always. Even so, there were sterling silver place-card holders, shaped like tiny acorns—gleaming nuts to mark their spots. The placement never varied here, but her mother set out acorns every time.

And now we've got Benjamin's crunchy girlfriend too, Cassy thought.

She felt aggrieved.

Her mother had seated Melora between Benjamin and her father. Cassy was all alone on the long left side of the table—like a little orphan girl.

"That's the craziest thing I've ever heard!"

It was her father's voice, booming out with good cheer.

He was homed in on Melora, as he had been for most of the evening.

"Something tells me you've heard crazier," the girl replied, sounding cagey.

Melora was smiling at Cassy's father, egging him on. She'd been explaining her vegan diet—which seemed to take up half the night, everyone worrying whether the girl was getting enough to eat. Her father was playing it willfully obtuse, as if he'd never heard of vegetarianism before.

"Don't you miss a good steak?" he asked, a little louche.

Cassy felt embarrassed for him, until she saw Melora wriggling to the edge of her seat—all wide-eyed and perfectly erect—as if she were aroused by the old man's pervy banter.

"I always found steak a little overrated," Melora said, looking Bobby straight in the eye. Cassy could hear the wink in her voice. She suspected they were both half drunk. The bottle of red wine in front of her father was drained to its dregs, and the one beside Melora was only half full.

"You just haven't had the right cut yet," Bobby said, staring at Melora as if he were famished. He hadn't taken his eyes off the girl since the soup bowls were cleared away.

Cassy felt invisible.

Still, she was careful not to stare. She let her gaze wander back to the antique mirror—one of four large panels her mother had installed on the dining room walls—with fancy beveling all around the edges and splotchy patches of black where the ancient silver had worn away. Those mirrors freckled just about everything they reflected with dark age spots. Cassy let the mirrors do her staring for her. She fixed on Melora's reflection in the panel across the table, studying the girl's profile—her puffy lips and ample cheeks, nearly everything about her just slightly engorged.

She was luscious. Cassy had to give her that.

She'd tried entering into their conversation a little earlier, while Melora was explaining the spiritual aspects of her yoga practice, but Cassy had felt like an intruder. She saw, in a flash, how it would all play out—the unmistakable twinkle in her father's eyes.

She withdrew on the spot, before she lost outright.

Cassy's father hadn't so much as glanced in her direction since.

"And red meat's a terrible waste of energy," Melora said, striking a more serious tone. "Did you know it takes eight pounds of corn to produce a single pound of beef?" she told him. "That's a huge waste of resources."

"But I like meat," Bobby said, grinning like a fool.

Cassy couldn't remember the last time he'd joked with her.

She thought back to those ancient Sunday nights, when it was just the three of them around the dining table—her mother and father and little-girl self—before her father left them, all those years before.

He hadn't had nearly so much to say back then.

Of course, they hadn't had these brilliant conversationalists at the table with them either. Benjamin and Melora were like a couple of tag-team lotharios—claiming her parents from the moment they sat down, regaling them both with endless talk.

"So eat meat then!" Melora told him, as if she were exasperated. She threw her hands up in frustration, even as she smiled. "Be an energy hog, if that's what you want."

"Careful, young lady," Bobby replied, mock strict. "You're not too old for me to take you over my knee," he said.

"Don't you wish?" Melora shot back, and the two of them dissolved in gales of laughter, their boozy red faces growing brighter with every guffaw.

They were loaded.

Cassy watched her father lean into the girl, placing his hand lightly on her upper arm.

"Oh, God," Melora groaned, as their laughter subsided. "You're a funny one, Bobby," she said. She seemed to mean it too.

Cassy watched her father leaning closer in.

She wanted this foolishness to stop right now. She was surprised, in fact, that her mother hadn't put an end to it already, but Cassy saw that her mother was thoroughly engaged with Benjamin, at the other end of the table, going over some business from the office, no doubt.

She wondered why she bothered coming to these dinners at all.

Cassy wanted to be patient, but she was breathtakingly tired—operating on about ten minutes' sleep from the night before. She looked down at her wristwatch peeking out from the cuff of her turtleneck sweater, but she couldn't quite make out the time; she brushed her fingers across her green sleeve, lifting it just high enough to see the face.

As if anyone else cares, she thought.

No one had spoken to Cassy in a long, long time.

It was almost nine thirty. She'd been there for three hours already, and they weren't finished yet. Cassy began to dread her Monday. Having to go back into her mother's offices and begin another stifling week, suffering the worst fallout from her debauched weekend too, sadness falling all around her like thick velvet drapes—the inevitable result, she supposed, of her sleep deprivation, and the copious disco drugs.

Her father seemed to be growing even more animated.

It made her angry, and hurt her feelings too. She turned to her mother at the other end of the table, hoping to commiserate over what a bastard Bobby Sutton was.

"Take some chutney," she heard her mother say, offering the gravy boat to Benjamin. She sounded strangely cheerful about it, Cassy thought—as if the chutney were some kind of unexpected good news.

"I came up with it today," she added—all hopped up, like a hostess on speed. Emma held the sterling gravy boat aloft, just waiting for Benjamin to dip the silver ladle in.

"I'd love some," he said, spooning a hearty serving onto his plate.

Benjamin dipped his index finger into the lumpy red pool, and brought it straight to his mouth. "What *is* that?" he asked, humming ecstatically, as if he'd flown straight to heaven.

"Cardamom," Emma whispered, her eyes opened wide. "Isn't it wonderful?"

Their ridiculous animation was nearly enough to make Cassy turn back to the pole dance at the other end of the table. She wondered what ecstasies they'd reach with a pinch of allspice thrown in.

"Have you tasted the chutney, Cassy?" Benjamin asked.

She must have been staring.

Cassy shook her head.

"It's sensational!" he said.

"Cassy doesn't like chutney," her mother told him, a tight little smile etched onto her face. "Do you, dear?"

Cassy couldn't think of *anything* she liked at that moment.

"More for us then," Benjamin said, beaming at Emma, who smiled right back.

Emma popped up from her seat at the table. "I'll be right back," she announced. "I want to get the recipe for you, before I forget."

Cassy watched her mother circling the room.

"Everything all right down here?" Emma asked, looking at her husband through slightly squinted eyes.

"Jim dandy," he replied, smiling back up at her.

Cassy watched her mother push briskly through the swinging service door. She gazed down at her plate. She hadn't eaten much.

She knew these dinners were a waste of time. Her mother had her precious meal to obsess over: the staging of the courses and all her various sauceboats, decanting more wine than they could possibly drink; her father floating off at the first opportunity—just like always.

His coming back hadn't changed a thing.

Cassy heard the housekeeper pushing through the service door—on the return swing from her mother, it seemed—as if they were running a relay race: one efficient woman passing the baton to another; this second one stacking dishes on the sleeve of her plain white blouse.

As a little girl, Cassy had been responsible for clearing the dishes and loading them into the dishwasher, for scrubbing the pots and pans—just like kids all over America, she supposed. But her mother always turned it up a notch: standing guard, like a sentry on the sidelines, studying the girl through a rifle scope. Her mother had strict ideas about clearing up, from the scraping of the dishes to the filling of the sink. She wanted clockwise spongework on the enameled pans, and special handling of her good knives. She wouldn't stand for deviation.

"Put some muscle into it" was her standard refrain.

Cassy knew it was crazy, but she felt a nostalgic tug for the olden days, for those years when it was just them—their lurching talk and all the tense silences that followed.

They weren't so bad, she thought.

For Cassy, those awkward spells were all suffused with hope, like a backlit doorway—glowing with invitation, holding out the quiet possibility that she might finally reach the place she wanted to be. Cassy wanted to love her parents, not just deep down, beneath it all, but in a daily way too—and she wanted them to love her back. She wanted to talk to them—*really* talk—but something in her simply wouldn't allow it. The girl could never just reach across the table and begin. There always seemed to be some impediment, some mild annoyance or petty jealousy. And when it came right down to it, she couldn't find a single pathway leading back to them that wasn't blocked up with rage—at her mother, who chose her public life over the girl at every turn, and her father too, loving her indifferently, until the day he ran away.

"I couldn't disagree with you more," Benjamin said heartily.

Cassy snapped her head up, as if he were disagreeing with her, but she saw that he was merely joining in the fun with Melora and Cassy's father. She listened in on their conversation—which might have turned to global warming.

"Something, something, overheated Gulf Stream," she thought she heard Melora say.

That explains the summer top, Cassy thought, begrudging Melora her loveliness, not to mention the hold she had over Cassy's father. It was nearly enough to make her wish she read the newspaper; she scoured her brain for something brilliant to toss into the conversation. She knew the long odds she was facing, wanting to claim her father back.

She suspected, in fact, that it was hopeless.

Cassy didn't know a thing about the environment, and she couldn't compete on the real battleground either—not for her father anyway. She'd watched him eyeing Melora's plump breasts all night, as if they might pop straight through the gauzy fabric of her cheap peasant blouse.

Cassy fiddled with the soft wrists of her modest turtleneck.

She wished for a plunging neckline too, but she knew she couldn't beat her in that department. "Melora," she grumbled, beneath her breath—as if that's her real name even.

"I see you're as crazy as your girlfriend," Bobby called out merrily, to Benjamin this time. They were all three grinning like idiots.

No more awkward pauses, Cassy noted—not with these two chatterboxes around.

"You're missing the point completely," Benjamin said.

Will you shut the fuck up?

Cassy wanted to scream it down the table—at Benjamin and his beautiful girlfriend—neither of whom, she knew, had a thing in the world to do with the unbridgeable gaps around that table.

GRACIE FLOPPED DOWN ONTO THE WINE-RED RUG that covered up most of her bedroom floor. She counted the number of tiles she could make out still, the alternating squares of black and white that circled the room; they were only visible at the edges though, peeking out from beneath that big burgundy rug.

It used to be a giant checkerboard in here.

The little girl missed the covered-up tiles beneath that rug—even the loose ones that moved when she stepped on them, and the ones she could pick right up off the floor.

Fifteen, she counted, then checked her work.

Gracie made herself a bargain. She'd count straight up to fifteen, then backward down to one again, and if she did it just right—without one tiny mistake—her mother would open the door on the very last count, just as she whispered "one" that second time, all finished with her reverse-counting. Her mother would have the bag of swim things over her shoulder, her winter coat buttoned up tight.

It seemed almost possible to the girl—her choreographed waltz of backward counting and opening doors, the seedling hope that perfect behavior might bring perfect control—especially when she considered all the things that had to go right before anyone actually opened that door. She stared hard at it then, wooden and white, closed up tight.

She knew how hard it was to count backward.

Still, she began. She counted straight up to fifteen, and perfectly too, but that was no surprise. Counting up is the easy part, she thought, taking a breather before the trickier descent, and wondering, in fairness, if she ought to have made the target number a little higher.

"A deal's a deal," her grandfather always said.

"Fifteen, fourteen, thirteen," she whispered, knowing that the hardest part was just around the corner, when she waved those "teens" good-bye. "Twelve," she whispered, struggling, then "eleven"—but the little girl was losing heart. She stopped counting then, abandoning the effort altogether, and just when she'd gotten to the easy part too—the ten-nine-eight.

It wasn't that she couldn't finish. Gracie knew she could, in fact.

The little girl had a different concern: What if I do my counting, she wondered, and the door doesn't open? She was fearful that whoever she'd made her bargain with, whatever witch or good fairy controlled the opening of bedroom doors, wouldn't hold up their end of things.

That's why she stopped. Gracie would rather throw in the towel herself than be disappointed by somebody else.

"Please *hurry*," she whispered—to her mother, she supposed, but she wasn't exactly sure. She didn't know where to send her prayers anymore.

Gracie looked up to the ceiling, then down at the floor. She saw her tummy folding in on itself, sitting cross-legged like that—like a fat staircase, she thought, gazing at the flight of flabby steps that led from her breastbone straight down to her hips. She tried sucking them in, but that didn't work. So she pulled her shirt taut—hiding every last stair. She knew they were there still, but at least she didn't see them now, hidden behind a veil of white cotton. That was almost as good.

Almost, she thought, but not quite.

She shifted onto her side and pulled her legs beneath her, sitting on her feet and ankles, raising her torso tall. "Ta-da!" she sang, like a tricky magician in a silky black cape: every step of fat had disappeared! Her torso was as smooth as glass.

Gracie propped her hands on either side of her then, burying them deep in the burgundy pile. Her grandfather had trimmed it from a larger stretch of wall-to-wall; its unfinished edges, cut as straight as he could make them with a razor blade and an old wooden yardstick, were forever sprouting strands that popped out sideways like weeds, as troubling to the little girl as coloring outside the lines, or that ugly lost-and-found bin at school: notebooks and shirtsleeves and lunchboxes in a jumble, a tossed salad of carelessness.

Gracie crawled to the edge of the rug and plucked a couple of wayward strands; she pushed them deep into her pants pocket.

The thought of school made her sink like a stone.

And Valentine's Day was just days away.

She had to go back to school tomorrow, become "Gracie S." all over again—the fattest girl in the whole third grade. She tried putting the thought right out of her head, but she didn't get very far. Mondays were the worst of all—with five straight days to go—and Valentine's Day on Friday, when all the cards would be exchanged.

Gracie began raking her fingers through the shaggy carpeting on either side of her.

And it's not just the girls, she admitted to herself, her fingers scratching back and forth. She was the fattest one in the whole third grade. *Boys included*, she thought, shaking her head, as if she could scarcely take in her terrible luck.

She kept moving her hands back and forth, soothing herself with the rocking motion. She watched the rug turn a lighter shade when she pushed her hands away from herself. *Scarlet*, she thought, a little proudly. Gracie was a real expert at naming colors—nearly every crayon from the sixty-four-pack at her immediate disposal. The rug turned dark again when she pulled her hands back to herself.

Pink would be her first choice.

She closed her eyes and dreamed up the palest shade, an accidental pink almost, as if a tiny red shirt had been laundered in a big load of whites. She'd seen it happen once, in the laundry room downstairs.

She kept her eyes closed just a beat longer—giving the magic time to happen—then she opened them again: the wine-red rug just as dark as ever.

Maybe even darker, she thought.

She didn't allow a trace of disappointment to register on her face.

We'll be going out soon, she thought, as light as a feather. Just as soon as her mother was ready—looking down at her hands again, and the dark red carpeting beneath her knees. She wanted to avoid the sight of any roadblocks that might be standing in her path.

She flipped onto her tummy, just killing time, and pretended that the rug was like the bottom of a pool: all pale, pale blue beneath a million cups of crystal clear water. She wriggled her legs straight out behind her and lifted her stocking feet high. She began flutter-kicking, as if she were in the pool already—slowly at first, and then a little faster. She concentrated on all the things she loved about the water: the lightness in her limbs when she swam underneath, and the way her curly hair grew long and silky. Gracie felt safe underwater, as if her ugly body were invisible beneath its clear skin.

Most of her fellow Beginners needed to be coaxed to wet their faces. The babyish ones wore water wings. She rolled her eyes at the prospect.

But not me, she thought. I dive down deep.

She brimmed with a bold stripe of confidence—lying face-down on a patch of red carpeting, her fat chin pressed into the scratchy nylon pile. She could touch the bottom of the pool whenever she wanted.

Gracie closed her eyes then, trying to keep some burgeoning unpleasantness at bay. She pictured herself racing through the pool instead. "Best in Class," and she knew it. She was lit up from the inside out—as if a three-way lightbulb had been turned to its highest setting, as if it were blazing from deep inside her.

I wish I was jumping into that pool right now, she thought, letting herself get carried away.

And then it was gone: all her easy flutter-kicking overtaken, in a flash, by the showstopper that had taken clear shape in her mind. My bathing suit, she thought—one click more was all it took to turn that lightbulb off—the worst one in the whole world. It had been so long since she'd been swimming that the awful suit had slipped her mind: plain and large and navy blue. An unvarnished picture of the thing—as big as a tent—blazed across her eyes, her confidence dissolving into the pool's chlorinated water. The proud picture she'd had of herself, just a moment before, standing tall at the shallow end, turned out to be nothing but a watery illusion. The bottom of that pool was much deeper than it looked.

Gracie could picture its tag, sewn sturdily in—"14H," it read, Fourteen Husky, and everybody knew it—its white stitches holding fast as the little girl sank deeper and deeper down.

Her bathing suit was nothing like the sweet little confections her fellow Beginners wore, with their pastel ribbons and strappy straps. Nothing like the suits the Advanced Beginners or Intermediates wore either, for that matter. Gracie went stock-still with shame, just picturing that suit—the kind old ladies wore.

She felt a burning heat around her neck.

She began raking her fingers through the carpeting again: back and forth, back and forth. She had no sense of changing shades this time though; she didn't even bother looking down. Just moved her hands back and forth, like a machine, staring off into the middle distance.

She found another image there, an even worse one: her swimming lesson over, she stood in the big square room with concrete floors and gray metal lockers all around the edges. She had to change out of her ugly swimsuit then—clinging tighter to her body, all soaking wet, showing every last roll.

She had to change in front of the other girls.

She was surrounded by girls on every side.

So she waited and waited, for as long as she could—wrapped up in her big white towel, stalling in front of the open locker, just staring in. She didn't let her eyes wander, not even once; only pretended to be very, very busy with some time-consuming business on the gray inside. Gracie stood like that until the other girls had gone, or a critical number of them anyway; until the roar of chattering and giggling and whispering had died down into something that felt almost manageable to her; or until the swimming teacher came back in and told her she'd better hurry; or worst of all, until one of the other little girls—slim as a reed, of course—turned to face her, with a tight little smile, letting her know, in advance, that she was only asking to be mean: "What are you waiting for, Gracie?"

They all laughed at her then.

Those girls would never give her Valentine cards.

I'm so stupid, she thought—having almost convinced herself that they might. Of course they wouldn't, and still she'd made a card for every last one of them—cutting paper hearts and pasting pictures onto every single one.

Gracie caught fire then, in the middle of her bedroom, in the dead of winter. She felt the whoosh straight through her; and she thought she'd die of shame. She thrust her hand beneath her bed, reaching it back as far as she could—her fat arm waving like a searchlight on black water, her chubby fingers wriggling.

"Yes!" she hissed when she seized on her prize—as close to the wall as she could possibly manage, her fleshy shoulder pressed up hard against the wooden frame of the bed. She pulled the thing from underneath, the perfect cure for what ailed her: a package of chocolaty cupcakes, a pretty pair, in fact, with thick chocolate icing, and swirling giggles of white decoration on top of that—even the icing had icing!

She'd found them in the lunchroom at school, left there by some careless boy who'd been too busy rushing off to recess to understand the value of what he was leaving behind. Gracie knew to stash them for a rainy day, and here it was, just a few days later.

She tore into the plastic and pulled a cupcake out—*hurry*! She had to be quick about it; her mother would be coming any second. *Now*!—taking an enormous bite. The moist chocolate cake filled her mouth, its sweet, dark icing up toward the roof, and the airy white cream from the cupcake's deepest center sitting lightly on her tongue. Her mouth exploded with the pleasure of it all. She gobbled it up as fast as she could, and swallowed it down even faster. Then she took another bite. *More*!—not a moment to lose, that second bite just as big and beautiful as the first. Then she licked every trace of chocolate from her fingers—so hungry.

And just like that, her horrible bathing suit was gone. It had disappeared without a trace, along with the wine-red rug that would never be pink, and the staircase of tummy she could never really hide, the Valentine cards that would never be delivered to her. All her aches and pains were buried away, for the moment anyway, in that moist brown cake—as far off then as the pool's damp changing room, its sharp smell of chlorine: the chemical source of so much pride, and even greater shame.

THE SUTTON PARTY WAS WINDING DOWN—THE ebonized chairs pulled back slightly, the snow-white cloth dotted with errant droplets of Emma's spicy chutney. The table was mostly denuded by then of all the bone china and sterling silver that their hostess had laid out. Just one small plate left before each of them—like a game of musical chairs that was grinding to a halt.

Only this last one to go, Benjamin thought.

He felt as tired as if he'd been jitterbugging all night in one of those old-time dance contests from the Depression era, sweaty from exertion and nearly spent; still, he kept his feet shuffling. He felt a little euphoric too, the adrenaline of all that fancy footwork racing through his body still. He'd managed to keep Emma entertained, and Melora had been such a hit. He was foolish to have underestimated her appeal, especially where Bobby Sutton was concerned—like a big bad wolf at the head of the table, ready to gobble her up.

He watched Emma push back in through the swinging service door, the large tray of coffee things in her hands.

We'll be out of here in no time, he thought.

Emma walked directly to Cassy's seat, just as she always did with that red lacquered tray. It was her daughter's job to help Emma serve the coffees. No words exchanged between them, none needed. He'd watched it happen a hundred times: Cassy taking the tray from Emma's hands and following her mother around the dining table, like a little kitten on the heels of an imperious cat; Emma lifting china cups and saucers from the tray and placing them down, without a sound, before each of her guests.

She made it her business to know who took decaf and who preferred tea.

But Cassy didn't stand up.

She just sat there, pouting like a sullen child, her mother standing right behind her. Benjamin watched Emma's face move from confusion to displeasure. He saw her eyes squinting and her lips begin to purse.

Bobby and Melora kept chatting at the other end of the table.

What's *wrong* with her? Benjamin wondered.

He kept staring at the girl as he jumped to his feet, scurrying to take the tray from Emma's hands. He liked to skirt trouble, where he could. Emma let him take it, but he could see she wasn't pleased. She didn't like unauthorized changes to her scripts; still, she tolerated this one—for the moment anyway.

Benjamin followed her around the table, holding the tray as steady as he could, while Emma served the coffees.

"Tired, dear?" she asked—pointedly, he thought—when she placed the cup and saucer in front of her daughter, pouring out the coffee from the silver carafe.

"Exhausted," Cassy replied, smirking a little. "It's lucky you've got paid help tonight," she said cheerfully. "Isn't it?" she added, smiling up at Benjamin.

Cassy had always reminded him of his older sister, Marie, and the epic battles she used to wage against him: the two of them grappling over his ball on the lawn or dunking heads in the swimming pool. "Truce," she'd yell, but Benjamin knew not to believe her. "I swear," she'd add, and he'd go along with her then—against his better judgment.

They were truces of a sort, he supposed—as soon as his sister got one last slug in, or kick, or pinch of tender skin between her sharp fingernails.

Cassy was a lot like Marie, he thought—his mere existence an affront to them both—unaccountably jealous of the three seconds of attention he might claim from their chilly mothers.

He knew to avoid them.

Benjamin walked quickly toward Bobby at the head of the table, the china clattering on the lacquered tray. He wanted to hurry Emma past the turbulence of her daughter's airspace.

They finished serving without incident, and Emma took the tray from his hands, nodding with a slightly exaggerated courtesy. She went back to the kitchen for a large plate of biscotti, all dappled with icing and drizzled with jam.

She took her seat again.

It looked to Benjamin as if she'd recovered.

"I read a fascinating article in the *Times* this morning," Emma said, addressing the table, rallying her troops.

Benjamin smiled in her direction and bit into a delicate cookie. It was soft and delicious, tasting of sweet almond paste and the crunchy pine nuts that dotted the top. He suspected that she'd made them herself.

"It was about this group called Doctors without Borders," she said.

Benjamin nodded briskly, wanting to help her along.

"Did you see it?" she asked.

"I must have missed it," he said, shaking his head.

No one else at the table had seen it either.

Benjamin rarely got much further with the Sunday paper than the crossword puzzle. He'd begun trying his hand at it—with Melora's help—several months before, after hearing the Sutton women comparing triumphant notes one night. They carried the puzzle around with them for most of the day, printed on an onionskinned page of the *New York Times Magazine*. Even so, they rarely got very far.

Benjamin squeezed Melora's hand beneath the table. They were nearly finished here, he meant to tell her; she smiled right back.

They could always find a few easy clues: the five-letter "Tatum" from *Paper Moon*, the obligatory African plains, beginning with a *v*; but there were always boxes and boxes that he couldn't begin to fill in, pristine and empty on that slightly crinkled page. He never had so much as an inkling of the special theme that tied those impossibly long answers together, stretching from one end of the tidy grid clear across to the other: that clever homophone whose discovery would unlock the whole thing, that cunning use of the letter *x*.

Benjamin knew that Emma finished those puzzles in a single go, her clever daughter just thirty-five seconds behind her.

Yes, he thought, they're quite a twosome.

"Doctors without Borders?" Cassy said, a little contemptuously. "You mean those goody-two-shoes volunteers?"

Emma nodded, but Benjamin could see that she didn't like her daughter's tone.

"The ones who go to third-world countries?" Melora asked.

Benjamin had heard of them too—leaving their cushy private practices at home, and ministering to the poor in far-off places. They'd always seemed so noble to him; he couldn't imagine what Cassy could have against them.

"The article was about this young woman," Emma told them, "a plastic surgeon who spends half her time in Malawi. She's set up a clinic there to operate on kids with birth defects."

"Where the hell is Malawi?" Bobby asked, a little drunkenly.

"In Africa," Emma replied, waving him off. That wasn't her point.

"People come from hundreds of miles away to see her," she continued, "some of them on foot. The clinic's gotten incredibly busy, but she's only got a few pieces of makeshift furniture. People are sitting on boxes."

Melora passed Benjamin the cookie plate again. She didn't take any herself, of course; those cookies were loaded with white sugar. Benjamin felt grateful to her for leaving it at that, simply going without.

"Maybe we should donate some furniture?" Benjamin said. He was always calculating his boss's angle.

"That's just what I was thinking," Emma replied. "What do you think, Cassy?" She turned to her daughter, the titular head of her charitable foundation.

Cassy didn't look impressed.

"In my experience," she said—as hard-boiled as any pundit on a Sunday-morning news show—"those volunteers are much better at making themselves feel good than they are at actually helping people on the ground."

Benjamin knew that Cassy was only resisting the idea because he'd suggested it. It had to be better than all those stupid "show houses" where they were always donating furniture—designers gussying up an apartment to hell and back, allegedly raising money for charity by charging admission at the door.

"I think you should check it out," Emma told her.

"Go to Malawi?" Cassy asked.

"Or call the woman up, at least," Benjamin suggested.

"Exactly," Emma said.

Everyone at the table turned to Cassy then—her mother and father, Melora even. Benjamin watched their reflections, staring at the girl in the ancient mirrors. He wondered if they could see, as clearly as he did, that the topic was rubbing Cassy terribly wrong. Benjamin watched her hardening in her seat. She didn't have the softest face to begin with—all whippet-sharp features and steely gray eyes—but it was pure rock salt now, suitable for the iciest of winter roads.

"Sounds like you should give Benjamin my job," Cassy said, glaring back at her mother.

"What are you talking about?" Emma replied.

He could hear that she was losing her patience with the girl.

Why hadn't she just stood up and helped her mother with that stupid coffee tray? he wondered.

"I wasn't complaining," Emma said.

"And I've already got a job," Benjamin added, smiling at Cassy, as if to defuse the situation. He saw right away that he hadn't.

"That's right," Cassy said, the contempt dripping off her like a leaky faucet. "In an elementary school."

"Come on," Bobby said, as if to nip her offensive in the bud. "Be nice, Cassy."

Benjamin appreciated the gesture, but he knew it was about as useful as asking an apple not to ripen on its leafy branch. It reminded him of those long-ago car trips he used to take with his family, sitting in the backseat, taunted by his older sister to the brink of tears. He refused to give in to them though; he was stoic to the end, but his sister was just as relentless, clamped on like a pit bull on the vinyl seat beside him.

"Be nice," their father always told her.

Benjamin knew that "nice" was out of the question.

He decided to look straight past Cassy's insult. "Just training the furniture buyers of tomorrow," he said, smiling still, as if to show he didn't hold a grudge. He thought it was rather charming of him, under the circumstances.

Benjamin finished his coffee and looked around the table.

He wanted to get the hell out of there. He knew from experience that it would be a fragile cease-fire. He began to calculate how long it would be before he could collect their coats from the front closet and leave this place.

"Maybe you should just write a check to Doctors without Borders," Cassy said, turning back to Emma.

Benjamin felt safely off the hook.

"I could do that," Emma replied. "If I wanted to." She wasn't the type to run scared from her daughter, or anyone else, for that matter.

"I know you could," Cassy said. "Although you're not exactly known for charity."

"Is that so?" Emma replied calmly, nodding her head a little as she did. He could see that she was officially out of patience. "Would you care to tell me what I *am* known for?" she asked, throwing the gauntlet down.

Benjamin nearly jumped into the fray, interposing himself between the women warriors. "Why, you're the queen of interior design," he might have said. "That's what you're known for, Emma."

But it was too late by then. He could see from the set of Cassy's jaw that she was moving in for the kill.

Benjamin wrapped his arms loosely around himself, as if he were chilly in that temperate dining room. He felt like a passenger in a slow-moving vehicle, heading straight for a six-car pileup. He could see it all.

" 'Convicted felon' would probably top the list," Cassy said, as lightly as if she were telling the time.

"That's enough of that," Bobby barked at the girl.

Benjamin watched her shrug her father off, just like his sister always had.

He turned to Emma, who looked frozen in place. On closer inspection though, he could see that she was vibrating slightly—thrumming with rage like a red-tailed warbler, hovering in the air above its perch, wings aflutter.

Cassy had hit her mark.

Of course, it didn't take very long for Emma to recover herself. She crouched forward in her seat like an angry predator, but he couldn't help seeing that she looked a little shrunken too—a couple of inches smaller in every dimension.

Benjamin had forgotten all about Cassy's cutting remark to him.

He only had eyes for Emma now, the gaping wound her daughter was so happy to inflict. He'd never seen his boss at human scale before—not even when she'd stood on those courthouse steps, announcing to the world, via fifty-seven camera crews, that she'd be going away for a little while.

It was a brand-new experience for him, seeing Emma cut down to size.

He wasn't sure he liked it.

TINA COULDN'T BELIEVE HER EYES.

Something must have changed around here, she thought, standing inside the front door still, surveying the wide-open room before her, but she'd be damned if she could find the thing that had. Even the giant poster was there—straight ahead, on the tiled wall in front of her: a man with a prosthetic leg doing the long jump, or the broad jump, some kind of jump anyway, and landing roughly in a sandy pit, hardscrabble determination written all over his face.

"Yes, you can!" the caption blared.

Tina knew that poster as well as she knew her own name—and for almost as long, it seemed. The photograph made her just as squeamish as it always had. She felt a fluttering in her stomach and the jitters in her legs. She fixed on the spot where the man's fake shin met up with his stump of leg, a spiderweb of shiny metal somehow holding the thing in place.

She looked away from his awful landing, just as she always had—that jarring mash of metal and plastic and skin—but not before she wondered at the perfect uselessness of the man's left sneaker, its bright white laces done up tight, protecting a fake foot from whatever it needed protection from.

Gracie pulled her mother into the massive room.

And that smell, Tina marveled—like a roundhouse punch of chlorine bleach. She'd know it anywhere.

She showed her membership card to their local Y to the woman who sat at the entry desk. It was probably the same woman she'd spoken with earlier. Tina smiled at her when she asked Gracie her name. She'd called the branch closer to home, first, wanting to confirm the pool hours there, but found it closed for renovations. So she pulled out the phone book and located a replacement pool—the one near her parents' house in Forest Hills.

"You said we were going swimming," Gracie whined when they climbed up out of the subway, "not to Poppy's house." She must have recognized the landscape, Tina supposed—the Korean deli on the corner maybe, or the video store across the street.

"We *are* going swimming," Tina replied, pulling her winter coat tight.

She felt a little whiny herself, not exactly thrilled at the prospect of a chilly swim on a winter's evening, but she was the one who'd dreamed it up, after all—making amends to Gracie for a phony party at the Baptist church, a weight-loss meeting in drag.

"Good," Gracie said, looking up at her a little bashfully. She rarely whined.

They walked hand in hand, just five or six blocks more,

to the YMCA where Tina had gone as a child. It was her first visit back in what felt like ten thousand years.

On reflection, she supposed it was more like ten.

The woman at the front desk waved them past; they walked deeper into the building. Tina saw the skinny pools straight ahead: two of them, in fact, just ten feet wide and twenty-five yards long. They were laid out neatly, side by side, the indoor version beneath a cage of foggy glass, and the outdoor one right beside it, emptied out in the dead of winter, surrounded by patches of mangy snow.

"There are *two* pools here?" Gracie asked, barely containing herself.

She pulled her hand away from Tina's and scampered down the hall to take a better look—her flame red coat, all puffy with down, bouncing up and down with every step. Tina had wanted to buy her a cloth coat—navy and fitted, she thought, as slimming as possible—but Gracie wouldn't hear of it. The girls at school wore puffy coats.

Her daughter looked like a beefsteak tomato as she bobbed down the hall.

Tina tried to shake it off.

It wasn't so hard really. She felt a little excited to be there herself. When she recognized the sunbathing area—that tiny patch of concrete just beyond the outdoor pool—she nearly laughed out loud.

Was it really that small? she wondered.

An image of her eighteen-year-old self flashed before her eyes. And not like looking backward, not like turning around on a mountain path and gazing back down the hill you'd climbed to the pretty glade a mile or two back. No—for that moment, Tina *was* eighteen again, all oiled and shining at the water's edge, lazing a summer afternoon away. She was sprawled out on the tanning deck, as pretty as a floral centerpiece—a spray of white roses maybe, in a long, slim vase—nothing but her two-piece and a thin beach towel between her own soft skin and the rough concrete floor, its texture as prickly as a bed of thorns.

Tina could feel the sun bearing down on her—its hot, rough fingers grabbing tight. She closed her eyes lightly and lifted her face to the searing heat. How she loved that burning stillness, the wavy sizzle on soft eyelids.

It never lasted long, of course.

There was always some commotion there, a rush of testosterone from the boys in the pool. Tommy, probably, she thought—shaking her head at the memory of him, her great love in those silly years—the hair on his arms and legs bleached to blond, his frayed cutoffs riding low.

Her great love, period, she supposed.

But it might have been any of them. All the boys preened for their bikinied attention—jumping wildly into the shallow end, the lifeguard's whistle and the boys' whoops their only warning of the dousing splash to come.

Gracie tugged on Tina's sleeve.

"Mommy," she said, interrupting the ancient afternoon, "I think the changing rooms are over here"—as if Tina hadn't known for a thousand years already exactly where those changing rooms were.

"I think you're right," she replied, smiling down at Gracie, and letting her lead the way.

Tina felt the moment pass: the wavy heat and the golden light. It gave way, in a flash, to the solid little girl in her puffy red coat. Tina watched her waddling down the hall, over the creaky linoleum floor, and into the changing room at the very end.

Such a fool, she thought—her not-so-fond farewell to the beautiful girl on the prickly concrete.

But even as she turned away, Tina felt a whispering memory of her girlish optimism: so sure that she was only stopping at that Y for one last summer; that she'd be on her way again soon—to some place worth going. She'd been on her way to being someone.

Tina cringed at her youthful arrogance, nearly blushing for the girl in her pink two-piece—as if hope itself were some kind of vice. Not that it matters anymore, she thought, distancing herself from that hopeful girl, playing it all down. She was certain that she'd thrown all her chances away by then—just dumped, in big handfuls, like a bushel basket of dollar bills from a second-story window. She'd watched them flutter away already; she didn't expect to see any more.

Tina didn't blame anyone for the course her life had taken.

She'd made her peace with Tommy long before. She could no more blame him for her predicament than she could begrudge him his fine cheekbones, or the long white threads that ran down his strong thighs.

Tina reserved the blame for herself.

She felt overheated by the time she reached the locker room; the memory of her youthful missteps had her metabolism racing.

She pulled off her coat as fast as she could.

"There's no one here!" Gracie cried, galloping all around the changing room. Tina shushed her in case she was wrong, but she didn't seem to be. She hoped the girl wouldn't be too disappointed. "I bet there'll be plenty of kids in the pool," she said, trying to reassure her.

"Maybe not," the girl replied—as if to reassure herself.

Tina hung her coat in a rusty old locker at the edge of the room. "Do you want to take your coat off, sweetie?"

"Can I have my own?" Gracie asked, pointing to another locker, just two or three down.

"Sure," Tina said. There were hundreds of empty lockers there.

The two of them sat down, side by side, on a long wooden bench.

"What's that say?" Gracie asked, pointing to a rusty steel tag on the outside of the locker.

"It says, 'Mr. and Mrs. Mitchell Pitt,'" Tina told her. She knew the name itself wouldn't answer her daughter's question. "They helped to pay for the lockers," she explained.

"Am I allowed to use it?" Gracie asked.

Tina nodded.

"But what if Mrs. Pitt comes in?" she wondered.

Tina decided not to tell her that Mrs. Pitt was probably long dead by then. She took off her sweater instead, and watched as the little girl did the same. "We'll just ask her to use another one," Tina said. "I'm sure she won't mind."

She untied her shoelaces and slipped off her pants, watching Gracie in close pursuit, never much more than a beat or two behind. They stood in unison finally—two girls in clean white underpants and warm wool socks, looking each other up and down.

"I'm so pale," Tina muttered, raising her arm to inspect her skin.

"Me too," Gracie said, lifting her arm the very same way.

Tina handed her a swimsuit. They both grew a little more furtive then. They finished undressing quickly—their eyes averted—and pulled on their swimsuits fast.

Tina had to admit that Blackman was right about the Diet Club.

Gracie barely fit into her swimsuit from the summer before. There were big handfuls of flesh, like yeasty dough, popping out from the edges of her Lycra suit—a fleshy jack-in-the-box all around.

"Almost time for a new bathing suit," she said, trying to sound upbeat.

"Do I have to have blue again?" Gracie asked.

"Not if you don't want," Tina said. "What color would you like?"

"Guess!" the girl cried. She loved a guessing game.

Tina knew, of course; all roads led to pink, but she took the long way there. "Purple?" she asked. Gracie shook her head. "How about yellow?" She shook some more. "Green?" Tina asked. The girl began shaking her head vehemently; she didn't stop either, not even between colors.

"Brown?" Tina asked.

"Eww," Gracie cried, hopping from one foot to the other.

Tina heard a dull thud every time she landed.

"I give up," she said finally, having named every color she could think of, some of them several times. "What color would you like?" she asked.

"Pink, silly!"

"Good choice!" Tina said, smiling down at the girl. "I had a pink swimsuit once."

"I know," Gracie said. "I saw it."

Tina couldn't imagine that she had, but she let it pass.

She closed their lockers firmly and led them to a large communal shower. It was a huge white cube—fifteen feet in every dimension—with old porcelain tiles on all the walls, and slightly larger ones on the ceiling and floor. They were beautiful too, like glassy white eggshells, all sparkling clean, but if you looked close, you could see a million cracks. Every tile was a shadowy network of them—the most delicate road maps in history.

Tina turned on the tap, one of a handful of shiny silver handles protruding from the wall. She waited for the water to warm up.

"Why are we taking a shower now?" Gracie asked.

"So we'll be clean when we get into the pool," Tina said, looking straight into the tangle of confusion on her daughter's face. "It's a rule," she said, trying again, "so that *everybody's* clean when they get into the pool."

"But we'll be clean as soon as we jump in," Gracie said. "Won't we?"

Tina let the matter drop. Better that, she decided, than getting too specific about other people's filth. "Let's have a quick rinse anyway," she said. She hopped under the warm spray—like a rain shower almost, that old showerhead so high above her head, three or four feet at least. The water gathered some heft on the way down, pinging hard against her pale skin.

She saw Gracie on the sidelines still, giving herself a big bear hug.

"Brrr," she shivered.

Tina coaxed her under the showerhead.

Gracie looked up skeptically.

Tina thought of Tommy for the second time that afternoon. She watched the water rolling down her legs, trailing off to the silver drain. They used to do it right here, she remembered—she and Tommy, in this little place—sneaking off to make love on the shower-room floor. Late in the day, after the little girls had gone home, but before the women came in from their offices.

She marveled at their never getting caught. It seemed so risky to her now.

They were short on pleasure, those shower-room trysts—more about boredom than sexual heat. Gracie was conceived right here, she thought, staring down at the tiles in front of her toes, the very ones she'd pronounced sparkling clean a moment before.

Tina felt ashamed of herself.

She turned to the wall, so Gracie couldn't see.

"Such a fool!" she hissed, growing angry at the memory of it—at turning up pregnant by the end of August, all hope of college dashed, and her parents so hurt and disappointed. Even junior college went by the boards, with a baby coming and all the extra expense.

She was no better than dirty water herself.

She watched it trailing down the silver drain.

They went as far as marrying—she and Tommy—in the autumn of that year. They found a small apartment in Woodside, but no one was very optimistic. Tommy was just a kid, she thought, only too happy to let him off the hook. He was no more ready for marriage than the man in the moon.

Tina didn't spare a kind thought for herself though. Somehow she couldn't, not even all these years later.

The marriage only lasted a couple of years. Tina cut him loose as soon as she could support herself. Her parents had helped her—straight through her mother's cancer and death—and Tina moved up quickly at the plant, rising from secretary to bookkeeper much faster than anyone would have thought.

She gave Tommy permission to leave as soon as she could afford the rent on her own. "Really," she told him, "it's all right."

He took her up on it too, running off like a boy on the last day of school, hurtling toward the summer days to come.

"I'll be back," he'd told her. "Wait for me."

But Tommy ran and ran and never looked back.

She'd heard he'd moved to California a couple of years before; they hadn't heard from him in ages. It was hard for her to say, just then, whether she was waiting for him still, or merely stuck in a rut.

Tina didn't blame him though.

I might have done the same thing myself, she thought—if she'd been in his place anyway, if she hadn't fallen in love with Gracie already. But she had, of course, so she wasn't going anywhere.

"Mommy," Gracie said, touching her lightly on the wrist.

Tina looked down at the girl, bursting out of her navy swimsuit—her face as wide as a movie screen, a picture of confusion pushing through the flab.

"What is it, sweetie?" Tina said.

"Are we clean yet?"

Chapter 6

MONDAY MORNING:
Milky Cereal and Cookie Crumbs

IT'S YOUR OWN DAMNED FAULT, EMMA THOUGHT, addressing herself like a critic that morning, a finger wagging in her voice. She wouldn't be in this mess right now if she weren't such an eagle eye.

It was a strange kind of criticism though—like a cube of sugar hiding in the salt cellar, just a compliment in disguise. Emma could be as backhanded with herself as everyone else in the world was with her. She was almost used to it by then. People always made their compliments sound suspiciously critical to her.

"Oh, Emma!" she'd heard, more swooning times than she could count. "I wish I could be half as cutthroat as you!"

She didn't have time to dwell on hit-and-run drivers that morning though.

Emma had more pressing business.

"Don't you ever miss a trick?" she mumbled, picking up the

phone and dialing it briskly, striking the numbers as roughly as typewriter keys: 4-1-1.

"Hello, operator," she said.

She'd waited until ten of nine to call—until Bobby had left for his office. She wanted the place to herself, and she had to wait for someone to be there, of course—for someone to pick up at the other end of the line.

Emma had woken up at five that morning, a full half hour later than she normally did. She didn't feel any better rested though—more like a dime-store thief with those few extra minutes slipped into her pocket. She put it down to the wine she'd drunk the night before, two or three glasses, at least—twice as much as she usually did.

At least *that* was tasty, she thought, berating herself once again for the overcooked pork and those awful vegetables that had turned out nearly raw.

"Hard as rocks," she grumbled—as if anyone ever cut rocks into neat little cubes and doused them with too much olive oil. She'd hardly been able to drop off to sleep the night before, what with her frustration at the terrible meal.

She didn't let herself so much as think of her daughter.

Emma was an expert at ignoring the elephant in the room. She focused on the terrible meal instead of Cassy's cruelty—first to Benjamin, like a warm-up pitch, then a fastball hurled straight at her own head.

"Convicted felon," Cassy had snarled—scarcely able to suppress her pleasure.

Emma pretended it had never happened.

She marched back over her dinner preparations instead—task by task—hunting in vain for the terrible error, the misstep that had cost her success. Failure tasted a lot like pork, she thought—as dry as dust.

Everyone ate, of course, just as if nothing were wrong. Benjamin took seconds even, but Emma couldn't forgive herself. She saw the way they heaped that chutney on.

But all that had to wait for now—her dinner and her daughter, her work even. "May I have the number for Forty-four West Realty Corp.?" she asked, the silver receiver pressed up against her ear, her rich brown hair falling all around it.

Emma was meant to be working up a clever variation on a guest room that morning—one that could double as a home office. She was taping a segment for *Oprah* that afternoon. But she had some personal business to work out first.

She was sitting in Bobby's study, at his handsome mahogany desk, swiveling a little in that ugly ergonomic chair of his, her lower back and lumbar spine allegedly protected at every turn.

But Emma didn't feel safe at all.

"You've got no one to blame but yourself, Emmy"—that's what her father always said, once she'd crashed hard to earth after aiming too high: losing her bid for student body president, only a runner-up as homecoming queen.

"Damned eagle eyes," she muttered, scratching a spot of tarnish from the brass trim on Bobby's desk blotter.

Emma knew she wasn't entirely to blame for her difficulties that morning. She wouldn't have found anything, of course, if there'd been nothing there to find. But she didn't want to be angry with Bobby either.

She hated problems she couldn't solve on her own—especially so early in the morning.

She was growing annoyed with the operator too.

"No," she said, huffing out a little breath, "I don't have an address." If I had an address, she thought, I wouldn't be calling you.

Emma had left Bobby in bed that morning, sleeping as soundly as he always did, the rise and fall of his slumbering chest in perfect time with the little puffs of air he spat—*puh*, *puh*, *puh*—all night long, like a speech therapist demonstrating the most perfect *p* imaginable.

It didn't annoy her either.

She liked having her husband in bed beside her. She wasn't much of a sleeper still, but she slept much better since he'd come back home. No question about that. She didn't even mind it when he flung a sleeping arm over her chest, like a protective mother driving toward an amber light. It startled her awake every time, but it was something like a comfort to her too.

She'd slipped out of bed as gently as she could and walked straight to the dining room. She wanted to see how the new housekeeper had made out—her inspection like a consolation prize, a gift-wrapped package with a silky white bow. She might not be able to lie in bed with her husband, like every other woman in the world, but she could do this, at least: she could see if the new girl had returned the place to any semblance of order.

She hadn't, of course—not at all.

There were water marks on the sideboard, and a brand-new chip in the Limoges. She saw cookie crumbs on the carpet as big as her fist, and a cell phone beneath the chair where Benjamin sat.

"Perfect!" she growled. "The only blind housekeeper in America."

She felt herself spinning out of control.

Emma scoured the room for something—*anything*—the girl might have done right, but there was nothing. She climbed down onto her hands and knees, fingering up a bushel of cookie crumbs and a gargantuan piece of roasted carrot.

She'd have to vacuum later.

Then she picked up the cell phone from beneath Benjamin's chair, lying dark as an iguana, blending into the faded pattern of the old Persian rug. It didn't blend near well enough to elude Emma though. That phone called out to her as loudly as if it were ringing.

Benjamin was in such a rush to get out of here, she remembered—wanting to flee the dustup that Cassy caused—that she wouldn't be surprised to find his hat and coat in the hall closet. He would have left his shoes, she thought, if it would have gotten him out of here any faster.

Emma walked back to Bobby's office with the cell phone in her hands. She'd have her husband messenger it to him later—at the elementary school, she thought, nearly rolling her eyes at the thought of the place.

Cassy might have had a point—about that, at least.

Emma wouldn't be seeing Benjamin again until Friday afternoon. He'd need his phone by then. She laid it down on Bobby's desk, at the center of the green leather blotter, then turned to leave, walking as far as the doorway before she changed her mind.

He'll just leave it there, she thought—Bobby would—if it's just sitting out like that. Emma didn't know *how* such a thing could happen—with the phone sitting there as plain as day—but she had more than enough experience with her husband to know that he would. So she walked back to the desk and slipped the phone into Bobby's briefcase, which was standing open on the desk chair in front of her.

A silky lining caught her eye, its bright red fabric gnashed between zipper teeth, as painful to her as a bloody wound. Emma opened the zipper, naturally, and pushed the lining back down inside. She found two silver keys there, on a steely ring. She pulled them out like a fairy-tale princess, as if they were the keys to the kingdom maybe, or to the handsome prince, locked away in some stony tower.

She turned them slowly in her hands, studying them from every angle. They weren't the keys to her apartment, she knew that much; or to the place in the country either. They didn't unlock the storage bins in the basement or the wine cellar either. They didn't look familiar at all. She kept gazing at the long silver prongs—the pattern of raised dots that ran down their shafts—like keys for the blind almost, written out neatly in Braille.

Emma had never seen them before.

She felt a queasy fluttering in her stomach and chest. They weren't the keys to Bobby's office. He had one of those electronic card keys that you pressed up against a glassy box. Maybe for his old apartment, the one he lived in before moving back in with her? But she didn't think so: he'd sold that place months ago. Wouldn't he have straightened out that lining after all this time?

Of course he would have, she thought.

From there, it was a rather quick jump—for Emma anyway—to Bobby's checkbook inside his briefcase, and her discovery of the regular monthly checks. They'd begun as soon as he moved back in with her, and they continued straight through to the first of February, just ten days before: checks like Swiss clockwork, written to "44 West Realty Corp." in the amount of $3,253.

Emma knew.

"Damn that Benjamin!" she muttered, as if to pin this mess on him, for dropping his phone the night before, but she knew in a blink that it would never stick. Benjamin didn't have a cruel bone in his body; he didn't want to hurt her.

"Lazy maid!" she grumbled then, trying another tack—like a slipper that fit a little bit better. If she'd straightened up the dining room like I asked her to, she thought, I wouldn't have found that phone at all.

The maid was toast, but Emma didn't feel much better.

If only I wasn't so damned observant, she thought with a sad shake of her sleepy head. She brought the chickens home to roost, just like her father had always taught her: no one to blame but herself.

It was six fifteen on Monday morning.

Emma plucked Benjamin's phone from out of Bobby's bag. She took the silver keys too, and walked to the kitchen—where the maid had somehow done an even worse job cleaning up.

"Thank God," she said. It gave her something to do, at least.

She set about cleaning the place as it ought to have been done, starting with the roasting pan and the silvery wire rack. The girl had left them—only halfheartedly clean—on the draining board beside the sink.

"Just filthy," she whispered, with a song in her heart.

Emma's mind wandered as she scrubbed. She'd be the first to acknowledge that her keen powers of observation had never served her quite as well as she would have imagined. Little details, she thought—that's all she ever managed to see. The big picture always eluded her somehow. She hadn't had so much as an inkling, for instance, that Bobby was going to walk out on her all those years before, much less that he'd come strolling back so many years later. She'd never seen it coming. Or that foolish business with her daughter last night—Emma had no idea she'd raised such a cruel child.

Of course, those were just the hors d'oeuvres, leading Emma straight to the main course, her tried-and-true entrée: an entire nation turning against her in such lockstep that they'd throw her into prison for an entire year—for something that happened in accountants' offices every day. Just a measly tax return, she thought, and no one in the world to save her. Emma shook her head, marveling at just how clueless an observant woman could be.

She scrubbed that roasting rack until it shone like new—better than new, in fact—grunting out her muscular exertions as she worked.

Is it me, she wondered, staring at the sparkling pan, or am I feeling a little better?

She moved directly to the salad bowl, which looked clean enough, but Emma washed it again for good measure, and all the serving platters too—even the ones she hadn't used the night before.

Bobby came in for coffee at seven.

"Morning, dear," he said, hugging her sleepily from behind—his stale breath ruffling the hair at the nape of her neck.

It didn't interrupt her scrubbing for a second.

"Sleep well?" he asked, giving her shoulders a gentle rub.

Emma flexed her body tight, humming out that she had, "thank you very much." She was glad he couldn't see her face.

"Bastard," she mumbled, the moment he left.

She opened the dishwasher door, moaning aloud as she looked inside, as if she were gazing into a bloody wound, straight through the red and the muck and the dirt.

"Look at this mess," she whispered, a real agony in her voice.

The disarray was breathtaking: plates and cups and saucers strewn in every direction—sizes and shapes in a riot of clutter, not to mention the jumble of cutlery. It looked to Emma as if a madwoman had loaded the thing.

She took out every single item.

Could the girl possibly think these things were clean? She reloaded the machine properly, the way it ought to have been done in the first place. There was loads of room to spare.

She has to learn, she thought, seething.

Bobby left for the office at eight thirty. "Have a nice day," he called.

Probably too late for that, she thought.

She wiped down every surface twice.

At five of nine, she dialed the number—44 West Realty Corp.—sitting at the phone in her husband's study. "Hello?" she said, when a man's voice answered. The super, she supposed, or the doorman maybe. "I'm calling from Bobby Sutton's office," she said. "One of your tenants," she added, bluffing.

Emma paused for a second. There were any number of

paths she could take. "He's asked me to messenger a package over," she said—choosing her route. "Can you give me the address, please?"

She scribbled it down: 44 West Seventy-eighth Street.

"And the apartment number?" she asked.

She waited while the man looked it up, turning the contraband keys in her hand. "Sutton," she repeated. "Robert Sutton." She wrote the apartment number down and hung up the phone.

That didn't take very long, she thought.

Emma supposed she should start in on her work. They'd be taping the home-office segment that afternoon.

Maybe next time, she thought, you could miss a trick or two?

But there was a soft note of sadness built into her tune that time. Emma knew very well that she'd be the prime victim of her discoveries that morning: the cell phone, that checkbook, those keys.

WHEN TINA WOKE UP, SHE FELT NEARLY INSPIRED, from the moment she opened her eyes practically, shielding them fast with the crook of her arm. She smelled the chlorine that was lingering on her skin, the residue of their swim outing the night before. Not even a long, soapy shower had erased it entirely.

Smells like medicine, she thought. And then she knew!—before she'd thrown back the covers even, inspiration coming straight through her nostrils.

We're going to the Free Clinic, she thought.

At her meeting with Benjamin the Friday before, he'd

recommended that she take Gracie to see a particular nurse there, a woman he'd worked with several times. Tina had her name stowed away in her purse, written on a piece of notebook paper in Benjamin's tiny hand. He'd promised to call ahead, to let the woman know that they'd be coming.

Maybe now we'll get somewhere, Tina thought.

She woke Gracie up the way she always did—standing by her bedside and whispering her name. "Gracie Grace," she called. Her daughter always pretended to be sleeping a little longer than she was—clamping her eyes shut, as if to fool her.

"Gracie Grace," she called again, a little louder this time, a swirling loop-de-loop built right in. Gracie closed her eyes even tighter as a smile broke out on her pudgy face. Tina smiled too.

"We're going to the doctor's today," she said—softly still, though her daughter was wide awake by then. She tried to make it sound like good news—opening her eyes as wide as she could—but Gracie wasn't fooled for a second.

"Are you sick?" she shot back. Gracie was terrified of needles.

Tina could hear that she was on the lookout for one already, hoping it might be meant for her mother instead.

"No, sweetie," she said, "I'm fine."

"Am I fine too?" Gracie asked, a little nervously.

"Yes," Tina told her. "You're fine too."

She jostled her daughter's shoulders, hidden beneath the covers still. "It's just a checkup, silly," she said, smiling down at the girl. But Tina could see that she wasn't convinced; Gracie studied her closely, as if searching for clues.

"It's time to get up now," she said. "Okay?"

She got her daughter dressed quickly and served up milky

bowls of cereal all around, without so much as a teaspoon of sugar on top—the way she herself would have liked it. Then she called in sick, which she hated to do.

They were just finishing up the January invoices.

"Don't worry," she told her boss—a pleasant enough man who owned the place. He sounded concerned. "I'll be fine," she promised, twinging with guilt before she hung up the phone, and coughing once more after she had—as if sickness really were a possibility.

She could already picture the mess she'd return to the very next day—her desk piled high with papers, and littered with errors that her well-meaning colleagues would make. Her just deserts, she supposed. Tina liked to do things right, but there'd be plenty of time to deal with her work, she thought, shrugging into her heavy winter coat. She was taking care of Gracie today.

She bundled the girl up, and herded them out the door.

I'm getting to the bottom of this, she pledged, closing the door so firmly behind her that anyone else might have mistaken it for a slam. Her mind was made up. She now had the name of Benjamin's nurse in her hip pocket, and determination enough for an army of men. Tina was ready to go—and fast!—all fueled up with that propulsive will that only comes first thing in the morning, before anything like a roadblock has had time to appear.

This is *not* about what I'm feeding her, she thought.

"Come on, Gracie," Tina said, prodding the girl, who was already walking as if she were destined to fall behind. "Let's go, go, go," she called, swinging her arms briskly as she walked down the subway platform.

Tina pretended not to hear the rustling of Gracie's labored

movements—the endless swooshing of puffy sleeves against that nylon trunk of coat, or the lower-pitched rubbing of thigh against thigh, the sound track of friction that accompanied her daughter's every step.

Tina just wanted a sensible explanation of what was wrong with the girl.

It was all she'd ever wanted—for someone to explain why Gracie was so fat—and Benjamin's nurse might be the answer to her prayers. Tina pledged to start off on the right foot with her too. Make it absolutely clear that her daughter wasn't overeating. She could almost picture the long, sad chapter brought to a merciful end: a diagnosis and prescription—a sharp needle maybe or a handful of pills. She'd take any solution though, so long as it included an explanation, and a course of treatment that shrank her daughter down to normal size again.

Her fantasy unspooled like a reel of silky ribbon beneath her feet.

And what's more, her brave, new mood held, even as she pushed through the clean glass doors of the Free Clinic—sauntering in, like the new cowgirl in town.

Tina headed straight for the reception desk and checked them in.

"We're here to see Mary Lane," she said—the name of Benjamin's nurse. "We were referred by Benjamin Blackman," she added, smiling at the red-haired woman behind the reception desk.

Today could be the day, she thought, sitting down to wait.

Half an hour later, Tina wasn't so sure.

"She'd be pretty," she heard an old woman mumble.

The woman was sitting off by herself, but Tina heard her

perfectly; she knew precisely where the woman was headed. She'd been down this road a thousand times before.

"If she wasn't so fat," the old woman croaked, folding her bony arms like an indictment, and letting her voice grow louder as she went—as if daring mother and daughter to hear her.

Tina looked down quickly. She saw Gracie in her big red coat, playing at her feet with the same old Mr. Potato Head set she always chose when they came here, poking a variety of candy-colored features—a yellow eye and a baby blue nose—onto a dull lump of plastic that was supposed to look like a potato.

"Don't you want to take your coat off, sweetie?"

Gracie looked up at her, but Tina couldn't tell whether she'd heard the old woman or not. Her face was as impassive as ever, like a costume mask from the five-and-dime, with its chubby cheeks of coated paper and heavy double chin, her eyes as mysterious to Tina as holes that were meant for peeking through.

"Do I have to?" she asked, hugging herself and her puffy red coat.

"Of course not," Tina said. "I thought you might be hot."

She felt a stab of helplessness; she was never quite sure what the little girl was feeling. Still, Tina decided—right on the spot—that Gracie *had* heard the old woman. She was only pretending she hadn't—her big red coat like a protective shield, keeping her safe from mean old women in waiting rooms and even meaner boys on macadam playgrounds.

Tina glared at the old woman, sitting off by herself. For good reason, it turned out. She wasn't reading a magazine or a newspaper, like the rest of them. The woman just sat there like a skinny old tuning fork, a torrent of mumbles humming out of her as if she were passing the time in lively conversation. Her face was puffy and purplish, and her skinny arms looked as brittle as fallen twigs. She was wearing an old black turtleneck, stretched to shapeless and faded to gray. But it was the belly that told the story, Tina thought—so big and bloated on her spindly frame, like a black warrior ant, all bulbous middle and threadlike limbs.

Mean old drunk.

She'd come in earlier with a younger woman and a pretty little girl in tow—her daughter and granddaughter, Tina supposed—not long after she and Gracie had arrived themselves. But the old woman's kin had been ushered into one of the treatment rooms already, a smiling nurse to lead the way.

No one ever smiles at us, Tina thought.

They just sat there—mother and daughter—waiting patiently as Tina's mood began to sink. She could feel the optimism leaching out of her like air from a punctured bicycle tire. She tried pretending it was the old woman's fault—her mean comment like a handful of rusty nails, puncturing her straight through—but Tina knew better.

In fact, she knew the old woman was right: Gracie *would* be pretty if she weren't so fat; and once she made that single admission—her first of the morning—the others came at her hard and fast. It shocked her to tally up all the things she knew just then, the little truths raining down as hard as hailstones. She knew she'd been foolish to come to the clinic. Of course she did. No one there—including Benjamin's nurse—was going to tell her anything she hadn't heard a hundred times before—a thousand times, more likely. Tina knew something even more frightening: no matter what happened in those little treatment rooms that morning, no matter what the diagnosis or lack thereof, Gracie wouldn't be shrinking down to normal anytime soon.

There wasn't any hope of that.

Tina looked down at Gracie, playing still in her huge red coat.

Soon that coat won't be big enough, she thought, gripping the arms of her chair tight, her eyes darting up to the clock on the wall.

Tina was running out of time, and she knew it.

But time for what? she wanted to know.

She saw the old woman trying to catch her eye.

Tina wouldn't give her the satisfaction of looking back, but she felt grateful to her all the same. The appearance of a real-life enemy—in flesh and blood—came as a small relief. She was only too happy to close the lid on her own box of demons, all nameless and shapeless and whirling so fast. The old woman was as welcome as a paperweight in a windy room; she kept Tina from blowing away.

"That your little girl?" the woman asked—indifferent, in the end, to Tina's refusal to meet her gaze. She didn't sound so mean, at least, speaking in a normal tone of voice.

Tina nodded, warily.

"How old is she?" the woman asked, friendly sounding, smiling through crooked, yellow teeth.

"Almost ten," Tina told her, as nicely as she could manage. "Aren't you, Gracie?" she said, placing her hands on her daughter's puffy shoulders, pressing down through the marshmallow of coat to the fat girl beneath.

Gracie nodded and looked back down at the plastic potato in her lap, its colorful features strewn all across the floor.

The old woman looked away—satisfied, apparently.

Tina was glad to have done her part, restoring peace to their little section of the waiting room. She looked back down at the magazine in her lap.

"Looks a lot older than that," she heard, a moment later.

Tina snapped her head up fast.

It was the old woman again—she was sure of it—returned to her nasty grumbling. She watched the woman wagging her head in hearty disapproval, a vicious smirk screwed onto rough lips.

"God knows what she's feeding her," the woman croaked. "Fat little cow."

Tina was stunned.

She felt her body surge with power, as if she were plugged into an electrical outlet, a million volts of energy careening through her.

Hadn't she just made up with the old woman?

The room felt brighter, as if the wattage that was coursing through her had no option but to spill out into the room, blaring floodlights all around. Tina could see everything then: she saw herself—not two minutes before—forgiving the old woman, and tossing her annoyance down like a harmless match onto a pile of wet leaves. It may have smoldered for a second, but that match had gone out.

So why this? she wondered.

And why now—an even more aggressive insult, coming on the heels of their friendly chat?

Tina's body was blazing hot, as if she were the one who'd kept her parka on. She closed her eyes and took a deep, deep breath, wanting to tamp those flames back down, but she didn't need to see the fire to know that it raged on still.

What the hell am I going to do? she wondered.

She looked back at the old woman, who was grinning like a loon.

Tina saw that she was crazy. It helped her settle down.

It's not her fault, she tried to think.

She didn't believe it, not at first, but she felt the heat subsiding in spite of herself. It really wasn't the old woman's fault. She couldn't have started a fire like that, no matter what kind of arsonist she might be.

Tina's body began cooling fast.

She knew what everyone thought. Of course she did—the old woman in the waiting room, and the red-haired girl behind the desk. They all blamed her—Gracie's teacher and Benjamin too.

She could read their minds.

She'd probably think the same thing herself, mulling over the unanimous vote against her. But it's not true, she thought, wanting to shout it from the rooftops. She knew it wouldn't do a bit of good.

Tina would never convince a soul.

Look at her, she thought, gazing down at Gracie again—the prime evidence against her, her daughter like a smoking gun. That mother must be force-feeding her, she heard them think—like a poor veal calf in a tiny wire pen—not slicing up vegetables, the way she claimed.

But I'm not, Tina insisted.

She knew it was true, and even she had a hard time believing it. She kept gazing down at the girl in her big red parka, at that full-moon face with its features stretched out wide.

Tina couldn't stand what she saw.

I'm not to blame, she thought.

She couldn't stand herself either, made up of selfishness and shame. She might not be to blame—not for the girl's fat tummy or face—but she knew that her innocence was long gone too.

BENJAMIN BEGAN TO GATHER UP HIS THINGS—AN armful of manila folders and a fresh legal pad, a mechanical pencil and a pen, just in case. He'd been waiting in his boss's office for nearly ten minutes by then, in a creaky wooden chair whose wheels wouldn't roll an inch—not on top of all that gray industrial carpeting anyway.

Dick Spooner—the principal at PS 431—was chatting on the phone.

Benjamin shifted in the guest chair and bumped his knee against the back of the metal desk. It made a hollow sound like a drumbeat.

He'd made the appointment for nine o'clock, and he turned up at the stroke of the hour, all ready to go—but he found his boss on the telephone, with a coffee and bagel spread out in front of him, the *New York Times*, in sections, underneath. Spooner waved him in.

Benjamin took a seat and waited.

He let his eyes roam around the room.

Spooner had worked in the public school system for nearly twenty-five years. And this is where you get, Benjamin thought: to a smallish office, with a respectably sized window, and a removable nameplate outside your door. "Principal," it read—a nameplate without a name—just a plaque on a door in an elementary school in Queens.

Maybe Cassy was right to turn up her nose?

Spooner didn't seem to notice him at all. He was much too busy quibbling over an apartment renovation he'd been planning for as long as Benjamin worked there.

"That is *not* what we agreed," he barked into the receiver.

He was a middle-aged man who kept extra-fit.

Benjamin watched him flex his biceps and admire it as he spoke. He pretended to be engaged with his file folders, as if he couldn't hear a single word the older man was saying. He wanted to spare him the embarrassment.

"In the master bath?" Spooner yelled.

He didn't sound embarrassed at all.

Benjamin opened his folders, one by one, and began thumbing through the papers he'd organized so carefully, in reverse chronological order—punching three holes into the top of every page, pinning them down, safe and secure. He was only playacting though. He was entirely familiar with their contents already.

Benjamin didn't approve of personal calls at the office.

"I suppose you're right," Spooner said, more softly then—fiddling with the ends of his navy blue tie, a pond's worth of kelly green frogs embroidered on it. "That's a big problem," he said, his voice laced with something like sorrow.

The change in tone reeled Benjamin in.

He looked back at his boss with concern, in time to watch him turn away, placing his mouth on top of the receiver. "The dining room is *so* small," he murmured—scarcely whispering his secret shame.

Benjamin felt like a fool.

He felt sorry for Spooner too. This was no racket for people who aspired to grandeur. He pictured the silvered mirrors in Emma's dining room.

Benjamin shifted forward in his seat, on the verge of standing up. Then he thought of the miserable dinner the night before. I suppose I can wait a little longer, he decided.

He couldn't afford to alienate both of his bosses.

Benjamin felt responsible for Cassy's rude behavior at dinner. He must have made her jealous. That's how it worked with his sister anyway—if he made any kind of claim on their mother's attention.

He waited a few minutes more, but Spooner's call seemed no more likely to end. That's it, he thought, standing up to leave.

His boss frowned back in annoyance and squinting confusion, as if he had no earthly idea why Benjamin would choose such an inopportune moment to stand. He shook his head briskly, and lifted his free hand, nearly touching thumb to forefinger: not much longer.

Benjamin sat down again.

He thought of Gracie—the reason he was there—of that cold afternoon, a month or so back, when he'd arranged to pick her up at her classroom.

He'd poked his head inside, interrupting a lesson in long division.

"Get your coat," he whispered, when Gracie came to the door.

She seemed confused, but went along with him all the same, plucking a bright red parka from the cloakroom at the back. Her classmates looked blind with boredom as the teacher scribbled on the blackboard, little explosions of chalk dust all around her.

He hoped Gracie would like the reprieve.

"Remember to carry the two," he heard, as Gracie joined him in the hall.

"Do you mind if we take a little walk?" he asked, starting down the long corridor. Gracie looked back at him, more warily than before.

"Do we have to?" she asked.

"No," he said, shaking his head. "We don't have to, but I'd like to get a little fresh air—if you wouldn't mind too much?"

Gracie supposed she didn't mind. "Not too much," she told him.

He smiled at her.

They put their coats on, and Benjamin pushed down on the silver bar that opened the school's back door, a gust of wintry air rushing in to meet them. Gracie looked up at him again, hopeful that the frigid weather might cause him to reconsider, but Benjamin soldiered on, guiding her back to the dangerous playground—where a small gang of boys routinely bullied her, pushing her onto the pavement and making squealing animal noises. And for some strange reason, none that Benjamin could work out anyway, Gracie refused to admit that it happened.

He wondered what else she was denying.

Benjamin made sure they'd be alone on the playground when he brought her outside, all the other students tucked safely into their classrooms—no one to bother her, for a change. He thought it might be useful.

"Don't you have a hat?" he asked, looking down at her bare head.

It was a bitter afternoon.

She shook her head. "I left it in my desk," she said.

Benjamin took the hat from his own head and handed it to the girl. "No cooties," he said, smiling down at her. "Word of honor."

She took the hat from his hands. "It's so soft," she said, pulling it over the crown of her head—a navy cashmere watch cap, a Christmas gift from Emma.

"It looks nice on you," he told her.

Gracie smiled up shyly.

They began walking around the playground.

The girl kept to its perimeter as if she might be safer there, beside the chain-link fence on two sides, and the school itself on the others. Benjamin let her choose the path and set the pace. She walked very slowly.

"Did you forget your mittens too?" he asked.

She nodded. "But I can use my pockets," she said, as if to keep him from taking off his gloves.

"We won't stay out long," he told her. "I just needed a little break."

Gracie looked as if she didn't understand.

"A break from what?" she asked.

"Don't you ever want to get away from all the people inside?" he said, canting his head back to the redbrick building. "Or is that just me?" he asked.

Gracie smiled up at him again.

"Sometimes," she said, softly.

They walked in silence for a few moments more. Benjamin heard their shoes touching down on the pavement, their leather soles clapping in perfect time.

"I like it out here," he told her. "When it's quiet like this."

Gracie mulled it over. "Me too," she said, nodding her agreement. It looked like she meant it. They walked a few steps more, and the girl continued, unprompted: "I don't like it at all during recess."

Benjamin kept on walking.

"Why's that?" he asked eventually, without any sense of urgency.

Gracie didn't reply right away.

"It's too . . . ," she started, but then her voice trailed off, as if she didn't know how to finish.

Benjamin was careful to keep looking straight ahead. He suspected she was on the verge of a painful admission, an acknowledgment—for the first time—of the terrible bullying she suffered there.

"Too many kids," she said finally.

Benjamin nodded his head. He supposed she was right.

When he looked down at her again, he saw she'd only put one hand in a coat pocket. Her other was exposed to the air, looking red and raw. Her left pocket was filled with something already. He saw it bulging.

"Want me to hold what's in your pocket?" he asked.

"No, thank you," she said.

"So you can put your hand inside?" he offered.

She shook her head. Benjamin decided not to press it.

Once they'd made two complete laps around the playground, he ferried her back inside. That's enough for one day, he thought. He knew that working with Gracie was going to take time. They took their coats off when they walked into the building. He headed them back in the direction of her classroom.

"Can I go to the bathroom first?" she asked.

"Of course," he said. "I'll wait for you right here."

He took the coat from her hands. It was Benjamin's responsibility to return the girl safely to her classroom. Gracie walked into the girls' room, and Benjamin opened her coat pocket as soon as she did. It was filled with golden coins—just a little bigger than quarters—the kind that had discs of cheap chocolate inside.

He knew that Gracie's mother worked for an outfit that made these candy coins. He'd seen it in the girl's file.

He remembered the box of gingersnaps, tucked away in Gracie's knapsack, and the girl's halfhearted denial that her mother had given them to her.

Benjamin shook his head. Strike two, he thought.

He remembered the unconvincing denials of his own childhood. Standing outside his grade school in the dead of winter, pretending—to anyone within earshot—that his mother had had car trouble, rather than admit the shameful truth, that she'd forgotten to pick him up again.

Why can't mothers just do their jobs? he wondered.

"Sorry about that," Spooner said, hanging up the phone finally. "You know how it is," he added, smiling across the desk.

But Benjamin didn't know how it was at all.

"We're finally closing in on demolition," Spooner told him, "and we've got to nail everything down."

They'd been closing in on demolition for years.

"So what can I do for you, Blackman?" Spooner asked—like a military man, or a sixth-former at some posh English school. He called the women by their first names.

"It's one of my students," Benjamin said.

Spooner nodded briskly, but Benjamin saw the wattage of his eyes dimming slightly. "Okay," his boss replied, landing hard on that second syllable.

Let's get this over with, he meant.

"It's Gracie Santiago," Benjamin said.

Spooner looked back blankly.

"The third-grader in Alice Watson's section," he added, but there was still no light of recognition in Spooner's eyes. "We met with the mother right after Christmas," he said. "The fat girl who was being taunted on the playground."

Spooner nodded vaguely, but Benjamin could see that he didn't remember her at all. There were a thousand students at the school, he supposed, and the principal couldn't be expected to remember every one of them.

Benjamin wondered if he tried even.

"I've been working with her for a month or so," Benjamin reported. "It's a clear case of neglect," he said. "And I suspect it may be worse."

Spooner didn't look impressed.

Benjamin knew that Gracie's case wasn't near as dire as most of the ones that reached his desk. There were no emergency-room visits in her file, no suspicious bruising or signs of abuse. She was barely a case at all. In fact, if it hadn't been for the playground incident, Benjamin would never have heard of her.

"For starters," he said, "she refuses to admit the bullying."

"So?" Spooner asked.

Benjamin might have known. He was all too familiar with his boss's view that kids should toughen up. "I believe it points to more pervasive abuse," he replied. "The girl's used to being victimized."

Spooner rolled his eyes.

Benjamin knew he'd better get to the heart of the matter.

"I've checked Gracie's medical records," he said. "She's

twenty pounds overweight, and there's no medical reason for it. There's nothing physically wrong with the girl."

Spooner looked back at him, a little confused.

"So she eats too much," he said. "That's not a crime."

"It's more than that, Dick," Benjamin replied. "The mother is allowing this to happen." He told him about the box of gingersnaps in Gracie's backpack, her pockets brimming with chocolate coins. "The mother is causing the obesity," he said.

Spooner looked at him skeptically. "You want to accuse the mother of giving the girl a bad diet?" he asked. Benjamin heard the contempt dripping off him. "Come on, Blackman," he said. "Half our students are—"

"I believe she's doing it *on purpose*," he announced, sitting up tall in the wobbly guest chair. Benjamin wondered if Spooner's indifference was causing him to dig his heels in deeper than he meant to.

"What are you talking about?" Spooner spat back, squinting across the desk as if he had trouble seeing, his eyes filled up with disgust.

It didn't matter to Benjamin though. He wasn't going to give up.

"I've met with the mother twice already," Benjamin said. "And I've never seen such a guilty-acting woman in my life. She's responsible for this," he said. "I know it." Benjamin decided he was justified in digging in his heels as deeply as he needed to: in the very best light, Tina was ignoring her daughter's interests, allowing her to get so fat.

"That's ridiculous," Spooner said. "Who wants a fat kid?"

"I know there's something here, Dick."

Benjamin was adamant about it. He'd convinced himself that the pretty young mother was acting out her anger on the little girl—probably furious with her, he thought, for stealing the attention away from herself. That's why she plies the girl with sweets, he decided: to make Gracie as unappealing as she could.

Spooner rolled his eyes. "So what do you want from me?" he asked.

"I want to make a psychiatric referral," Benjamin told him. "I need your sign-off."

"It sounds like a waste of time," Spooner said, huffing out a little breath.

Benjamin didn't say another word, but he didn't look away either. He held his ground.

The phone rang, and Spooner scrambled to pick it up.

Shit, Benjamin thought. He couldn't let his boss slip away. "Dick?" he said, with an insistence that surprised him.

"Hang on a second," Spooner said into the receiver. He looked back at Benjamin as if he were so much asbestos hiding in the walls of his tiny dining room.

"Okay, Blackman," he said. "Just don't let this get in the way of any real emergencies."

Like your drapes? Benjamin thought.

AT THE VERY MOMENT OF WAKING, CASSY PLUCKED the miserable scene at her mother's apartment from all the others at her dreamy disposal—like bobbing for just the wrong apple in a wooden barrel filled up with them.

It was too late for turning back.

She pictured last night's dinner in painful detail. She could see it breaking up fast—once the name-calling began anyway. She watched Benjamin running for the door like a white-tailed deer, in just five or six leaping strides—as if it were hunting season still.

Calling her mother a felon had pretty well spoiled the evening.

Why am I so mean? Cassy wondered, turning over in bed.

"We all have our nights," her father had told her as he walked her from the dining room into the foyer. He'd forgiven her already. Cassy appreciated his kindness, but she only had eyes for her mother.

She stared at Emma, and Emma stared right back.

She saw anger and hurt—in nearly equal measure—in the tight purse of her mother's lips, and the softness of her cloudy eyes.

Cassy wanted to apologize right away.

Of course she did; it was the least she could do, but something inside her held her back. Cassy waited instead, wanting to see how her mother would respond.

Emma kept looking and looking, as if she'd never laid eyes on her before.

It's a little late for that, Cassy thought.

She felt even more abandoned then, seething as her mother stared, as if she were a piece of gold jewelry. Was it precious to her, Cassy wondered, or merely paste? Her mother's gaze gave no hint.

Emma reached out and took her daughter's hand.

And still neither of them spoke. They let the moment pass.

Cassy pulled her hand away.

She might have relished the attention once—when she was twelve maybe, or thirteen: her mother's eyes on her, at least, if not a soothing hand at the nape of her neck, or a kind word on her way out to school. She wouldn't have minded the public squabbling even—not back then, not if it jolted her mother into something like attentiveness. Provocation had been one of the only weapons in the girl's arsenal, after all. She'd dragged irrelevant boyfriends home, nearly begging to be caught in the act, trailing the evidence of misbehavior behind her like so many neon breadcrumbs in the forest. There were ziplock packets of powdery drugs and condoms wrapped in golden foil; there were glittering piles of shoplifted jewelry, sprinkled like fairy dust all around her room.

But her mother never said a word.

"We'll talk later," her mother said—as late as last night, when Cassy walked to the door.

Probably not, she thought, waiting for the elevator that would take her downstairs—but that's okay too.

Cassy had almost stopped hoping for her mother to pay attention by then. She'd learned to make do with what was on hand instead: her anger, for starters. There was always plenty of that. She hoarded her mother's failure to inquire, the relentlessness of her self-regard, as if they were faceted rubies in a black velvet case. Her anger was more than enough by then.

Cassy was accustomed to inattention.

It's not the end of the world, she supposed, rousing herself in bed that morning. She could apologize later, at the office maybe. Or maybe not, she thought, smiling a little as she stretched out long.

She *is* a convicted felon, after all.

Cassy sat up and rested her head against the plush mohair headboard. She noticed a little fur hat down by her feet.

I don't have a fur hat, she thought, watching—dumbstruck— as the thing sprang to life, turning into a tiny brown dog before her very eyes. But I don't—she started—yet there it was: like a curly brown lamb shrunk down to size, no bigger than a furry shoe.

Its eyes glinted back at her.

The two of them sat frozen in place, sizing each other up. Then the little thing was on her in a flash, frisking onto her tired chest and licking her face with gusto.

Cassy screamed out.

Now she remembered—the featherweight of its little body, and the silky fur against her skin. She huddled at the edge of her bed, and the puppy scampered to a neutral corner, squeaking out a tiny bark. It was her impulse purchase from the night before.

Cassy had walked past the pet store on her way home from her mother's—just in from the corner where the cab dropped her off. Le Petit Puppy, it was called, next door to the deli where she bought her milk. There were always a handful of dogs in the window—little white ones usually, tumbling in the bay that was strewn with ashy wood chips and three tons of confetti.

She could smell the filth right through the glass.

Cassy wasn't a dog person.

There was just one puppy in the window last night—a little brown one with curly hair. Cute enough, she supposed, but she only stopped because the little thing was all alone, looking every bit as defeated as she felt. They might have been the only two puppies in the whole wide world that hadn't been claimed after a weekend of brisk trade.

Cassy saw the confetti, but she knew the party was over.

It was nearly ten o'clock on Sunday night.

She walked into the shop and asked a sour-looking man behind the counter where the dogs slept at night. She had a hunch that everything would be fine if she could just lay her eyes on a comfy little dog bed, or a fluffy pillow at the back—a mother dog somewhere in the vicinity.

"What's it to you?" he asked, scowling at her rudely.

He's not very nice, she thought—with his scowling face and nasty disposition. She wasn't quite sure how to respond to him either: what *was* it to her, in fact? The two of them stared each other down like quick-fingered gunslingers at the OK Corral, neither of them moving a muscle, but ready to draw in the blink of an eye.

The man behind the counter looked as if he'd said everything he was going to say.

"I'll take it," Cassy told him.

She'd never considered such a thing in all her life. I don't *want* a dog, she thought—not two seconds after she'd offered to buy his.

"Suit yourself," the man replied. He didn't sound impressed.

The man retrieved the puppy from the window. Cassy didn't know its age or sex; she didn't even know its breed. The man put together a little "care package" for her—they came free with purchase at Le Petit Puppy. She didn't know the first thing about dogs, but she wasn't going to ask the man behind the counter a single question more: look where the first one had gotten her.

"That'll be eight hundred dollars," he said.

Cassy watched the puppy peering over the edge of the bed, its furry little face hungry for the floor. It stretched its skinny back legs long, a bony ballast to its head's strong desire.

She recognized the warring impulse.

She cowered in a neutral corner, the bedcovers pulled up around her ears as if she needed protection from the little thing. She was impressed when it jumped off the bed finally, landing front legs first without a sound on the wooden floor. She watched it scamper out of the room.

Thank God, she thought, in pure relief, as if all her troubles had vanished with it, a poisonous wasp flown out the bedroom window.

It took her that long to realize that the puppy was on the loose.

She scrambled out of bed, chasing after the thing, peeking into the bathroom first, but the dog wasn't there. She nearly stopped to pee, but didn't, fearful that the little thing might have something similar in mind. Cassy ran through the foyer and into the living room, but the puppy was nowhere in sight. Just the kitchen to go, and she was heading straight for it when she heard the sound of water pouring beneath the dining room table.

"Oh, no," she moaned.

She saw the puppy then, squatting a stream of urine across her leopard-skin rug. "Not the leopard!" she cried.

The dog looked up at her, its head cocked slightly. It finished its business and walked right off. It didn't look sorry at all.

Cassy contemplated the yellow puddle, like a shallow bowl of consommé. It didn't seem to sink into the rug. I guess that's good, she thought, running to the kitchen for a roll of paper towels. She supposed it made a kind of sense. It was *skin*, after all—a leopard's skin; a dog's pee shouldn't sink into it any more than a burst of rain on the African plains. Cassy fell to her hands and knees and began sponging up the urine with a magnificent wad of paper towels. She didn't want a hint of the stuff seeping into her own skin. It was more than enough that the poor old leopard had been doused with it. She noticed that it didn't leave a trace—no circle of darkness or moistness at all. She ran her palm over the soft leopard, combing her fingers through its stiff black mane.

That's lucky, she thought.

But it was a strange kind of luck; she knew that too—the need for which might have been so easily avoided if she'd just left the damned dog in the store window where she'd found it.

Cassy got rid of the pee-soaked towels and came back to the living room with what remained of the roll tucked beneath her arm, just in case. She saw that the little dog had burrowed its way beneath the living room sofa, a chic Florence Knoll number in navy blue, just six inches or so off the floor.

It was awfully cute, she had to admit, smiling at the dog in spite of herself—a tiny camper beneath a blue pup tent. The puppy lay its head down on its two front paws and yawned wide.

Maybe this wouldn't be so bad?

Then it began to gnaw on a sofa leg.

"No!" she screamed, throwing the roll of paper towels straight at its little brown head. She missed, and the dog squeaked out another bark, darting from its perch beneath the sofa and knocking into the small side table, upsetting the little blue teardrop that Cassy had only just placed there with care, the one she'd stolen from her hostess on Sunday afternoon.

The teardrop fell to the floor and shattered into pieces.

Serves me right, she thought, giving chase.

The little thing had a funny run: more up-and-down than she would have thought, and practically no forward momentum at all—more like a curly brown rabbit than any kind of dog.

It made it easy to catch, at least.

She scooped it up and placed it in the crook of her arm. It felt soft and warm there. She couldn't help but bring her cheek down to its silken curls.

"Oh, God," she moaned, trying to resist it—visualizing the puddle of pee on the dining room rug, and the smashed-up teardrop, and the gnawed sofa leg. She tried to picture all the havoc it would wreak, but her visions were useless to her then. The dog felt like heaven in her arms, soothing even after her mad dash through the apartment.

And it wasn't so much brown, she noticed, as cinnamon-colored—just the nicest shade of auburn. Russet, she thought, and once she'd named it, she knew she was done for.

Cassy carried the dog into the bathroom, for lack of any better plan. She placed it down at the bottom of the tub and sat herself on the toilet seat. She needed to collect her thoughts.

The dog's ruddy fur looked even prettier against the shiny porcelain.

She felt exhausted.

The dog scratched all around the porcelain, trying to scamper up its shiny sides, but it never made it very far. The tub was too slippery and deep for that; the puppy kept tumbling down to the bottom again.

"Just relax," she said, in a quiet voice.

They were her first kind words in a very long time.

Cassy tried to relax too, picking up the dog again and settling it snugly into her arms. She felt her body unwinding at the puppy's perfect fit, her heartbeat slowing with its warm, soothing touch.

She supposed there were worse things than a little urine on her leopard-skin rug.

Chapter 7

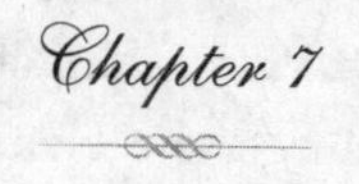

MONDAY LUNCH: *Beef Lung and Anise Biscuits*

EMMA SWANNED PAST THE DOORMAN ON HER WAY inside, a benevolent smile on her lips and a slightly distracted air—like the queen of a small European country. Her silver fur hung from her shoulders as she sailed quietly onward. She read the freestanding sign on its thin black pole: "All Visitors Must Be Announced."

She walked straight past it.

Emma had no business in this place.

"Good morning, ma'am." The doorman smiled, as if he'd seen her there ten thousand times. He probably has, she thought, nodding back at him, so regal, a fresh coat of lipstick lying heavy on her mouth. He'd have seen her on all those magazine covers when he sorted the mail, or on his television set every time he turned around. Just one of the advantages of being me, she thought, her tongue almost in cheek: she was free to walk into strange buildings with impunity.

Emma didn't kid herself though; there'd have been hell to

pay if that doorman hadn't let her pass. She had half a mind to call Bobby, in fact—to warn him about the lax security of the place—but she wanted the element of surprise on her side still.

She'd been more than a little surprised herself when the car pulled up in front of the building, 44 West Seventy-eighth Street—her husband's secret hideaway. It was one of those huge residential towers, a developer building that had been slapped up in about fifteen minutes and christened with a fancy name to compensate for the overwhelming cheapness of its construction—"The Vanderbilt," she'd bet, or, better still, "Ardsley Hall."

"Is this it?" she'd asked the driver. It looked so ordinary.

He confirmed the address.

"Wait here," Emma said. "I'll just be a minute."

The driver hopped out of the car and opened her door. She thanked him sweetly. She always seemed to manage sweetness best when she was a little afraid.

She glided past the doorman.

Every surface in the lobby was slick and shiny. There was a sea of cheap terrazzo on the floor, and ugly panels of milky glass attached to every wall. She walked on tiptoe; she didn't want to make a racket.

What were they thinking? she wondered, tapping past a small arrangement of Mies-inspired furniture. Vinyl would be a step up for these cushions, she thought.

Emma was conscious of her every step, of lifting her feet so carefully up and placing them down again even more so; she didn't want to slip.

Wouldn't that be the icing on the cake—breaking her neck in her husband's love nest?

Ex-husband, she reminded herself.

She sailed past the mailroom and into a waiting elevator, which carried her straight to the twelfth floor. She found Bobby's apartment at the end of the hall—number 12G. She fished the keys from a deep chinchilla pocket and pushed straight past the stubborn lock.

I should remind him about pockets, she thought, rolling her eyes at Bobby's carelessness.

She prepared herself before she opened the door, as if composing a face for the television cameras. "Here we go," she said, lifting her head high as she walked directly in.

Emma felt her heart drop down to her knees as she took in the scenery, all hollowed out inside; there was nothing to keep that broken, beating thing in place. She'd expected something from a Crate and Barrel catalog, generic and a little low-down, suitable for a college student, maybe, or a little better than that—a suite in a business hotel perhaps. But her husband's apartment defied her expectations. Every item looked chosen with care—fabrics rich and tweedy, the tables cut from a forest of burnished wood. She recognized some of the pieces from so long ago that she had only the vaguest memories of them; others she didn't remember at all.

And I've got a mind like a steel trap, she thought—when it comes to furniture.

She opened the velvet drapes in the living room and looked down onto a pretty playground across the street. She spent more time gazing out that window, at the splintery seesaws and metallic swings, than she ever had looking out her own windows, onto her spectacular view of Central Park.

Emma needed to sit down.

She made her way to a club chair in the corner. It was upholstered in old kilim rug. Too much, she thought at first—all that color and pattern colliding—but she knew it was only wishful thinking. The fabric had softened beautifully with age, and it was perfect for the chair, she hated to admit.

She picked up a section of the newspaper from a stack on the floor beside her. February 9, she read: just the day before.

Bobby had told her he was going to the office.

I need an Advil, she thought—maybe two.

Emma rustled for a bottle of pills in her handbag. She choked a couple down, dry—even though the kitchen and its sink were just ten paces away. She tasted the sugary coating on her tongue, and fingered a loose button on the chair's armrest.

She wondered where the kilim chair had come from.

Back when he was happy, she supposed.

Emma stood up again and wandered all around the place—strolling through the kitchen and peeking into the tidy bath. She walked into the small bedroom just beyond it.

This is worse than I thought, she decided.

There was an old oak suite from somewhere in their pasts—a tartan spread and matching drapes. She was sure she recognized it.

"From his mother's house!" she gasped.

This was no hot-sheets hideaway. Emma got the picture then: this was where Bobby really lived.

She wanted to be furious; she expected at least that much of herself, but for the life of her, Emma couldn't rip a single picture down or slash even one upholstered cushion. A sharp knife would be no use to her here.

I can't compete with this, she thought.

She sat down on the corduroy sofa in the living room.

It was camel colored, with crisp little arms and thin walnut legs. "And would you look at that picture?" she murmured, shaking her head at a breathtaking landscape on the opposite wall. She remembered Bobby's admiring it—at a Sotheby's auction, she thought, a million years before.

"Absolutely not," she'd said at the time. She'd never have a nineteenth-century landscape. Emma liked her art fashionable and contemporary.

Now, all these years later, she admired it, and its hand-wrought frame too.

Solid mahogany, she suspected.

Emma was forced to unlearn, in a stroke, what she'd spent half her life believing to be the case. He *does* care, she thought—having convinced herself, long before, that all her home improvements sailed right over his head. Bobby cared plenty—just not about the home he shared with her.

Emma wasn't sure what to do next.

All those vain promises he'd made when he came back to her weren't worth a damn, she saw. She wouldn't let herself wallow in hurt feelings though. Emma might feel frail at heart, but she'd be cast iron for the world to see.

She stood up again, and settled on the familiar: she rearranged the furniture. She dragged the kilim chair from out of its corner—pulling it forward, toward the center of the room. Then she inched the sofa away from the wall—letting it breathe a little. She moved the velvet ottoman to the other side of the room.

Much better, she thought, admiring her handiwork.

She'd opened up the room.

It was time for Emma to leave.

She stepped into the hallway and nearly bumped into a

girl who was rushing in the opposite direction. Looks like a prostitute, she sneered, fixing on her short, short coat and her tall black boots that shone a little cheaply. So much for the neighborhood, she sniffed—but she knew the girl was just young.

"Emma Sutton," the girl called out, as if it were the beginning of a playground rhyme.

Emma nodded heavily and kept on walking.

A few minutes later, she pushed through the revolving doors again, walking out to the street. She found her car waiting at the curb, right where she'd left it. She saw her weekday assistant—Allison—waiting in the backseat, her driver scrambling from the car once he'd seen her on the sidewalk.

"Too late, Danny," she said, in a punishing mood.

Emma opened the door for herself. She stepped into the car and took her seat, waited for the driver to close the door behind her.

"Everything all right?" her assistant asked. She sounded a little nervous.

"Perfectly," Emma said, settling into her seat again, as if she weren't terribly hurt. She shrugged the fur from around her shoulders and sank back into the upholstery leather. "Why wouldn't it be?" she asked, looking back at the girl through gimlet eyes.

Allison looked down fast.

Emma was sure she must be wondering what the hell her boss had been doing in some mediocre apartment building on the Upper West Side—for twenty minutes, no less—but she wouldn't confide a thing in the girl. She'd already learned her lesson on that front. She'd already sat by, stunned, as nearly every last one of the boys and girls who'd ever worked for her sang their hearts out to the *New York Post*, back in the thick of her legal woes. People would say just about anything, she'd learned, for the prospect of seeing their names on Page Six.

She wasn't going to give the girl the ammunition.

"Any calls?" she asked.

Allison ran down a list of three or four, but Emma didn't care about any of them really. "And a Mr. Tanaguchi called at noon."

"Who's that?" she said.

"He's from the UN?" Allison told her. She made it sound like a question; the girl made everything sound like a question. It annoyed Emma terribly. "Something about a Nakashima table?" she added.

Of course, Emma thought—the little man from the auction house, her losing bidder. "What did he want?" she asked.

"He said you knew where he could find a Nakashima table."

"I do," she replied, a little defensively.

She was on the verge of telling the girl to throw the message away.

Why bother? she wondered. But something in her balked at the impulse: Don't, she told herself, in no uncertain terms.

Don't what? Emma wondered.

She sat quietly in the back of her limousine, an index finger pressed softly against her lips and a wave of guilt flooding over her. She drew a perfectly straight line between her terrible behavior at the auction house and the betrayal she'd discovered upstairs, as if her thievery of the Nakashima table had prompted Bobby's abandonment of their life together.

It felt as causal to her then as if the tiny Japanese man—or George Nakashima himself—had placed those secret keys into the palm of her husband's hand.

Emma needed to undo it at once.

She'd make it up to Mr. What's-his-name.

"Call him back," Emma said. Then she changed her mind. "No," she continued. "Call Christina at Modern Edge first, and tell her that I'm coming by at five. Tell her I want a Nakashima table."

The girl was scribbling as fast as she could.

"If she's got anything for us to look at," Emma told the girl, "call Mr.—"

"Tanaguchi," Allison said.

"Yes," she said, all determination. "Call Mr. Tanaguchi and have him meet us there."

"At five?" she asked.

"Well, of course, at five," Emma said.

The car phone rang before the girl had finished transcribing her instructions. Emma had no doubt she'd botch the job. Allison answered the car phone, and turned to Emma.

"It's Benjamin," she said, her hand covering the mouthpiece.

"I'll take it," she replied, plucking the receiver from the girl's quivering grasp.

"Hello," she said, the way some ladies do—a tad softer and a half note higher than her normal speaking voice.

She was impressed with him for calling.

"I want to apologize for last night," he told her, without any warm-up or pleasantries at all. He sounded sincere.

"Whatever for?" she asked. She'd just expected him to thank her.

"Well," he said, "I think I rubbed Cassy the wrong way. I think that's why she snapped at us."

Emma didn't remember her snapping at him.

"That wasn't your fault," she said.

"Well, I think it was," he replied, contradicting her.

It was sweet, she thought—his trying to take Cassy off the hook.

"So I'm sorry," he said, repeating himself.

"She was just blowing off steam," Emma told him. That's all it was—a little sparring between girls. But she knew Benjamin wouldn't understand that. He never seemed to have any steam to blow off at all.

"By the way," she said, "I've got your cell phone."

"Did I leave it?" he asked.

"Well, I didn't steal it," she told him. Emma hated stupid questions. "We'll get it to you later," she said, handing the phone back to Allison, who looked at it as if she weren't quite sure what to do with it.

"Well, hang it up," she said—which the girl proceeded to do.

Emma sat back again, cradled in a sea of dark upholstery leather. She looked out the window to see how far they'd gotten—not very.

She was pleased that Benjamin had made the effort—not that he could do much to improve her black mood. She could have dealt with a mistress in three easy steps, but a secret life—a whole world apart—was something else altogether.

Emma felt beside herself.

Plus, her trip to the Upper West Side had made her late. She was supposed to be in the studio already, shooting her self-styled version of the perfect home office.

Emma was tired. And the day had lost its promise.

Getting into Bobby's apartment was the only item on her agenda that she cared about. And look how *that* went, she thought, a grim little smile baked onto her lips.

"ARE THE SANTIAGOS HERE?" A VOICE CALLED—A woman's voice. She sounded strict to Gracie.

Her mother stood up right away, but the little girl kept her head down low.

It was nearly ten thirty. They'd been waiting at the Free Clinic for a long time that morning.

"Let's go, sweetie," her mother said, reaching her hand down to her.

Gracie had watched her grow impatient long before: crossing her legs, then uncrossing them fast, flipping quickly through the big stack of magazines. Now that they'd been called at last, her mother was ready to get going.

Gracie hadn't minded the wait at all.

There was a big chest in the corner, filled up with toys. She'd studied them leisurely before making her careful choice, carrying Mr. Potato Head back to where they sat.

She liked the way people kept to themselves here.

Much nicer than at school, she thought, where people always seemed to be butting in. She could have gone on waiting, in fact, and she wasn't thinking of school then, or not *only* of school anyway—of waiting long enough to miss an entire day, or maybe gym class and recess, at least.

She wasn't trying to avoid a shot either.

No, Gracie would simply have liked to go on waiting. She liked being left alone.

"Sweetie," her mother said, a little louder that second time, wriggling her fingers down at her, like squirmy bait at the end of a fishing pole. She was trying to hurry her along.

Gracie looked up at the woman who had called their name. She was standing in the doorway that led back to the treatment rooms, a serious face to match her hard voice, and a clipboard held tightly in her hands.

She's old, Gracie thought, looking the woman up and down.

She was dressed all in white—like a lady snowman—with curly white hair and a loose white smock, a pair of pants that looked like pajama bottoms. I'll bet her shoes are white too, Gracie thought—resigning herself to her unhappy fate. She knew it didn't matter that the woman's shoes were blocked from view just then; she'd have her chance to see them soon enough.

"We're over here," her mother called, standing tall, all ready to go. Then she raised her hand like a teacher's pet, so quick to volunteer.

Gracie began gathering her things from the floor as slowly as she thought she could get away with, collecting the plastic potato head and all its colorful features. She placed them neatly in the cardboard box.

"I'm ready," she said finally, rising to her feet.

Gracie kept studying the woman with the clipboard in her hands. The more she looked, the less she worried. This might not be so bad, she decided, her nervousness melting like a strawful of Pixie Dust on her outstretched tongue.

"Let's go, sweetie," her mother said, sounding tense. She began walking toward the door, pulling Gracie behind her.

The woman in white was fat.

Sometimes that's all it took, Gracie found.

She was confident in her judgment too. Gracie was a real expert at reading people. She'd had to be—with grown-ups especially. Their looks told her a hundred times more than their words ever did. Gracie kept a book of them at home, in fact—a book of looks: a black-and-white notebook with white spills running down the front, and a circle at the center with two lines printed through. Gracie had written her name in between them, painstakingly careful not to let a single letter touch. Inside, there was a pair of long columns—page after page of two long columns: one of *X*'s, another of O's. They'd begun as a log of every compliment and criticism the girl received—an *X* for every admirer of her pink-and-white sneakers, or the cartoon book bag she carried down the hall; an O for every mean boy who called her "fatty" on the playground.

The O's outweighed the *X*'s by a large margin.

But that didn't dissuade her from her work.

Gracie was scrupulous at keeping track, and her record-keeping had grown subtler over time. She still logged all the overt comments, of course, but she'd begun tackling trickier exchanges too; her notebook had become a catalog of nearly inscrutable looks: an *X*, she decided, for the man on the subway, who'd pointed his finger at her and whispered to the lady beside him—all bad signs, she knew, but overridden somehow by his kindly smile; an O for the nasty woman with them in the waiting room, huffing and puffing like the Big Bad Wolf. Gracie wasn't sure those heaving breaths were meant for her, but she was sure enough.

The woman in white hadn't given herself away.

Not yet anyway, Gracie thought, studying that chubby, neutral face—neither an *X* nor an O at the moment.

The woman led them back to a room with a black leather bed at the center. She asked Gracie to take off her clothes—her sweater and her T-shirt, her beige corduroy pants. "You can leave your panties on," the woman said, just to be clear.

She opened the girl's file and began to read it.

Gracie hated the sight of naked flesh—her own especially.

She looked down at her feet as she began to undress, and she hoped her mother and the woman in white were doing the same. She folded each article of clothing the moment she removed it, then she laid it neatly on the chair before she took the next piece off.

"So you know Benjamin Blackman?" the woman said, closing the file and looking at the two of them.

"Yes," her mother responded. She didn't sound particularly happy about it though. "He was the one who suggested we come to see you."

"Mr. Blackman?" Gracie asked.

She was surprised to hear his name spoken here, so far away from school. Her mother hadn't mentioned anything about him. Gracie felt even more embarrassed of her nakedness then, as if Mr. Blackman might somehow see her.

The nurse nodded back at her. "Yes," she said, "Mr. Blackman."

"He's my friend at school," Gracie said.

Her mother looked surprised at that.

Gracie knew her mother didn't like Mr. Blackman at all. She'd known that for a long time already, but she suspected that her mother would change her mind once she got to know him better.

"He's very nice," Gracie said, to underscore the point. "We

make puzzles together sometimes," she reported. "And once he let me wear his hat."

Her mother didn't look impressed.

Gracie didn't say a word more; she wasn't usually so chatty.

"I think he's nice too," the woman added, nodding her head in agreement.

Gracie didn't like to see her mother in the minority, but it was clear that she'd been outvoted where Mr. Blackman was concerned.

"Gracie?" the woman said, calling her back to business then. "Can you skip around the room for me, please?"

Of course I can, she thought.

She kept quiet though; she didn't like to brag. It was a good start, she suspected, that the woman in white liked Mr. Blackman, but that didn't guarantee she'd be nice to her.

Gracie began skipping around the room, in just her underpants. She tried to do it as nicely as she could—lifting her feet high, the way they taught her to at school. She tried keeping the woman in sight, but she lost her for half of every skipping turn.

"That's fine," the woman said, once she'd made two complete laps around the room.

Gracie knew it wasn't a compliment, just a sign that she could stop her skipping. She was breathing hard.

"Can you come over here, please?" the woman asked.

She placed a chilly metal disc onto Gracie's naked chest. The disc connected to a black cord that snaked up around the woman's neck. She placed the earpieces into her ears.

"Do you know what I listen to with this?" she asked.

"My heart," Gracie replied. She looked down at the floor when she spoke, then back up at the woman.

"That's right," the woman told her, nearly smiling then.

Gracie studied the woman's chubby cheeks, the light-colored fuzz that sprouted all around them. She watched her squinting eyes. They seemed to look right past her as she listened to her heart. Gracie didn't mind at all.

"That's fine," the woman said, pulling the pieces from her ears and looping them around her neck again.

Gracie looked at her mother, hovering behind the woman in white. She watched her open the file folder that the woman was reading earlier. She looked a little sneaky about it.

"Can you step up on the scale for me?" the woman asked.

Gracie knew to be ashamed right away.

She wished she could go back to her skipping, but she knew she didn't have any choice in the matter. She walked to the scale and stepped right up, her white socks looking extra bright against the black metal tray she stood on. She watched her feet spread out wide.

Gracie liked shoes; they kept her feet in place.

The woman slid a chunky black weight across a silver bar, then inched a smaller one forward—tap, tap, tap—until she'd settled them both into little notches. The weights were staring Gracie in the eye. She wished this part would be over.

"That's fine," the woman said.

Gracie stepped off the scale quickly.

Her mother was turning pages in the folder still, scowling as she went.

At least she didn't see how much I weigh, Gracie thought. She felt grateful for that.

The woman turned around and caught her mother with the file. "That's not for you," she said angrily, snatching the folder from the table. She closed it roughly and huffed out a breath.

Her mother was in trouble.

"That's crazy!" her mother shouted back.

She was just as angry as the woman in white. "Where does Blackman get off," she said, "making accusations like that?"

My Mr. Blackman? Gracie wondered. She didn't make a peep.

"Why don't we discuss this outside?" the woman said calmly.

Gracie wasn't sure what to make of this development. She knew it couldn't be good—nothing so hidden ever was. She knew better than to ask.

"Why would he say such a thing?" her mother asked. She was very upset.

"You can get dressed now, Gracie," the woman said, giving her shoulder a gentle nudge.

It looked like she was getting away without a shot.

She pulled her T-shirt and sweater back on as fast as she could. She felt almost safe again with her arms covered up. She pulled her pants on too, just in case.

"We came here for *help*," her mother said, only slightly less agitated than before. "Not for abuse."

Gracie couldn't understand what had gone so wrong.

It wasn't her weight, at least; her mother hadn't seemed to notice that. Did she *want* her to have a shot? Gracie wondered.

She knew to keep quiet. It was the only way she learned anything: by disappearing and listening in.

"Why don't you come with me?" the woman said to her mother. "We can go to my office."

Her mother nodded.

"Will you wait for us here?" the woman asked, smiling at Gracie at last.

I knew it! she thought.

Gracie smiled back at the woman and nodded her head. She had nothing to fear from the woman in white.

Her mother left the room without another word.

I hope she doesn't need a shot, Gracie thought—though she knew by then that a shot couldn't sour her mother's mood much more than it already was.

BY ONE O'CLOCK THAT AFTERNOON, AND TWO small puddles of urine later, Cassy was settled into a conference room at her mother's offices. Russet was sitting in her lap, his furry chin resting on the arm of her swivel chair. Cassy combed her fingers through the soft crown at the top of his head.

She'd be happy to sit like this for a very long time.

There was a knock at the door, and the puppy sat up tall.

The two of them—dog and girl alike—stared, wide-eyed, at the homely stranger who was ushered in, summoned there from God-knows-where by her mother's trusty lieutenant, Ruth—a middle-aged woman of deep complaint, with a busy career and not much else to occupy her time.

"This is Pete Peters," Ruth said by way of introduction, wrinkling her nose at the silly name. "He's *supposed* to be the best dog trainer in town." It was no compliment though, not the way Ruth said it, with all her skepticism seeping out.

And right in front of him too, Cassy thought.

Ruth closed the door behind her as she left.

To Pete's credit, he acted as if he hadn't heard a thing. He let the rudeness roll right off. It may have been what made him the best. *That,* she thought, and his poor, poor face—which only a dog could love. It was deeply pitted with acne scars, and topped off with a massive nose. His skin seemed to be stretched a little tighter than it ought to be.

Maybe it's the scarring? Cassy wondered.

It looked painful to her, in any event.

Pete shook her hand firmly and nodded pleasantly.

He was about her age, she decided—somewhere between thirty-two and thirty-six. Cassy liked to keep track.

"So who do we have here?" Pete asked, smiling brightly and crouching down low, homing in on the puppy in Cassy's lap.

She offered the dog up gingerly, as if he were made of spun sugar—her thumbs and forefingers wrapped lightly around his middle, those little legs dangling down. Cassy was afraid of hurting him.

"Let me show you how to pick him up," Pete said, sounding genial.

He held the dog's stomach firmly in one hand, and let its bottom rest in the palm of the other. "He's more comfortable like this," Pete said, matter-of-fact, and smiling still.

Cassy had to admit, the dog looked happier with him. Maybe this wasn't going to work out after all?

"So what's his name?" Pete asked, handing the dog back to her.

Cassy was surprised.

She'd assumed that her failure to hold the dog properly would mean a suspension, for the time being anyway, of any further dog-holding privileges.

Pete wasn't her mother, she supposed.

"He's called Russet," she said, smiling back at him—holding the puppy correctly this time.

"Rusty," Pete called, in a lively voice, having misheard her, apparently.

But Cassy preferred that name, in fact—less precious, she thought—and the little dog did too, snapping his head up when Pete called it out.

"Look," he said. "Rusty knows his name."

"And he's only had it since the morning," Cassy replied. She was only too happy to join into the fantasy of her dog's prodigious intelligence.

"He's a poodle," he asked her, "right?"

"I think so," Cassy replied, nodding her head hopefully. In truth, she hadn't the faintest idea.

Pete gazed back at her, his brow furrowed quizzically.

Cassy felt chastened again.

"Well, of course it's a poodle," she said, tilting her head and smiling back, as if she'd been making a little joke. Most people would know what kind of dog they have, she supposed.

Pete walked back toward the swivel chair.

Cassy felt a flash of fear.

Was he going to take the dog away from her again, just because she hadn't known its breed? She held its soft body a little tighter.

Pete leaned in and scratched the puppy beneath its furry shoulders. "Hey, little poodle," he sang, his voice so calm and low.

Rusty responded immediately: stretching his front legs long and sliding them forward on Cassy's thighs, reaching his skinny bottom straight up into the air.

"Look!" she said. "It's Downward Dog!"

Her puppy knew yoga, it turned out.

"Where do you think the name came from?" Pete asked with a grin.

They were like a little family almost, she thought—a doting mommy and daddy, a pretty baby boy. Cassy looked all around the conference room as if to shake herself awake. She marveled at the persistence of such ludicrous fantasies in the face of her own family life, not to mention the three thousand photos of Emma on the wall, a persistent reminder if ever there was one.

The conference room they were sitting in was her favorite one, by far: just two walls of glass, with crisp white Sheetrock on either side. It was barely twelve feet square, only room enough for a wooden table and four conference chairs, the obligatory pictures of her mother on the wall—all in matching frames, of course. The room looked onto the executive suite on one side, and the great outdoors on the other, a quiet side street on the Upper East Side.

Her mother's operation took up an entire limestone mansion.

Through the outer pane of glass, Cassy looked down to the street. She admired the pretty town houses across the way.

Still, most people complained about this conference room. Like sitting in a fishbowl, they said, with its wall of windows right onto the hallway. It was the last to be booked generally, but it was always Cassy's very first choice, nestled between her own small office and her mother's Winter Palace, right next door.

That's probably another reason people don't like it, she thought: the proximity to Emma's lair.

Cassy hadn't seen her mother all day. She'd been looking for her too.

Her mother was the reason she'd dressed up that morning. All in dove gray, from head to toe, a chic silk blouse that was just right for her coloring—a sea of pale neutral to set off her shiny brown hair.

She knew her mother would approve.

Cassy wanted to make it up to her for the fracas she'd caused the night before: her rudeness at the table, and the pall she'd cast. She wouldn't skate away scot-free, of course. There'd be consequences to pay for ruining her mother's dinner. So she dressed herself up as nicely as she could, and came into the office not so terribly late, ready to fulfill her duties as head of the Emma Sutton Charitable Foundation.

Cassy heard a knock at the door.

She straightened her collar right away, preparing herself for her mother's gaze, but it was only Ruth again, with a tray in her arms: a pitcher of coffee and a plate of those anise biscuits that Cassy liked so much.

It was another reason she liked this conference room so well: her mother's fawning underlings. Emma might not give her the time of day, but her employees sure as hell did, swarming all around her like a hive full of bees, buzzing in and out, attentive to her every need.

Ruth set the tray on the conference table.

"Everything okay?" she asked. She sounded just as skeptical as before.

Cassy nodded. She thanked her too.

"Want to get down to work?" Pete asked.

Cassy wouldn't have minded a coffee and a few of those anise biscuits first. "Sure," she said as she watched Pete unzip his silvery backpack and pull all manner of strange equipment out. He looked like a magician with a pair of mourning doves and twelve long feet of fluttering chiffon. There was a brown leather strap with a shiny brass buckle, and a matching leash with a topstitched loop; a tangled web of black nylon straps; and a ziplock bag filled to the gills with what looked—to Cassy anyway—like dried-up pieces of poo, brown and wafery thin.

Rusty perked up at the sight of it.

"What's that?" she asked.

"Beef lung," Pete told her, very matter-of-fact.

"The lung of an *actual* cow?" she asked.

Cassy had never imagined such a thing.

"Air dried," he told her—just one of several preparations. "Do you mind?" he asked, extending the bag toward her.

Cassy backed away slightly. She didn't know precisely what he intended to do with those lung bits, but she nodded her head anyway.

Pete broke a small triangle from a larger piece of lung. Then he crouched down to Rusty, who gobbled it fast.

Cassy could hear it crackling in his mouth.

Like potato chips, she thought.

"You're hungry," Pete said, "aren't you, boy?"—ruffling the top of Rusty's head. The dog stared back at him intently. It was obvious to Cassy that the little thing was desperate for more.

"So what have you been feeding him?" Pete asked.

Cassy felt a flash of panic. She'd shared a slice of toast with him that morning, and a little bit of cheese. She knew that couldn't be the right answer though, so she settled on vagueness instead. "I didn't have any dog food at the apartment," she told him. "So I fed him what was in the fridge."

She looked up at Pete to survey the damage, but she didn't see any on his homely face.

"Was I wrong?" she asked, bracing for the worst.

"Of course not," Pete said. "Dogs have lived on table scraps for hundreds of years."

Cassy felt a wave of relief as she watched him break off a much larger piece of lung and hold it out to the dog.

She appreciated his tact.

"There's a great pet store just a block or two away," he said. "We can get everything you need there."

Cassy began to get the picture: Pete wasn't going to criticize her for being a lousy pet owner—no matter how lousy she turned out to be.

Not to my face anyway, she thought.

Cassy rarely trusted a generous impulse, especially one directed toward herself. He probably keeps more clients this way, she thought, rolling her eyes as if she'd seen straight through him.

She watched Pete fasten a collar around the dog's skinny neck, and the collar, in turn, to a leather leash. "We should practice walking on lead," he said, "before we head down to the street."

She nodded back at him.

He made a show of lacing the leash around his long fingers.

She could tell that she was meant to be studying his method for later use. He has beautiful hands, she thought—at least. She peeked up again at his scarred face.

"Let's go, Rusty," he called, a little singsong in his voice, as if they were headed to the candy store. Pete began to walk around the conference table, and the little dog went willingly at first, only balking after a few steps more and looking up at Pete—a little aggrieved, it seemed to her.

The trainer flicked the leash gently, but Rusty refused to take another step. The dog sat decidedly down.

Pete flicked the leash again—to no avail.

"We'll try later," he said, bending down to unclip the leash from Rusty's collar.

The puppy ran straight to Cassy the moment he was free.

She smiled at the odd little gait, that funny, hopping run—every step nearly as high as it was long. She felt proud of the puppy's return to her too.

"Look," she said, taking the dog onto her lap again. "Rusty loves me."

"That's not love," Pete replied. "That's just running away from the leash."

Cassy supposed he had a point.

"Believe me," he told her, with confidence to spare, "after two or three weeks of treating him right, that's when you'll really begin to love Rusty, and that's when he'll be loving you back."

Cassy felt her stomach lurch. Still, she looked at the trainer as if she weren't impressed, as if she already knew how the whole world worked.

AFTER THEY LEFT THE FREE CLINIC, TINA BROUGHT Gracie back to school. She'd planned on a full day off for both of them, but she was too upset by what she'd read in Gracie's file. She needed to address the charge right away.

The two of them walked down the long corridor that led to Gracie's classroom, the girl moving slower with every step.

"Is it lunchtime, do you think?" Gracie asked.

Tina had just given the girl a sandwich.

"Are you hungry again?" she asked, surprised and annoyed in nearly equal measure: It's no wonder she's so big. Tina hadn't eaten a bite herself; and after the morning they'd had, she couldn't imagine ever eating again.

Gracie shook her head.

Her daughter was such a riddle. "Then why did you ask, sweetie?"

"Because recess comes after lunch," she said, looking down at her pink sneakers as she walked.

Tina could feel her dread mounting with every squeaking step.

"I'm pretty sure recess is over," she replied.

"Really?" Gracie asked, smiling up at her mother, relief blooming on those chubby cheeks, her eyes half a ton lighter.

Tina nodded back at her. She thought her heart might break.

They were both relieved to find class in session when they reached the classroom door. Tina gave her daughter a hug, and told her she'd be back for her at the end of the day. She wasn't going back to the office herself. She had another errand in mind, walking back down the long corridor, her anger growing with every step: she was going to confront Benjamin Blackman.

Where the hell does he get off? she wondered.

Tina had only been hoping for insight when she peeked into Gracie's medical chart—for some additional information.

They'd told her that her daughter's metabolism was "slow-normal," that she'd always have trouble with her weight—they promised her that much—but Tina could keep it under control, they said, if she'd just stick to the diet she'd been given.

She heard the accusation like a door slamming in her face.

She tried convincing herself that she was being oversensitive. She'd always suspected that people held her accountable for Gracie's weight, but she never imagined anything like what she found in that file—written on a pink message pad, with Benjamin's name on the "from" line, his horrible accusation down below: "Suspects mother of making girl fat—*intentionally*."

She could see the heavy underlining on that pink paper still.

Tina nearly screamed at the memory of it.

But facts were facts, she knew that too: her nine-year-old daughter, barely four and a half feet tall, had weighed in at one hundred and fourteen pounds that morning, in her stocking feet. She'd gained three pounds more after six weeks of strict dieting. Gracie was literally off the charts; there wasn't even a place for her on the height/weight graph that hung on the treatment room wall.

It was a double mystery to her: How was Gracie gaining weight on so little food, and why would anyone think she wanted it to happen?

Even the nurse there, Benjamin's friend, who'd seemed sympathetic at first, had a hard time keeping her doubts in check. "You're sure you're following the diet properly?" she asked, when Tina pulled out the Xeroxed copy of the program she'd been following.

"Down to the letter," she swore.

"The portions too?" the nurse asked, her voice rising up at the end—the disbelief audible.

Tina had trouble believing it herself.

As luck would have it, she saw Benjamin walking toward her in the hallway—as inevitable as a winter cold. She felt herself growing agitated at the sight of him. "What a coincidence," he said, when they met, as if he were pleased to see her. "I was just about to—"

"Save it, Blackman," Tina said brusquely.

She had no patience for small talk, no further use for his charm.

What had they gotten her, after all, the progress meetings and the endless chat? Nothing more than a false accusation in her daughter's records. She was finished with Benjamin—with the phony smile that was plastered onto his face, and the clean white hand that was extended to her still, as if she might actually shake it.

"Excuse me?" he said—polite still, but stunned.

"No," she replied, shaking her head from side to side. "I can't think of a single excuse *for* you," she said. Benjamin was a snake in the grass, nothing more, as far as she was concerned—faking concern, but betraying them in the end.

"What are you talking about?" he asked. He sounded surprised.

Benjamin looked all around them in the corridor, as if he were afraid of making a scene. "Can we go to my office?" he asked. It sounded like begging.

Tina didn't care who heard her anymore.

She followed him back to his tiny office, next door to the

gym. She peeked into that wide-open room and found an army of boys inside, divided into two camps—each one hurling bouncy red balls at the other, throwing them ferociously, with all their might. The gym teacher blew his whistle, but the boys didn't care. They kept beaning each other just as hard. She heard balls whizzing through the open air, and the splat of stinging contact.

"That's enough!" the teacher cried finally.

Tina wished for a bouncy red ball herself. She could feel the pleasure of whipping it at Benjamin's face. She'd put everything she had into it too—just like those little boys did.

Benjamin stood outside his office door, waiting for her to enter first.

More of his phoniness, Tina thought with annoyance.

She pulled roughly at the guest chair and took her regular seat.

"Tell me what's going on," he said. He looked confused.

She'd always suspected Benjamin of disliking her, ever since their first meeting, when she watched him flirt, then turn against her in a flash. She hadn't the vaguest idea what she'd done to deserve his ill will, but all that seemed beside the point now—now that she'd read the cruel note in Gracie's file.

"I took Gracie to the Free Clinic this morning," she said.

Tina heard an unexpected flutter in her voice, as if she were running short of breath. She felt a quickening in her chest too: her anger shifting just a little, enough to let some nervousness in.

"Did you meet the nurse I was telling you about?" he asked.

"I know what you said about me," Tina replied, ignoring

his question—her voice trembling more than before, like the fast-beating wings of a tiny songbird.

"I'm sorry?" he said, polite but confused.

"Don't treat me like a fool," Tina snapped. "I read it in Gracie's file."

She let her voice grow loud and harsh. She was aiming for the antithesis of his. "You told them I'm to blame for Gracie's weight. You said that I'm making her fat on purpose."

Tina glared at him hard. She expected him to wilt on contact. That's what they said about standing up to bullies, wasn't it?

"Yes," Benjamin replied calmly, not wilting at all. "I did tell her that was one possibility."

Tina was impressed with his nerve, acting so cool in the face of confrontation, but she could be tough too. "What are you talking about?" she said, bringing her fists down hard onto his desk.

Benjamin didn't flinch.

Tina felt a flash of fear, a burgeoning sense of what she was up against. When she first met Benjamin—back in January—he'd told her that he wanted to work with Gracie because of some nasty business on the playground. She'd taken it all at face value then, but now she wondered if he'd suspected her all along.

"I wish there was a better explanation," he said, his voice measured still and calm. "But the people at the clinic assured me there's no medical reason for Gracie's obesity."

He wasn't backing off at all.

"That means," he continued, looking straight into her eyes, "that the people who've been entrusted with her care are letting her down."

That's me, Tina thought. He was blaming her without using her name.

"And I'm not going to let it continue," he said.

Neither was she. "Are you crazy?" Tina shot back at him, his calm demeanor like an accelerant to her own. "Do you have any idea what we go through," she cried, "Gracie and I? Do you know how many times I've dragged her to that Free Clinic, begging for help? How many times I've come in to see your useless school nurse?" Tina felt walls of frustration building all around her—as tall as mountains and pressing in close. "So you solve the problem by blaming me?" She was nearly shouting then.

"Please," Benjamin answered, bouncing his hands lightly in the air—a polite request for modulation.

"Please *what*?" she said, ignoring him and his sign language both.

Tina heard the trace of a sob breaking on that final word.

Please, God, she thought—don't let me cry. She begged herself not to, even as she felt her eyes welling up. She wanted to kick herself for being so weak.

Benjamin reached his hand across the desk, as if to comfort her.

It was just the push she needed.

"*Don't touch me*," she said—three hard pellets, fired at him fast.

She pulled her hands away from him and dug them into her purse instead, pulling out a sheaf of yellow papers.

She thrust them across the table at him, her hands trembling with anger and more than a trace of fear: six yellow pages—one for every week of Gracie's latest diet. She saw their pale blue lines through watery eyes; she watched them swimming across the pages.

Benjamin took the papers from her hands, turning them like a steering wheel in both of his—from vertical to horizontal—like some kind of treasure map that needed orienting to the west.

He kept his eyes fixed on them.

Tina had drawn vertical lines down every one. She'd used a ruler to make them straight: three lines making four columns, with underlined headings at the top: "Breakfast," "Lunch," "Dinner," and "Snack." She'd been meticulous about it, recording every morsel of food that Gracie had eaten since the diet began—even the gingersnaps she'd caught her with the day before.

The papers looked worn from all her constant handling, the folding and unfolding. Tina updated them all day long.

A nurse at the Free Clinic had suggested it: a food log.

Benjamin was quiet still, studying the pages one after the next.

Tina began to settle down then, breathing more easily as she watched him read. These papers would prove that he was wrong.

They will, she thought, won't they?

She summoned the determination she felt in making them. The breakfasts were easy, she remembered, the dinners too. She fed them to the girl herself, after all. Sometimes Tina recorded a meal before Gracie had even eaten it. Her bowl of cereal barely moistened with milk, the chicken breast cooling on the counter still, and Tina rushing to the bulletin board—so anxious to record every bite.

She saw the messy trail of tack holes running across the yellow pages, the pinpricks of light that came shining through.

They looked like track marks to her.

Benjamin sighed a long, deep breath. He looked up at her finally with a benign expression on his face.

"It's the lunches that give me trouble," she said, blurting it out in spite of herself. It was the one weak spot on her careful log. She wanted to admit it before he found her out. The school sent lunch menus home for the week, and Tina did the best she could: poking and prodding, as gently as possible, trying to work out what the little girl had eaten, without making a federal case of it.

The lunches may not have been complete.

"Thank you," he said, in a gentle voice, nodding his head a little.

For just a second, he looked—to Tina anyway—as if he weren't quite sure how to proceed, as if he'd been set down on the open road without a map or any clear directions for getting to the place he wanted to go.

Welcome to the club, she thought.

"Are you telling me that this is *everything* she's eating?" Benjamin asked, gesturing down to the papers in front of him.

Tina nodded her head. She told him it was.

"And you do all the grocery shopping?" he asked, as if to cover every angle.

"We live on our own," she replied.

With that, Tina watched him begin to harden on his side of the desk—like a lump of molding clay that had been left out in the open air. He sat a little taller in his chair.

"I appreciate your showing me this," he said; his voice sounded harder too. "I can see it took a lot of work."

Tina nodded her head.

"It shows me that some part of you wants to make things better," he said.

Tina kept nodding, straight through her confusion. It wasn't *some part of her* that wanted things better. It was every fiber of her being.

Doesn't he know that? she wondered.

Tina had to find a way to make herself known to this man. She thought she'd done that though, in their earlier meetings. She thought her food log would make things clear as day.

Tina began to feel a little helpless.

If Benjamin reached his hand to her again, she might not pull her own away so fast. She and Gracie needed all the help they could get.

"I'm confused," he said.

"How's that?" she asked. He didn't sound confused at all.

Tina stared across the desk at him like an animal in the wild: she was frozen in place, just waiting for the smallest twitch.

"It doesn't make sense," he said, "for Gracie to be eating as little as this, and still not losing weight."

It didn't make sense to her either. She stayed quiet.

"I *know* she's eating more than this," he said finally—laying the yellow papers down on the desk.

But how could he know that? Tina wondered.

She tried not jumping to conclusions, or landing on the accusation she heard so clearly in his voice. Tina picked up the yellow papers from the desk.

"*This* is what she's eating," she said. "I swear it."

Those yellow pages weren't wrong. They couldn't be: she'd kept such careful track.

"But I see her loaded down with junk food every time we meet," Benjamin said. He sounded exasperated. "That's not written down."

What junk food? she thought.

"And Gracie as much as told me you give her boxes of cookies," he said, "and candies from the place you work."

Tina was stunned. "Gracie wouldn't say that," she told him. "I never give her sweets."

There's something physically wrong with the girl, she thought—there has to be.

"Then where's she getting all that food?" he asked, his voice sharper than before. "I've seen it myself."

Tina didn't know the answer.

"She's only nine years old," he said, pounding away.

Tina shook her head.

She wasn't convinced that he was telling the truth about Gracie—her daughter never lied—or about the junk food either, for that matter, but it was clear enough that he was back to blaming her.

"I want to help you," Benjamin said. "I really do."

Tina stared back at him, as worn out as if she'd lain awake for three days running. She wanted desperately to believe him, in the prospect of some kind of help anyway, but he'd already made it plain enough that he couldn't be trusted—putting lies into Gracie's mouth, dismissing her careful food log.

Benjamin wasn't the help she needed.

"We're going to get to the root of this problem," he said. "I promise you that. We're going to find out *why* this is going on."

Tina breathed a long, deep breath.

That was all she'd ever wanted—from him or from anyone

else, for that matter. She only wanted to know why this was happening to her little girl.

"We think a psychiatrist might be helpful," Benjamin said.

"For Gracie?" she asked. "I don't understand how—"

"No," he said, shaking his head and interrupting her fast—as gently as possible, under the circumstances. "For you."

Chapter 8

MONDAY AFTERNOON:
Café con Leche

AT THE STROKE OF FIVE, EMMA'S DRIVER PULLED up to Modern Edge, the finest shop for mid-century furniture in the city. Its proprietress, Christina O'Dowd, stood in the doorway, a dark-haired woman in her middle forties. Emma could see, from behind her car's tinted windows, that the shopkeeper was already on high alert, looking out for her special guest like a duck hunter in a wooded blind—peering out through squinted eyes, searching for movement in the brush. Christina opened her glass door the moment Emma stepped out of her car, and she held it open too, taking careful aim as Emma crossed the busy sidewalk.

"*Querida,*" she sighed, once the eagle had landed.

It was some kind of Spanish endearment.

Emma knew that, but she couldn't say which exactly, and she couldn't imagine what prompted it either, suffering both her cheeks to be kissed by the woman.

Ridiculous, she thought—of the foolish kisses, and Christina's getup too. She was dressed as an Old World widow that afternoon, in a loose black shift with heavy brogues on her feet.

"*Café con leche*?" Christina offered—again, in Spanish.

Emma shook her head, brushing imaginary lint from the sleeve of her sweater. She'd left her fur in the back of the car. She couldn't imagine why a woman no more Hispanic than herself would cling so fiercely to a Latin identity. Emma studied the shopkeeper's ruddy cheeks and bright blue eyes.

What a fake, she thought—Christina's surname was O'Dowd!—but a consistent fake, at least: the woman had been doing this Spanish Rose routine for as long as Emma had known her, coming on twenty years now, with Spanish endearments pouring forth and that strong black coffee bathed in sweet milk.

Emma never cared quite enough to get to the bottom of it. Everyone's got their shtick, she supposed.

She began to look for Tanaguchi.

It was a sea of white inside the shop, with bright white walls and shiny bone floors, dozens of hot white lights burning down from above. The furniture couldn't help but blaze against so clean a canvas. Emma was impressed with the upkeep too. She knew that scuffs would be inevitable on a floor like that, but she didn't see a single one.

"Is my friend here yet?" she asked. The shop looked as empty as a graveyard—a tidy one, at least—giving the place its due.

Christina pointed to the back of the shop, to a massive globe that hung down from the ceiling. It was three or four feet in diameter, and made of woven rattan. Emma saw Mr. Tanaguchi then—his back, anyway—sitting inside the hanging chair, perched like a bird in a woven cage, his short legs dangling down.

"He likes the Nana Ditzel," Christina said, a sale blooming in her eyes.

Emma began to cross the room, the shopkeeper at a barely respectable distance. She didn't like being bird-dogged this way, but if anyone could help her, she suspected, it was going to be the senorita.

Christina had an excellent eye; there was no doubt about that. Her shop was filled with exquisite things—a Santa's workshop for the mid-century set. Any number of dealers could claim that much, Emma supposed, but Christina had more than inventory: she had a knack for moving it too. She sold every stick that came her way, and all at premium prices, her shop growing bigger and grander as the years wore on. Emma had seen the woman in action: making people hungry for the things she had, sprinkling them all with glittering appeal—the furniture and the shopkeep, the customer himself.

People wanted to join Christina's club; they couldn't wait to whip their checkbooks out. Emma had done it herself.

She knew you couldn't fake that.

Taste is easy, she thought, crossing the room—it's selling that's hard. Emma hoped she'd work her magic on Tanaguchi too.

He turned to her in the suspended chair.

He must have heard her shoes clacking hard against the lacquered floor. She planted her feet more gently down, smiling sweetly as she approached.

Emma couldn't help wondering if Christina had grown as tired of the grind as she had herself. She *created* this wave she's riding, Emma thought—she'd built the shop up from scratch, inspiring the hunger for all that furniture, growing it ravenous through will and hard work, the same way that Emma incited her much larger audience: all those women watching at home, yearning for her cozy sitting nooks and the festive accessories that she sprinkled throughout. Emma tended their desires with the greenest of thumbs, selling them every ingredient they could possibly need—fanning a seedling interest into a forest of cash flow and desire.

She felt dog-tired.

"I'm glad you could meet me," Emma said, extending her hand to him.

"Please," Mr. Tanaguchi said, wrestling himself free from the hanging chair, like an awkward boy on a jungle gym.

She admired his trim custom suit.

"It's for me to thank you," he said, "Ms. Sutton"—the hanging chair bumping softly against the back of his legs. His hand felt delicate in hers, like a sparrow she might inadvertently crush.

"Call me Emma," she said, smiling sweetly.

She wanted to be gentle with him. And she wanted penance for herself: a furniture outing to clear the slate from her double-cross at the auction house.

So *unnecessary*, she thought, begrudging her bad behavior.

She was always going to win that table; there'd been no need for any high jinks at all.

And if I hadn't won, she considered then, growing harder on herself with every passing second, would *that* have been the end of the world?

Emma felt a soft nudge of self-awareness. Small, but persistent, it had trailed her all day, flitting like a firefly on a summery lawn. She kept grabbing at it, over and over; she knew it was important, and here it was again, its faint light seeping from inside her cupped hands: she couldn't afford to be the kind of person who won at any cost—not anymore, she decided. She saw the terrible toll it took, every stolen victory another excuse to run herself down. Just as it had been since she was a girl—running endless laps around a cul de sac of sabotage and shame.

"Winning isn't everything," her father always told her. "It's the only thing"—barely suppressing a chuckle as he laid his winning cards down, collecting the last of her allowance dimes and gloating victorious every time.

Here's to new leaves, she thought.

Emma was determined to discredit her father once and for all. She was going to make amends to the man she'd wronged—or one of them, anyway. She thought of Bobby and his secret flat. On the surface, of course, it was she who was the injured party, but she wondered about that too, standing in the corner of Modern Edge.

Emma turned to Christina, who was lingering nearby—a light switch just waiting to be turned on. "We're looking for a Nakashima table," she told her.

"Of course, *querida*." Christina smiled. "Your office called ahead."

"It has to be spectacular," Emma announced, just stating the ground rules for everyone to hear: only a table better than hers could erase the stain of her bad behavior. "Mr. Tanaguchi is making a present to his wife," she said.

"What a generous husband!" Christina cooed, turning to the man with blushing cheeks. "You wouldn't like to marry me, would you?" she asked, with a flirty smile.

Mr. Tanaguchi stared back at her blankly, Emma too; they didn't like that kind of talk.

"I've got two tables down here," Christina said, recovering quickly—never one to keep a losing tack. "And one upstairs," she added, almost like an afterthought.

A phone rang inside Emma's bag. It didn't sound like hers.

What on earth? she thought.

But then she remembered: it was Benjamin's phone. She'd forgotten to give it to her assistant. "Sorry about that," she said, letting it ring through to voice mail.

Christina led them around the shop.

"*Fantástico*," she'd cry, from time to time, landing hard on that second syllable, admiring some irrelevant table or chair—in Spanish, no less.

Emma wished she'd get on with it already.

"Here's the first one," she said, pointing to the most ordinary dining table Emma had ever seen: just a single plank of dark wood and four doweled legs beneath it. It didn't look like Nakashima at all, not to Emma anyway.

"It's an early piece," Christina sighed—as if that made its dreariness something to aspire to.

Emma hoped their visit wouldn't be a waste of time.

"I have a client who's *desperate* for it," Christina whispered, with emphasis on the desperation. "But if you like it . . . ," she said, letting her voice trail off.

She'll screw the other client, Emma thought.

Mr. Tanaguchi looked appalled.

Don't worry, Emma wanted to tell him, as reassuring as a pat on the shoulder—there's no other client. It's an imaginary footrace.

"I don't care for this one," Mr. Tanaguchi announced.

Emma agreed entirely.

The second table was better, but not near enough: it had a gorgeous walnut top—no doubt about that, it stood gleaming before them. And it had the rosewood butterflies of Emma's table, those elegant insets that joined the planks together, but it was awkwardly shaped—too short somehow for its substantial width.

"It's a little stunted," Emma said. "Don't you think?"

Mr. Tanaguchi nodded quickly.

Christina didn't see it that way at all. "Oh no," she said, pointing to the table, as if there must be some confusion about the one in question, her loose black sleeve dangling down. "This is one of my favorite shapes," she said, with a gush in her voice, as if she were repairing an oily vinaigrette, adding as much balsamic as it took to make things right. "And the shorter length works like a charm in city apartments," she said, balancing Emma's criticism with an equal dose of praise.

"Do you live in the city, Mr. Tanaguchi?" Christina asked.

It was clear that he did—to Emma, anyway—from the frightened look on his face. Tanaguchi went mute, refusing to admit it, as if the wily shopkeeper might stick him with the table if she learned the hard truth.

"Mr. Tanaguchi lives at the Japanese embassy," Emma said.

She had no idea where the man lived, but she'd heard the bossy trap in Christina's voice too. She wanted to take him off the hook.

Mr. Tanaguchi's eyes widened with gratitude.

"We need something grander than this," Emma said. "And

more beautiful. I told you, Christina, we're in the market for an *exceptional* table." She didn't want to hear another word about the squat little thing in front of them.

Christina nodded thoughtfully, as if Emma had clarified an important point. "I may have just the thing," she said—never one to hold a grudge, not in the middle of a sale anyway.

Emma couldn't blame her for trying.

"It's just upstairs," she said.

Benjamin's cell phone rang again.

Somebody really wants to get through, she thought. The phone hadn't rung all day, and now it was ringing every five minutes.

Christina led them up a flight of stairs to a loft apartment above the shop. Everything was even whiter and cleaner up there. She walked them straight to the third Nakashima table, set off in a small anteroom. She made no introduction or preliminary comment. Just looked down at the table, then grinned up at them both.

It's perfect, Emma thought, the moment she saw it, like Goldilocks laying eyes on that third bowl of porridge: just the right size, and piping hot too! It was exactly what she'd been hoping for, every bit as elegant as the table from the auction house, its edges curving as gently as a coastline. The book-matched planks were perfectly symmetrical, and she counted four ebony butterflies joining them at the hip. Plus, this one had an extra feature—a gap at the center where the tree itself seemed to grow apart. So dramatic! And it looks to be the right size, she thought: ten feet long and four feet wide, just like the one she'd stolen at FitzCoopers.

Emma looked at Tanaguchi. He was no poker player.

She suspected then—thinking back—that Christina might

have choreographed the entire affair: showing them the ordinary tables first only to heighten the thrill of this last one, claiming even greater victory after the prospect of so much defeat. She might have had it *moved* upstairs, for all Emma knew, keeping it out of sight until the perfect moment.

Mr. Tanaguchi nodded his head in brisk little strokes.

"How much do you want for it?" Emma asked.

"Seventy-five thousand," Christina said, her Latin charm gone south of the border. She was all business now.

"That must be list," Emma replied, with a curt note in her voice. "How much for me?" she asked.

"I suppose," Christina warbled, ever so reluctantly—like a little bird peeking out from its nest—"that I could go to sixty-five," she said, "for you."

Emma looked at Tanaguchi one last time.

She saw the eyes of a birthday wish, flickering like waxy candles atop a chocolate cake. "We'll take it for sixty," Emma announced—her penance complete, or so she hoped.

"BOBBY?" HIS SECRETARY CALLED—THE WAY SHE did all day long—in through the open door that separated her desk from his.

"Yes," he replied.

He didn't care for the shouting back and forth. When he wanted to speak with her, he walked to the doorway.

Bobby was one of the named partners at an expensive law firm that specialized in real estate transactions. They made money hand over fist during those times of year when sunlight shone through glassy windows—at the height of spring and the beginning of fall—but it was February now, and things were decidedly slow. He had the corner office there, like Emma had hers, and his secretary, Susan, sat right outside, in a cluster of secretaries who worked for the higher-ups.

It was just after five o'clock on Monday afternoon.

"That was Emma's office," Susan called in. "She's not going to make it home tonight until seven." Emma's office phoned him all day long with little updates on her shifting whereabouts, and pointed inquiries—it seemed to him—regarding his. He found it mildly annoying.

"Thank you, Susan."

Bobby never asked his secretary to stop her shouting—to phone him on the intercom or walk to his doorway instead. He wasn't the sort of person who needed to express every last one of his preferences. He'd never said anything to Emma either, about her constant checking-in. She'd only get defensive, and he supposed she'd have every right to be. His determination to reconcile had caught him by surprise almost as much as it had her; he could hardly blame her for a little healthy skepticism. She probably thought he was leaving for good every time he walked out the front door.

Bobby had a capacity for taking the long view.

He laid down the document he'd been skimming, for the condo-ization of an old veterinary hospital. He was only too happy to set it aside.

The *smell*, he thought, wrinkling his nose as he pictured the putrid apartments that would result from his work.

He may have had the corner office, but he didn't take the proceedings there near as seriously as Emma took hers. Sometimes he wondered if his desire to reconcile with her was attributable, in part anyway, to professional boredom.

Could be, he thought, a little indecisively.

He knew that a much greater share of it had to do with Emma's fall from grace, the vulnerability he saw in all those newspaper photos, and on every channel of his television set. *That* was the woman he knew, looking out from all those pictures—the woman he loved. Bobby had been deeply moved by the backlash against Emma. It was so inevitable, he thought. Just when you get the taste for it—the power and the glory—they come after you with guns blazing. And it was just as inevitable, it seemed to him, that Emma would never have seen it coming.

He smiled at the notion of the *New York Post* bringing her back to him.

Bobby surveyed his cluttered desk, but nothing leaped out at him. He supposed he was finished for the day.

He checked his wristwatch. He had a couple of hours still.

Bobby was in no rush to head back to Emma's place, to wait by himself in those palatial rooms. So he ambled over to his briefcase instead, on the nearer of the lounge chairs in the corner, and unzipped the small compartment.

Bobby was headed back to the secret flat. He'd have a glass of wine and some *All Things Considered* on the radio. He'd make it back to Park Avenue in plenty of time for dinner with Emma.

He hadn't expected their reconciliation to be easy, not by any means, but he hadn't expected it to be quite so difficult either. Emma had begun to close herself off again as soon as he moved into the apartment with her, and he hadn't helped matters, he knew, by renting the place on Seventy-eight Street.

Something has to give, he supposed, but he knew full well that it wouldn't be Emma.

Bobby kept poking around the bag's small compartment, but to no avail: the keys weren't there. He felt himself snapping to attention, as if that silky lining were a live electrical outlet, and he was shocking himself, again and again, jamming his fingers in like that.

"Hang on," he mumbled, keeping calm.

He prided himself on his even temper in the face of small annoyances and terrible calamities, but he felt seriously challenged this time out. He kept running his finger all around that pocket, closing his eyes, as if to enhance his sense of touch; but it didn't matter how long he swirled his index finger, those keys were not to be found.

Bobby began to lose his nerve.

He walked straight to the coat closet in the corner, a little faster than usual, frisking his topcoat like a detective on TV, patting down the navy cashmere as if it were armed and dangerous. He didn't feel them. So he pushed his hands into those navy pockets—all the way down deep—the two at hip level first, lined in chamois. They were meant to keep his fingers warm on chilly days, but that wasn't his problem now: his palms felt clammy to the touch as he pulled them out again—empty. He checked the pocket up high—the one at his breast, where he kept his wallet sometimes, but never, once, his keys.

No one in the world had ever kept his keys up there.

Bobby rushed back to his desk and seized on the briefcase—his first hope and his last. He snatched out every folder and every single pad, shaking them as he did, just to be sure. He took the pencils out and the pens, the small roll of mints at the bottom of the bag, as if his keys might have wormed their way inside the silver foil. But no luck. He upended the bag, listening for the music of jangling keys, the metal rods clanging as they clattered to his desk, but Bobby wasn't much of a musician, it turned out. All he produced was a fair bit of dirt and three silver paper clips, a pile of white paper scraps that come from ripping sheets of paper from spiral-bound notebooks.

Where can they be? he wondered.

He ran his hands around the suede lining of the bag.

"Susan!" he called, as helpless as a child, nothing like the way he usually sounded. He didn't walk to the doorway either. He felt relieved when she appeared: a sensible woman of fifty or so, average in most every respect—save her extravagantly dyed hair. She'd turned sun-kissed blond a few years back, and was meticulous about keeping it up.

"I've lost my keys," he told her.

She looked back at him as if she weren't quite sure what he wanted her to do about it; she looked down at the pile of rubble on his desk.

"I'm sure they were here," he said, pointing into the bag. "But I can't find them now."

"I'm sorry," she said, a little uncertain still. "I haven't seen any keys."

Bobby kept looking at her, waiting for something more.

This was a job for Emma, he suspected. She'd have found those keys already; she'd have found them before he knew they were missing—the thought of which made him more nervous than before. Emma must never, ever find those keys.

It would be curtains for him if she did.

Susan walked to the desk and took the bag from his hands, like a mother who saw, at very long last, that there was no alternative to stepping in: her little boy would never do up those buttons all by himself. Bobby let her take it willingly. She made a thorough search of the bag, her eyes peering in. Then she sorted through the contents lying in a heap on top of his desk: there were no keys. She swept the dust and the paper clips into her open palm, the scraps of paper; she threw them all into the trash can beside his desk.

"Have you checked your coat?" she asked, as if she were inspired.

Bobby nodded.

"And your suit jacket?" she continued, looking up at him.

He walked back to the closet, all filled with hope—to his gray suit jacket, hanging beside his topcoat in the narrow closet. It was impossible, he knew, but it was a fresh thought, at least. He confirmed they weren't there.

Susan walked around the room, her eyes ranging high and low, like a pair of headlights on a dusky road.

"I'm sorry," she said. "I don't see them."

He thanked her kindly; he meant it too—for stepping in when he needed her. He sat down at his desk again. It was just a set of keys, he supposed, trying to settle himself down. It wasn't as if Emma would know what doors they unlocked even if she had found them. He knew it was true, but he couldn't tolerate lapses.

Bobby needed to be vigilant where Emma was concerned.

Susan called in again: "Should I let Emma's office know?" she asked.

"No!" he called back, startled and loud. "Don't do that."

"Well, you're locked out of the apartment, aren't you?" she asked, appearing in the doorway again, as if by magic. The emergency seemed to have had a salutary effect on her office etiquette.

"No," he said, "I've got those still"—in something like a normal tone of voice. He watched her looking back at him quizzically. "Don't worry," he said, cutting her off before she asked the question that he didn't want to hear. "I'll be fine," he said, nodding his head in brisk dismissal.

Bobby stared at the empty briefcase in front of him.

He remembered emptying his trouser pockets the night before; he remembered pulling out a delivery slip for a turkey sandwich. He'd made sure there was no address on it before he threw it away. I would have remembered a set of keys, he thought—especially with the tension from the dinner swirling all through the apartment, Cassy's bickering, and Emma stewing just a room away.

He could remember admonishing himself, earlier in the afternoon, as he stood in the peach-colored hallway, the girl across the way locking his apartment up tight: Be careful with those keys, he'd thought.

Still, he couldn't remember what he'd done with them.

Had the girl kept them, he wondered—the sexy one with the ugly face? He seized on the possibility. Maybe she hadn't given them back? It was unlikely, he thought, but his only hope.

He remembered the girl and her black go-go boots, her tight red coat and piercing stare.

Why couldn't he remember the one thing he needed to?

Bobby snatched up his briefcase and his blue overcoat. "Good night," he said, walking past Susan a little too fast, straight down the hall to the elevator landing.

"Don't stay too late," he said, the way he always did, but it sounded like an afterthought. He was busy pushing an arm through the sleeve of his navy coat, willing the elevator to arrive on the spot. He needed to get to the girl across the hall. He jumped into the elevator as soon as it came, pressing buttons right and left—lobby, door close, lobby, door close—his right sleeve dangling down behind him. He transferred the useless briefcase to his free hand, its zipped compartment as empty as his pockets. He finished putting on his coat and buttoned it up tight.

I'm sure I put them back, he thought.

When the elevator doors opened again, Bobby rushed through the lobby, just like everyone else in the world, hurrying to find that very first cab; he was heading uptown before he knew it.

Where could they be? he wondered.

Twenty minutes later, he walked into the secret building, straight to the elevator and onto his floor. He ran his hand tenderly over his beige metal door—no means of entry, but a foolish hope in his heart. She probably wouldn't be home from work yet. Bobby knocked on her door.

The girl answered it right away, just as fast as she did everything else—whipping it open as if a fierce wind were blowing through. She looked like a NASCAR racer that afternoon, in a short leather jacket with colorful patches and tight black leggings underneath.

"You're here!" he cried, so happy to see her. "I'm sorry to bother you," he said, "but I was—"

"Oh, my God," she interrupted—talking loud and fast, trampling over his every word—past his early jubilation and his polite apology too. "What was Emma Fucking Sutton doing here today?" That was the only thing she wanted to know.

Bobby dropped his chin to chest.

He supposed he'd known all along. He was sure he'd put

those keys back. So that's the end of that, he thought, closing his eyes for just a second. The hallway was quiet, but Bobby heard a riot of noise: the ticking of fluorescence overhead, and the water whooshing through pipes in the walls; he heard the girl breathing right in front of him, and his own heart beating, steady and slow.

He heard Emma in every decibel.

This time you've gone too far, he thought.

MELORA FLOATED HER ARMS UP INTO THE AIR—AS long and light as two helium balloons, touching palm to palm above her head, in perfect time with a long, deep breath.

Benjamin looked on in wonder.

They were facing each other in the open room, his own bare feet not twelve inches from hers. Then she dropped her arms in a slow, sweeping arc, her hands carving the open air, and bent forward at the waist like a pocketknife—a silvery blade retracting back to its sheath. She touched the top of her head right onto the floor, and placed her forearms flat as any stony sphinx.

It was a yoga class, for couples: Monday night at six o'clock.

Benjamin was meant to be doing the same, but he froze as he watched his girlfriend perform: her movements as smooth as a clock's second hand, ticking past each minute mark, no faster—or slower—than the one before.

I can't compete with that, he thought, lifting his arms half-heartedly up and bending over as far as he could go—which turned out to be not very far at all. His head hung down like a bunch of grapes.

He felt lucky to reach the floor with his fingertips.

It's not a competition, he reminded himself, as he often did on the brink of loss. Benjamin felt plenty competitive though: there was a teacher there, after all.

He strained his fingers farther down.

"Now melt deeper," the teacher called, in a soft monotone, that breathy voice that's used for reporting dreams to friends. He was a rough-looking man with tattoos running down his naked arms.

That voice didn't suit him at all.

There were pairs of men and women scattered all around the room—eight couples, he counted, plus the pair of women at the back who couldn't keep their hands to themselves.

Benjamin was having a rough time. He couldn't stop his whirring mind or concentrate on the poses at hand. His thoughts hopped from place to place like a grasshopper in a bed of Boston ivy, leaping high and covering improbable distances: from the rough confrontation with Tina Santiago at school, to Emma's squabble with her daughter the night before, then on to the rent that would be due in fifteen days. He had no idea where his thoughts might land.

"And deeper," the teacher purred.

Benjamin heard the sound of wings beating.

It was coming from the stereo: no music or lyrics, just the sound of beating wings, and an occasional bird cawing in the distance. He rolled his eyes, but he didn't bother with that sound track for long. The teacher was roaming all through the room, doling out little compliments and complaints. Benjamin strained to hear them all, like a boy with a drinking glass pressed up against the door. He made sure he knew the recipients too, begrudging every last one of them. Every word of encouragement to someone else was one less word of praise in the world, one fewer that he might win for himself. He knew it didn't make any rational sense, but resources were finite, in Benjamin's experience, and the world had a way of being miserly.

But in a yoga class even? he wondered.

There was just no avoiding himself, sometimes.

"That's beautiful, Melora," the teacher called, wandering over to their side of the room. It was only fair, he supposed. A blind man could see how good she was. Benjamin felt a little aggrieved all the same, longing for a word of praise himself, but the rough-looking man didn't have one to spare.

The birds don't caw for me here, he thought, sneering past his hurt feelings. He muscled his fingers farther down, until he felt a strain slicing through his lower back. He pushed straight through it—for as long as the teacher was in sight anyway. There was very little Benjamin wouldn't have done for the attention of that tattooed man. It was all he ever wanted really: for the person in charge to approve. He looked up from his stretch to find the man. It crimped his neck looking up like that, and made his back feel even worse. He watched the teacher walking away, his own heart sinking in perfect time.

"Why didn't you return my calls?" Melora whispered, breaking free of her perfect pose for just long enough to catch Benjamin's eye, then returning to it as effortlessly as before, as if laying her head and feet on the very same plane was her preferred posture.

She might have bent down deeper still.

"I told you I was busy," he replied, whispering back.

He heard the ice in his voice. Benjamin was annoyed with her for making him come to this yoga class.

"Remember to breathe," the teacher called.

In fairness, of course, he knew that Melora hadn't *made* him do anything. She'd only asked him if he wanted to come, but to Benjamin, it came down to the same thing.

It does, he thought, if I want to please her.

So he didn't return either of her calls—in a silent blaze of annoyance—then met her at the yoga studio at quarter to six.

"Listen for the sound of your breath," the teacher told them.

It was called *Ujjayi* breathing. Benjamin closed his mouth and breathed through his nose. He heard the raspy commotion at the back of his throat. It sounded like the sea, he thought, like the peaceful roar of distant waves. He could feel himself floating off—listening to the sound of his breath, nothing but that.

What if I did this always? he wondered.

He began to settle down, his heart beating slower with every breath.

"You're obviously upset about something," Melora hissed.

A bird squawked loudly on the stereo.

So much for seaside breathing, he thought. Benjamin wished she could be quiet. None of the other couples was making a peep.

"Now place your hands on the floor and kick back to Plank," the instructor called. "Gently, please. Beginners, walk back."

Benjamin was a beginner; there was no doubt about that. He felt a little stab of shame. He heard his classmates jumping their legs back behind them, landing heavily on the floor like so many sacks of potatoes. He knew they hadn't done it right, but he envied them all the same. Benjamin had to scuttle his own legs back: He didn't know how to jump. Still, he made his back as straight as a board—that plank of wood they were meant to emulate.

Just the beginning of a push-up, he thought.

He heard the teacher moving close. Benjamin locked his arms in place. The man stood above him, straddling his hips: "Just a little higher," the teacher whispered, lifting Benjamin's midsection from above. "Now relax your neck," he said, rubbing it gently, "and keep on breathing."

Benjamin exaggerated the sound of the sea.

He kept his stomach high and his neck down low. He tried so hard to keep it all straight.

"Very nice," the teacher said.

Benjamin felt a flush of pride.

See, he thought, that's all it takes. But he knew better than that: that's what it took, in fact, twenty-four hours a day. He was ever vigilant for that mumble of approval—hungry for it all day long—from Dick Spooner Monday to Friday, and Emma all weekend long. He turned to strangers in yoga rooms when no one better was around.

"Did you not want to come tonight?" Melora asked him.

The teacher had barely walked away, and here she was, ruining his moment in the sun.

Benjamin shushed her.

He knew he ought to stand up for himself, tell her that he didn't like yoga under the best of circumstances, much less after a long day at school. He felt his arms trembling as he clung to his push-up pose.

It didn't look as if it was taking Melora any effort at all.

Benjamin was reticent about speaking up. He'd always been extremely talented at figuring out what other people wanted, and frightened at the prospect of not giving it to them. That was his source of value in the world, he supposed—his utility.

The smallest lapse might cause a terrible rift.

"Now fold your left leg under your body," the teacher called, in his hushed voice, "as you lower yourself into Pigeon pose."

Benjamin hated this one. He bent his knee and jerked his ankle beneath his hips. When his leg was nearly in place, he began to lower his body down. He felt a searing pain spread through his buttocks and back.

"Remember to breathe," the teacher called.

Benjamin tried to, but his back and shoulders were too seized up for that. He flexed every muscle in his body instead, as if he might will himself straight through the pain. He was sweating profusely, and panicked that this moment would never end.

I can't, he thought finally, cheating his left leg lower down.

The pain subsided, and the sweating too; his leg was scarcely bent at all.

He looked over at Melora, folded into a compact little shape. More like a bug, he thought, than any kind of pigeon. She looked back at him, a question mark all over her face.

"I hate this," he said, surprising himself.

"What?" she asked.

"I hate yoga," he told her—from the bottom of his heart—"and I hate this couples class even more."

She smiled back at him.

"I'm serious," he said, resting his head onto folded arms. He was exhausted already, only twenty minutes in.

"I believe you," she replied.

It gave him a thrill to be so difficult. He waited for the fallout.

"Will you two be quiet, please?" It was the woman next to them. Her "please" didn't sound sincere at all.

"Let's get out of here," he said, with authority to spare. Their pissy neighbor was the very last straw.

Melora unfolded herself from her perfect pose and stood up just as gracefully as she did everything else. "Okay," she said.

Benjamin rolled up their yoga mats and walked to the door, with a fleeting glance at the yoga teacher. He couldn't help it. The two of them started down the narrow hallway, back to the lockers at the very end.

He supposed she'd be annoyed with him. "I'm sorry," he said. He really was.

"For what?" she asked. Melora didn't seem upset in the least.

"Leaving class," he replied.

"It's fine with me," she said, shrugging her shoulders.

Shouldn't she be upset? he wondered.

Benjamin felt confused. It was one of the extraordinary things about working so hard to please people, failing so rarely: he was always much more frightened of the consequences than he needed to be—as if the mountains might crumble down to the sea because of an aborted yoga class.

Melora didn't even care.

They kept walking down the hallway. Benjamin looked into an open classroom, at a bunch of women with babies in their arms.

"What's that?" he asked.

Melora peeked in. "It's new," she told him. "It's called Mommy and Me—a class for newborns."

"But they're just babies," he said. "They can't *do* anything."

Melora shrugged her shoulders. "It's very popular."

"They can't even sit up," he said, brimming over with frustration.

There couldn't be anything in it for those babies. It was all for the mothers, he suspected, with a flash of resentment.

"You're so funny," Melora said, turning away from the classroom and the women with babies in their arms.

Benjamin looked at her. He wasn't sure what she meant.

"What are you really upset about?" she asked.

Benjamin looked down at the ground, at his naked feet, so bony and fragile. He felt a bright flash of fear, as if those awful yoga mothers might come barreling out, their beanbag babies in their muscular arms, and trample his feet with their sensible shoes.

Benjamin didn't know what he was so upset about.

Melora reached out and touched his arm, the cotton sleeve of his sweaty yoga shirt. He thought he felt his eyes welling up.

Water everywhere, he thought.

He tried to locate that seaside breath again, somewhere at the very back of his throat. He needed to stay quiet for a minute. He was sure that the next word out of his mouth would slide into a sob.

They walked in silence to the locker rooms: the men's on the left side, the women's on the right.

"Are you taking a shower?" she asked.

"Is this working?" Benjamin blurted back, looking straight into Melora's bright blue eyes.

"Is what working?" she asked him.

"*This,*" he said, moving his index finger back and forth between them. "Us." He was more surprised than when he told her he wanted to leave the yoga class.

He hadn't meant to say anything so big.

"What do you think?" Melora asked softly.

She didn't sound upset at all.

Unfortunately, Benjamin didn't have the vaguest idea. It was why he'd asked her: he didn't begin to know himself. He was so busy trying to make her happy that he hadn't a clue whether their relationship was working for him.

He knew he felt terribly burdened.

Melora stood still as a stone, as if it were another yoga pose.

"I don't know," he said, a moment later. "It feels like too much for me sometimes—a complete disaster if I can't figure out what you want, and somehow even worse if I do. Then it's just on to the next thing," he told her.

It's true, he thought. He hadn't sugarcoated it for her. He felt as if he were walking on a treadmill with her, shifting always into higher gear.

"Maybe you should think about what *you* want," she told him. "Every once in a while, anyway," she added, after a pause. She smiled back at him.

It sounded like a tall order to Benjamin though. How could he possibly figure out what he wanted at this late date?

He didn't have much experience in that department.

They stood in silence for a moment longer.

"I feel like a kid sometimes," he said. "Just waiting to be told."

Melora looked back at him, a broad stripe of confusion painted across her face. "I'm not your mother," she told him. "And you're not eight years old anymore."

"I know that," he said, snapping back at her.

But Benjamin didn't know anything of the kind.

He didn't know what he knew anymore. "There's so much child in me still," he mumbled.

Melora looked at him kindly. "Well, I don't think you'll ever be eight again, Benny," she said, wrapping her arm around him, sweaty shirt and all.

Benjamin nodded heavily.

EMMA WALKED OUT OF THE FURNITURE SHOP, HER Japanese cohort in tow.

It was almost closing time—just before six.

They'd concluded all their business inside: they were both proud owners of Nakashima tables then, waving good-bye to the shopkeeper and sixty thousand of Mr. Tanaguchi's hard-earned dollars.

"*Adiós,*" Christina called—Spanish to the very end.

"I'm glad it worked out," Emma said, extending her hand to Tanaguchi.

Something in his formal mien had her shaking hands with him far more often than she would have thought strictly necessary. She was careful when she shook—marveling, again, over his tiny fingers, the bones as slim as a hummingbird's neck. Emma knew her strength; she knew to be frightened of it—but Tanaguchi didn't, pumping his gray-flanneled arm energetically, thanking her for going to so much trouble on his behalf.

"No trouble at all," she said, spotting her car over his left shoulder.

The driver had kept the engine idling.

In fact, it was a fair bit of trouble, beginning with her foolishness at the auction house. Emma was glad she'd put things right, or somewhat right, at least. The two tables were about a wash, she hoped—and once she figured in the auction premium, she realized, with a small flush of pleasure, that she'd actually ended up paying a little more for hers.

Still, correcting the problem hadn't erased the sting entirely.

I deserve what I get, she thought, pulling stunts like that.

She wondered if she'd learned her lesson at last, having repeated this mistake ten thousand times before: driven to win at any cost, only to find the price so high, her self-regard trampled underfoot.

And all for a stupid table, she thought, hoping against hope that there wouldn't need to be ten thousand errors more.

"Will you let me know what your wife thinks of it?" Emma asked, walking toward her car. Tanaguchi nodded quickly, his eyes glued to her as reverently as a national monument. He was keeping strangely close.

Does he want a ride from me too? Emma wondered.

She wasn't sure where her obligation ended. She owed the man something, she was sure of that, but hadn't she made it up to him already—the stunning table a perfect tit-for-tat? She wanted to get into her car and drive away, but she could see that Tanaguchi wasn't finished with her yet.

"I didn't call because of the table," he said, looking down

at the sidewalk between them. He sounded nervous, on the verge of a painful admission.

But hadn't he just bought a table?

"Or not *just* for the table," he said, clarifying a little.

Emma's car began to look extremely appealing to her. She suspected him of a low-grade crush or—worse—some kind of revved-up fandom.

"I spoke to the secretary general this morning," he said—the man who ran the United Nations. Tanaguchi looked back at her as forthrightly as a child. "I told him all about you," he said.

"Really?" she replied, as if she were flattered.

Emma wasn't interested in the least. She tried to signal her driver through the tinted windows, opening her eyes wide in their sockets. She'd had enough of conversations like these to last a lifetime, with their promising beginnings—her name dangled in front of some prominent man, the head of the United Nations, the chairman of Goldman Sachs—but they came to nothing soon enough. Those conversations were never about her, really.

Her fans had a way of placing themselves front and center.

"I told him how kind you were," he said.

Emma felt a pang. Her "kindness" was a sore spot still.

"It was nothing," she said. "Really." She'd changed her mind about the conversation though; she'd just as soon hear how it turned out.

What if the secretary general had pieced together what a scoundrel she was?

Emma looked down at the sidewalk herself.

Her alligator shoes looked beautiful—perfectly still on the concrete walk.

Mr. Tanaguchi grew more animated. "We've been asked," he said, his voice full of pep, "the Japanese delegation, I mean, to chair a commission on relief efforts in the wake of natural disasters." He sounded excited about it, as breathless as a teenage girl confessing a crush to her very best friend.

"The secretary general asked me to lead the charge." He had so much to say, the words came tumbling out.

Emma could see how proud he was.

She congratulated him, but she was confused as well. She wondered why he was telling her any of this. She took another step toward her car.

It's nothing to do with me, she thought.

"It's a serious problem," he said, looking straight at her.

"Yes, I know," she replied. "You can't open a paper these days without seeing something about it."

She was ready to leave, but Tanaguchi kept close to her.

"And it's not just here," he said, sounding desperate. "Not just Katrina. It's a worldwide problem."

He was shadowing her every step. He didn't want her to get away.

"It's affecting the welfare of people in nearly every country," he said, looking her square in the eyes.

Emma could see the sincerity. She wished she had a taste for public service herself—as if it were a living room arrangement she might whip up. Oh, well, she thought, shrugging it off—fresh out of sofas.

"And we could do so much more with a global response," he said. "In most cases anyway."

He was on natural disasters still.

Emma realized that she'd been a red herring in his conversation with the secretary general, just a boldfaced name to be dangled down, nothing to do with her at all. "I wish you good luck with it," she said, moving decidedly toward the car.

Her driver hopped out—*finally*, she thought—opening the door so she could slip inside.

"We were hoping—" he said, a little more quickly now, as if he saw his moment slipping past.

Emma heard it too: he was getting to the point.

She feared a dinner invitation.

"We'd like you to be the spokesman," he said.

"Of what?" she asked. "Your committee?"

Tanaguchi nodded. She watched his tiny head bouncing up and down.

"Why me?" she asked.

"We think you'd be perfect," he said, scarcely able to contain himself. "Reliable and trustworthy," he told her.

Emma could think of a few people at the Internal Revenue who might disagree.

"The media will cover anything you say," he continued. "And people will listen to you."

It didn't sound like a terrible idea, actually.

Emma thought of Elizabeth Taylor and her AIDS work; she thought of Audrey Hepburn and UNICEF. It couldn't hurt, she supposed.

"You know," she said, getting straight to the point, "I've had some trouble lately." She straightened her camel-haired posture and steeled her handsome face.

"I'm sure you heard about it," she added.

"We've all had our troubles," Tanaguchi told her. "They only make us stronger in the end," he said, smiling kindly.

He sounded as if he were sure of it.

Emma felt grateful to him—the stranger she'd screwed

just two days before. She knew, then and there, that she'd accept his offer.

"It's very kind of you," she said. "May I think about it?"

"Of course," he replied. "May I call you?"

Emma nodded as she stepped into the car. "I'll need to know what the job entails," she said. Her driver closed the door behind her. She saw Tanaguchi nodding through the tinted window. He looked as if he could make her out still, but she knew he couldn't. She smiled back at him anyway as she settled herself into her seat, wrapping the chinchilla around her shoulders. She'd grown chilly lingering outside.

Emma felt something like happy—for the first time in a long time.

Her Tanaguchi was like a gift that kept on giving, offering her so many chances to redeem herself: first with the table, she thought, and now with this—an opportunity to become a public servant, working on the side of the angels.

Tornado-ravaged angels, she thought, smiling to herself.

"Let's head home," she told the driver.

Benjamin's cell phone rang again—for the fourth time in half an hour.

Emma fished it out of her bag. She wanted to turn it off, but she didn't know how. All the buttons were so tiny. So she answered it instead. "Hello?"

"Is Benjamin Blackman there?" It was a woman's voice—youngish, by the sound of it. Not the girlfriend, at least; Emma was glad of that.

"I'm sorry," she said. "He's not here."

"I'd like to speak to his supervisor then," the woman continued.

Emma was confused—for about a tenth of a second.

But no one on earth would refer to *her* as Benjamin's supervisor. It must be someone from school.

She should take a message, and leave it at that. But the woman on the phone sounded plainly distraught, her voice fluttering toward the end of its rope, just a step or two away from an explosion of some kind—either in tears or in rage, Emma couldn't tell which.

Plus, today was a day for good deeds.

And God knows when that'll happen again, she thought.

"This is she," Emma spoke into the cell phone.

It wasn't a lie, not technically anyway.

"I need to make a complaint about Mr. Blackman," the woman said.

Emma was intrigued. She'd never had a moment's trouble with Benjamin herself; she couldn't imagine what a "complaint" against him might be.

"With whom am I speaking?" Emma asked.

"Tina Santiago," the woman said. She offered to spell it for her, as if Emma were taking notes, or looking her up on some official roll.

"Okay, Tina," Emma said softly, repeating her name back to her, the way she'd learned to do on all those daytime television shows—taking questions from the studio audience and creating a personal bond.

"Why don't you tell me what's going on?" she said.

Then she settled back into her seat, into her newfound career as a social worker. It was her third good deed of the day, and it wasn't even dark yet.

It wasn't much of a sacrifice either: the uptown traffic was terrible.

"It's my little girl," the woman began.

Emma felt out of her depth at once. She thought of her daughter and her mother; she thought of herself too, her father smirking from the sidelines. What Emma didn't know about little girls could fill a very thick book.

"Her name's Gracie," Tina said.

Emma might not know about girls, but she knew a kindred spirit when she heard one—the sound of a woman who was convinced she'd wrecked a life.

"Go on," she said.

Chapter 9

THE FOLLOWING SUNDAY:
Sweet 'n' Sours

BOBBY STRETCHED OUT IN HIS FAVORITE CHAIR, the soft one that was covered in old kilim rug. He reached his legs onto the ottoman in front of him—theoretically comfortable, but not.

He knew it should have been curtains for him: like the little red fox who steps into a steel trap, those ragged metal teeth springing down to bone. Bobby could almost picture Emma parading down the corridors of his not-so-secret apartment building. He winced at the thought of it.

But here he was still—all in one piece.

He fingered the kilim-covered button on the chair's armrest, trying to concentrate on the Sunday paper, plodding through the sections like a diligent schoolboy—even the slim afterthoughts of automotive and society news.

He couldn't pay attention to any of them.

Bobby was bewildered by his good luck still. Against all odds, a kindly farmer had set that red fox loose.

It doesn't make any sense, he thought, looking up from his paper to the rainy landscape hanging on the window wall, the very one that Emma had rejected all those years before.

"Would you like some more coffee?" the housekeeper asked, poking her head into the spacious room, careful to keep the rest of herself at bay.

"No, thanks," he said, smiling back.

Bobby looked back at the painting, at the pointillist clouds in its canvas sky. They were raining down still, just as they had for twenty years, even as wintry sun smiled into the room, pouring in through large casement windows and firing up the fancy rugs.

He felt a little warm.

He had half a mind to take his sweater off, but he was so satisfied with things as they were just then that he was loath to change a single one of them. So he stayed as he was, a little overheated beneath that layer of Shetland wool.

This wasn't Bobby's secret apartment.

It wasn't even the West Side, the longtime home to his kilim-covered chair and the horsehide ottoman beneath his feet. The sun had never poured into his secret rooms—not like this, he thought—and for all the times he'd moved that rainy landscape, from place to secret place, it had never once hung on such lushly paneled walls. Bobby was as confused as if he'd stumbled onto an old-time lover in a brand-new bed, smiling up at him from crisp white sheets.

He and his things were installed at Emma's place: the armchair and the ottoman, the secret landscape that was painted in oils.

It was all her idea too.

He was mystified by his brilliant wife, but thrilled at the outcome all the same.

Just then, he heard a crashing racket from down the hall—a rainstorm of clattering metal and a heavy, thudding fall. He jumped up from his chair with a heartfelt pang for the new housekeeper: he'd be sorry to see her go.

But it was Emma he found sprawled out on the dining room floor, a riot of silverware on the glass-topped table, and plenty more strewn on the rug around her.

"Are you hurt?" he asked.

"I'm fine," she said, sitting up and giving her head a rueful shake. "Other than being a clumsy ox," she added.

Bobby reached down and helped her up.

"You're Cyd Charisse in my book, kiddo."

He wasn't accustomed to seeing his wife in such disarray. Even in prison, she'd been so self-possessed. He had to admit that her clumsiness gave him a glinting pleasure.

Emma smiled as she struggled to her feet.

Bobby straightened the Persian rug she'd tripped over, and gathered up the chunks of a striped Venini vase. The housekeeper dashed in and snatched the ruined pieces from his hands, spiriting them away.

They knew how Emma loathed the evidence of carelessness.

He began to gather silverware from the table. The pieces felt cumbersome in his hands.

"Leave it," she said. "I can do that later"—rolling her neck a little gingerly and shaking out her arms.

"You're sure you're okay?" he asked.

"I'm fine," she nodded.

Still, he watched her closely; Bobby knew all too well his wife's propensity for marching past a sprained ankle or any number of bruised ribs.

She must have seen him looking. "Really," she said, "I'm fine."

He stayed to help her set the table. He found himself wanting to, though she'd made it clear enough—over the years—that she considered his help in such matters more in the nature of a handicap. He began with the large serving pieces, plucking them from the jumble of fallen cutlery.

Emma liked doing chores by herself.

"If you want a thing done right," he'd heard her say, often enough, "then go it alone."

But Bobby suspected she'd make an exception for him that afternoon. They'd been so accommodating to each other all week long. He picked up the salad forks, one by one—only the shorter ones, with three tines instead of four. Then he circled the table, and placed them down on the far left side of the white linen place mats.

She didn't object, which he took as a good sign.

"How's dinner coming?" he asked.

"Easy," she told him. "We're having paella from the seafood shop on Madison."

Bobby smiled back at her. It was unusual for Emma to delegate, especially where food was concerned. "I'm glad to hear you're taking it a little easier," he said, smoothing out a ruffled place mat.

They went back to their work.

"I found a beautiful table," she told him, worrying her finger over a scratch on the glass tabletop. "At auction," she said.

She seemed to have shaken her injuries off.

"For here?" he asked. He kept his head down low, concentrating on the dinner forks in hand.

She hummed that it was.

"What's the matter with—" But he stopped himself in plenty of time, checking his impulse to ask what was wrong with the one they had.

Emma squinted back at him, waiting for his conclusion.

He smiled at her instead, silent as a stone.

What difference does it make, he thought, as long as the damn thing isn't mirrored? Bobby despised the old mirrors she'd installed on the dining room walls. It was like a carnival fun house, those wavy distortions all freckled with black. He kept working the puzzle of cutlery, its pieces strewn across the defunct table.

"The auction you went to last weekend?" he asked.

Emma nodded back at him, her eyes a little wider.

"With Benjamin?" he added, grinning slyly.

She was surprised that he could marshal so much detail, but Bobby had always seen more than he'd let on.

"That's right," she replied, smiling as she nodded.

"Tell me about it," he said, starting in on the spoons his brow furrowed and his back a little tight. He was concentrating on his work and feigning interest in the table too—so many new activities all at once.

"It's Nakashima," she said.

He heard the trace of thrill in her voice.

Bobby knew that Nakashima was a Japanese designer; he could even summon up a vague image of a chunky-looking thing—the kind of table that looked as if the tree trunk were built right in.

"That's wonderful," he said. "I know you've been looking for one."

Emma smiled at him again.

Bobby was as determined to accommodate her new table as she was to tolerate his clumsy help with the settings—not to mention his egregious behavior, earlier in the week. They were a pair of red foxes, it turned out, only recently spared from that steely trap, a little bruised and timid, but sticking together all the same.

It was less than a week since Emma had discovered his secret apartment.

Bobby couldn't fathom that he was standing there still. He was sure that he'd destroyed their fledgling reconciliation, that it had been dashed into as many pieces as a porcelain teapot slipped from soapy hands.

But Emma had gone a different way instead.

He'd been frightened to come home that night—the Monday before—once he knew that Emma knew. So he'd killed time at the secret building, hunting for the super and a spare set of keys.

I'll be needing them, he'd thought.

But the super had gone home for the night, and the surly doorman told him he'd have to wait until after the dinner rush, so Bobby headed back to Emma's place, bracing himself for the very worst. He pictured china flying and drinks splashing wet, his suitcase packed and ready to go, but he found his ex-wife in a calmer state: her face drained of color, and looking every one of her sixty-two years. Emma was tired and hurt, not raging at all. She looked as if she'd walked all the way home from his secret building—via mainland China perhaps.

"Are you in this?" she asked him, when he walked in the

door. Her voice was quiet. "Are you in this or not?" she asked. "That's all I need to know."

It was a simple question, he supposed, but he studied her carefully, as if she might have buried a card trick deep inside it. Was she really leaving the answer up to him? He stared at her intently, as if to catch her sleight of hand, to see for himself how the trick was done, but all he saw was her navy ensemble, and a fair bit of sadness around the eyes.

"It's a yes-or-no question," she said.

"Yes," he told her. "Definitely, yes." He meant it.

Emma nodded back carefully, as if she were contemplating a roast in the oven. "So what's this all about then?" she asked, opening her fist and producing the secret keys.

Bobby looked down at his feet. There was nothing to do but apologize—which he did, again and again.

"I'm in this," he swore, more persuasively than before.

Emma looked a little skeptical, but she kept nodding.

"It's just that I need a little room sometimes," he told her.

"We have fourteen of them here," she replied briskly.

"And you've filled up every one of them," he said, more aggrieved than he would have expected. He was surprised to find his anger at such an inopportune moment.

Bobby was hurt at how little she'd taken him into account.

"I'm here too," he said.

She nodded back as if she understood; he thought it was unlikely though. "You're here too," she mumbled, repeating it back as if she were trying to remember it for a later date.

"I know I should have said something," he told her. "But . . ."

"But what?" she asked. She didn't sound angry; she only wanted to know.

"I didn't think you'd care," he said.

But Emma cared plenty, and she proved it too: the very next day, she had her driver ferry them to the West Side. They walked the secret rooms of Bobby's apartment as if they were tourists—or better yet, shoppers, choosing which pieces to ship across town.

"Anything you want," she said. "Within reason."

Bobby smiled at that.

Emma complimented his eye, and she deferred to him too, only sticking yellow Post-its onto everything he liked. They were solicitous of each other—like children at a scary movie, keeping each other close.

"Are you sure?" he asked hesitantly, circling the kilim-covered chair.

"Absolutely," she said, sounding certain.

It was as big a gesture as she'd ever made, and by the time he got home from the office that night, the pieces were already sprinkled through the apartment—like a greatest hits album of Bobby's secret life, all his furniture married up with hers.

And now she was letting him set the table.

Would wonders never cease?

"I know who's coming to dinner," he said, a teasing note in his voice.

"You do?" she said, playing along.

"Well, it *is* Sunday night, after all," he told her. "What more is there to know?"

AS BENJAMIN CLIMBED THE STAIRS FROM THE SUBway and onto the street, he watched the sun sinking low in the afternoon sky. He'd only been underground for twenty minutes, riding the train uptown again. But there's no arguing with a sunset, he supposed. He saw trails of orange and gold streaking through the sky, leading straight to the sun that hovered off in the west, burning orange and red through the gaps in Central Park.

He felt nostalgic for the weekend already.

It was colder now. He pulled a brown woolen cap over the crown of his head. He was on his way to Emma's place to make his Sunday presentation and join the Suttons for dinner.

Melora had pleaded a previous engagement.

He'd left her at home, watching *The Virgin Queen* on television.

He screwed up his courage and walked into Emma's building, smiling at the liveried doorman in bright white gloves and brassy buttons as big as golden doorknobs. The old man greeted him like he always did, clapping him hard on the back and crooning a line or two from some topical song.

"*Don't change a hair for me*," he sang, "*not if you care for me*."

Benjamin paused a moment, as if he were thinking hard, but he knew right away it was a hopeless case. He never knew the doorman's songs.

"*Stay, little Valentine*," the doorman sang, even louder, "*stay*."

"Sorry," Benjamin said, shaking his head. "You got me again."

"Jesus," the old man moaned. "Don't you know any songs at all?"

Benjamin shrugged his shoulders and walked sheepishly on. Everyone knew where he was headed. He found a younger man in the elevator, dressed just like the first. This one's job was to press the button for Emma's floor, and keep him company on the ride upstairs.

He couldn't be trusted to go alone.

He let himself into Emma's place through the back door, just like always, walking straight into her big white kitchen, all clean and clear and swabbed down with disinfectant—those bright white tiles as ready for an emergency appendectomy as any bowl of corn flakes.

He smelled an herb roasting in the oven.

Rosemary, he thought, or maybe thyme.

Benjamin turned up at four thirty every Sunday, biding his time until Emma came to collect him. Sometimes he rehearsed his weekly report, but he didn't need to today. He was thoroughly prepared already. He wasn't much interested in the rest of the apartment: her high-tech library and the countless formal rooms, all that Bauhaus like so much upholstered currency—only traded at auctions, but never sat in at all.

Benjamin preferred the kitchen by far.

He'd always preferred kitchens, ever since he was a boy; and he was hopeful still of stumbling onto the kitchen of his dreams: a snug little room no bigger than a minute, with flowery paper on the walls and steamy windows from the everlasting warmth—a batch of muffins in the oven maybe, or a pot of soup on the boil.

It must have been from a movie, or some television show.

He could picture the nook where the family took its cozy suppers. It wasn't about architecture though; he knew that.

Benjamin resigned himself to Emma's breakfast table—a chilly sea of white Carrera marble in the corner of the room.

He found Tina Santiago sitting on the navy banquette.

"Whoa!" he cried.

Tina rolled her eyes as if he'd made a bad joke.

Benjamin couldn't have been more surprised if he'd found his own mother sitting there—or June Cleaver, raised up from the dead. "Jesus, Tina," he said. "What are you doing here?!"

She couldn't possibly have any business with Emma, could she?

"Are you here for me?" he asked.

"Why would I be here for you?" she replied.

He heard the trace of backbone in her voice; he saw it in the set of her mouth too, as if she'd applied a steely coat of lipstick. Benjamin was confused, and impressed by her nerve. He felt more than a little guilty at the sight of her: he'd thought so often of her yellow papers since their difficult meeting at the beginning of the week—Tina's battered food log. They came back to him, over and over; he couldn't get them out of his eyes, those six wrinkled pages with their pale blue lines.

He'd begun to second-guess himself almost as soon as he'd gotten home that night. Tina was clearly the likeliest source of Gracie's junk food—he wasn't discounting that—but he'd behaved as if it were a foregone conclusion. He owed his clients better than that—the benefit of the doubt, at least.

Benjamin knew he'd fallen down on the job.

He'd let himself become identified with Gracie, turning the girl into a chubby little version of himself, and Tina into his own mother—her attention fixed firmly on herself. His compassion had evaporated like a puddle of water in high desert air. But Tina was suffering too, her scrupulous food log should have made that plain, and his proposed solution—shuttling her off to a shrink with a sharp elbow of blame—had no doubt hurt her even more.

He pledged to make it up to her.

"Are you here to see Emma?" he asked her kindly.

"Didn't she tell you?" Tina replied.

"Tell me what?" he said. "Who?"

He heard a laugh track tumbling out of the maid's room next door, all saccharine and canned. He peeked in, expecting to find the housekeeper, but he saw Gracie instead, sitting cross-legged in an easy chair, watching cartoons in a shiny yellow dress. She looked like a taffeta piñata, stuffed to bursting with sweets.

Nothing was making any sense.

"I work here now," Tina announced.

Benjamin wondered if she was lying. But there she was, as plain as day. She'd never have made it past Emma's building security if it wasn't true.

But doesn't she work at a candy factory? he thought.

He was sure she did, that he'd read it in Gracie's file.

"What's going on here?" he asked finally, staring at her as if he were lost in the forest and she a vaguely familiar elm.

"Didn't she tell you I was coming?" Tina asked.

He shook his head from side to side.

But he'd heard the ring of truth in her voice. Benjamin didn't say another word; he waited for Tina to explain.

"After our last meeting," she told him, her eyes flashing at the memory of it, "I was crawling out of my skin. I didn't know what to do."

Benjamin nodded his head.

He could picture that. He hadn't been nice to her at all.

"It was after hours," she told him. "So I called your emergency number, the one you wrote on the back of your card. I had to speak to you."

Benjamin could understand that too, but it still didn't account for her turning up here.

"I called four or five times," she said, "and finally a woman picked up. She said she was your boss."

But Spooner's my boss, he thought.

It took him a moment longer to understand: it was Emma—his tiny cell phone in her capable hands. He remembered the night she'd found it.

"I told her everything," she said, "and she offered to meet us the next day." Just my luck, he thought. "I couldn't believe it was Emma Sutton," she told him, cracking a smile, in spite of herself. "And she believed me," Tina said. "She knew I didn't do anything to Gracie."

She paused then—waiting for him to jump in.

"I didn't, you know," she said, looking straight at him.

"I know," he mumbled—so softly that she might not have heard him.

The expression in her eyes was the final argument in her favor. No one could fake despair like that. "I know," he repeated, a little louder that time.

Better safe than sorry, he decided. He didn't want to hurt her any more than he already had.

"She promised to get to the bottom of it," Tina said.

He heard the blind faith in her voice. He didn't blame her. If he were in her place, he might feel just the same.

If anyone can fix a problem, he thought, it's Emma.

He gazed across the table at her—trim and pretty in a black sweater, her wavy hair long and loose. It was as if he hadn't seen her since that very first day at the principal's office, when he tried to pick her up on that long wooden bench.

He smiled at the thought of how differently all this might have turned out.

"She gave me a job too," Tina said.

"As what?" he asked. Now she was hitting close to home.

"Her assistant," she said, smiling up at him.

My job, Benjamin thought, the resignation weighing him down. He'd been sacked already by the sound of things. His feelings were hurt, of course, but he couldn't help seeing the justice of it.

"I gave notice at the plant already," she told him.

Benjamin looked across the room, gazing deep into Emma's fancy oven—a light glowing softly from the inside. It looked like a long tunnel to him—like a passage to China, or the end of the world. He wished he could crawl inside it.

"Congratulations," he said, trying for cheerful. He wouldn't go down as a poor loser, at least.

"And she's made an appointment for us already," Tina said. "With the best endocrinologist in town." She rolled right past him, like a rubber ball down a red dirt road. "He's going to run every test there is," she added, her pure excitement shining through. "And if that doesn't work," she said, "Emma promised that we'll keep going until we find the thing that does."

Benjamin walked to the sink for a glass of water.

"I owe you an apology," he said, letting the cool water run over his fingers. He looked down the drain as he spoke.

"You think?" she asked, dripping with sarcasm.

"I know you won't believe it," he said, turning back to her, "but I was only trying to help."

Tina's look confirmed that he was right: she didn't believe him at all.

Benjamin stayed right where he was—in watery exile at

the stainless steel sink. This kitchen was Tina's kingdom now. They looked each other up and down, neither of them knowing quite what to do—not until Gracie settled the question for them, walking in with a big crystal bowl in her hands. It was filled up with candy.

"Mr. Blackman!" she said, walking straight up to him and presenting the bowl. "The reds are sweet," she explained, "and the greens are sour."

Benjamin saw her fingertips dyed to match—sweet and sour both.

He took a green one.

"Where did you get those?" Tina asked sharply.

"From the lady," Gracie said, sounding a little vague. She looked down at her patent leather shoes.

"Put them back where you found them," Tina said. "Please."

Gracie pouted her way out of the room. "And no more candy," Tina added, turning back to Benjamin and blushing fiercely.

"I didn't give them to her," she said, looking guilty all over again.

"I know that," he told her.

"You do?" she asked, a little surprised.

"Of course I do," he said. He watched the relief washing down her face. He studied it for a moment longer. "I made a real hash of it with Gracie," he said. "I'm sorry for that."

Tina walked to the oven and peeked inside.

He felt a pang of nostalgia: he'd probably never set foot in this kitchen again.

"We're a tough case," Tina told him, gazing into the oven still. "I know that."

"Who isn't?" Benjamin replied.

She smiled a little.

"I don't know what scares me more," Tina said, turning around to face him then. "The prospect of your beating up on me still, or your leaving us alone."

She leaned up against Emma's fancy blue oven.

"I don't know how to help her," she admitted.

Benjamin couldn't believe he'd ever doubted her. He saw then—as plain as day—that Tina felt guilty because she couldn't *fix* her daughter's problems, not because she'd caused them.

"Stick with Emma," he told her. "She'll get you the help you need."

Benjamin supposed he should probably get going. No one there had much use for him anymore.

"I didn't want her at first," Tina told him. "The baby, I mean. I was only eighteen years old," she said, "just a baby myself. I wasn't near ready to be a mother."

Benjamin stood where he was. Tina wasn't finished with him yet.

"I was furious at her father," she said. "And at myself even more."

Tina didn't owe him any explanation, but Benjamin supposed she was entitled to tell her side of the story.

"But that all changed as soon as we got her home," she said. "It all made perfect sense to me then. *Gracie* was the reason I'd worked hard in school, the reason I'd kept my nose clean."

Benjamin hadn't imagined any of this.

"I could never hurt her," she said, sounding mystified at the very notion.

He hadn't even tried to imagine it.

"I wanted to help her so badly," he said. Benjamin looked Tina straight in the eye. He needed her to know it was the truth. "I know that's no excuse," he said. "Meaning well."

"It's a start," she told him.

Benjamin felt his face softening and his shoulders wilting down. He didn't understand why she was being so nice. *I wouldn't be,* he thought, *if our places were reversed.*

He supposed it was the mother in her.

"You screwed up," she said. "That's all. It could have been bad, but it turned out fine." Tina looked around the fancy kitchen. "I wouldn't be here," she said, "if it wasn't for you."

She walked back to the marble table.

"A new job for me," she said. "And specialists for Gracie."

"I know," he replied. "But it shouldn't have to work like that."

"Listen," she said, sitting down at the banquette. "You should take my old job if you only want things to go right."

Benjamin squinted back at her. He didn't understand.

"Those chocolates come out perfect every time," she said.

She was very beautiful.

"But the rest of the world isn't like that—all cut-and-dried, good or bad."

Benjamin sat down too.

"So we keep on going," she said. "You patch yourself up and move along." She made it sound nearly true. "It's not like we have a choice," she told him, shrugging her shoulders and wrinkling her nose.

Benjamin looked out the kitchen window onto Emma's stunning view of Central Park. He wished he could take Tina and Gracie outside for a walk. It turned out he liked Tina Santiago—very much, in fact.

He almost forgave her for stealing his job right out from under him.

"So you're taking over this weekend?" he asked.

"No," she replied, as if she were surprised. "The weekends are *yours*," she told him.

Now Benjamin was confused.

"I'm Monday to Friday," she said. "*You've* got the weekends, just like before."

"Then why are you here?" he asked—if he hadn't been fired.

"Because Emma asked me to come," she said, a little proudly. "She wants me to hear your weekly report and join you all for dinner."

BY THE TIME CASSY WALKED INTO CENTRAL PARK—about an hour or so later—the dusky afternoon was settling into darkness. The swooping succession of silver-toned streetlamps, dotted over hill and dale, flickered on in a single stroke. Cassy was nearly breathless at the abracadabra of so many lights switching on at once. She'd never suspected Central Park of any showmanship at all. To her, it was like a big, fake plant—a rubber tree made of rubber, or an orchid cut from silk: just more of the city masquerading as countryside.

She could count on one hand the number of times she'd actually set foot in the place—usually at someone else's behest, and never, of course, at night. But she had to admit, the effect was amazing: all those lamps interrupting the darkness, like dozens of moons glowing overhead.

She nearly slipped on a patch of ice.

Cassy glared down at the fancy shoes she was wearing in

honor of the occasion: they were pointy-toed with a kitten heel. Her mother had sent them to her a few weeks before.

She'd failed to see the maze of slushy puddles that was freezing over for the night. She was careful to avoid them, but her puppy marched straight ahead, pulling hard from his end of the leash.

"Slow down, Rusty," she called.

And still he pulled, turning every iced-over puddle into an Olympic rink. He took the ice in a flurry of slippery paws and tumbledown steps, like a red-haired Abbott or Costello with a banana peel underfoot.

"Look at him," she said, turning to Pete, the homely trainer.

They watched in unison as Rusty righted himself, finding his footing on solid ground. The little dog turned back to them every time—a flash of eye contact, then on to the next puddle.

"He's so proud of himself," she said, projecting.

Cassy leaned lightly into Pete as they walked.

She hadn't seen him dressed up before, his heavy brown boots traded in for loafers, his long legs draped in gray flannel. He looks pretty good, she thought. There was still no getting around that face of his—the deep scars and tremendous nose—but Cassy noticed it less and less.

And handsome faces had always been her weakness.

"He just wants to make sure we're still here," Pete said, squeezing her hand as he spoke. They watched the dog slip and slide, then turn around to face them.

She gazed at Pete, in profile, until he caught her looking, and then she turned away.

"Hey, Rusty," she called, in a hissing whisper, the only

voice the dog responded to. The little thing stopped dead in his tracks and turned around to face her. "I'm not going anywhere," she promised, whispering still.

The puppy cocked its head at a rakish angle.

They're both looking at me now, she saw: Rusty and Pete. Two nice boys, she thought. She wondered if she could get used to that.

And still the puppy stared.

Cassy took it as a sign of devotion.

"He wants a treat," Pete told her, sounding knowledgeable as he dashed her loving fantasy into sharp little pieces.

"How do you know?" she asked, a little peevish.

He was always so quick to turn her dog into a pragmatic little beast. Maybe Rusty was staring because he loved her?

"I don't," he said, sounding startled. "Not for a fact anyway."

Cassy wondered how long Pete would stay in the picture, if he'd be there with them the very next week. Typically, she'd have moved on by now—at the first sign of trouble.

"I do have some experience with dogs though," he said, smiling at her.

Cassy appreciated the minor backpedaling.

And she hoped, for the record, that he'd be with them next week, and the one after that. The little dog stared at her still, sitting politely, but not moving an inch. She knew Pete was right: he wanted a treat.

She reached into her pocket and bent down to the dog.

Pete leaned into her when she stood up again, as if he'd grown lonely in her absence. "Look at the lights over there," he said, pointing past the skeletal trees at the perimeter of the park, his eyes lifted to the windows on Fifth Avenue. They twinkled yellow in the velvet sky, like a jeweler's case filled up with canary diamonds. "They look like stars," he said. "Don't they?"

They did, in fact, but she drew the line at his mushy tone. "Sure," she said, a little harder than she meant. "If stars paid a light bill."

She watched Pete's face fall. Cassy reached for his hand.

"No light bill," he muttered, shaking his head. "Well, you got me there, I guess."

She wondered at the syncopated rhythm of their courtship: the lavender-scented love notes floated up high, only to be dragged down to earth again—laced into a pair of gravity boots. Rusty wasn't staring because he loved her, he said; he was a hungry little brute. And the apartments in the distance were just that, she told him, not any kind of North Star at all.

Should all these missed connections be telling her something?

But the longer Cassy gazed into the blackish night, the more she thought Pete had a point. Those glittering buildings—with some lights on, and others off—did look a bit like constellations, glinting diagrams in the evening sky.

"Star light," she whispered, right into Pete's ear. "Star bright," she said.

She wanted to make it up to him.

He smiled back at her. "Who's from Con Edison now?" he asked.

Cassy didn't get to finish her wish though: just then, a hearty squirrel with an elaborate tail skittered in front of them on the macadam path. Rusty yanked his leash right out of her hands, running loose and giving chase, barking wildly as he went. He might have gotten away altogether if Pete hadn't stepped on the leash—in quick order too.

"You have to wrap it around your fingers," he snarled at her. "I've told you that a hundred times."

Cassy nearly crumbled under the weight of his criticism.

"Relax," she said, as if her feelings weren't hurt, as if she were shrugging the whole thing off. The crisis had been averted, after all. Rusty's leash was safely underfoot, and the squirrel had bobbled up some barky trunk, its luxurious tail trailing behind it.

"No," Pete said, angry with her still.

The dog made soft growling noises beneath its breath.

"It's *your* job to keep him safe," he told her. The fact that it had worked out—this time, anyway—didn't take her off the hook, not in his book.

Cassy felt terrible.

Oh, well, she thought, bidding Pete a silent farewell.

"Show me," he said, very serious still.

Cassy was confused.

"The leash," he said. "Show me how you wrap it."

She wound the leash around her fingers, securing it in place just like he'd shown her so many times before. "Better?" she asked, looking up at him.

She cared enough to get it right.

For a split second, she could actually picture the long through-line of a real relationship: the screwing up and the moving on.

She lost it just as quickly.

Pete tried reaching an arm around her waist, but Cassy pulled away.

This was a brand-new leaf for her—sticking with it, with

anything—the nice man and the little dog, all these trees. She wanted to get it right, but she had no particular faith that she could.

She couldn't even remember to twine the leash around her fingers.

She liked Pete—a lot—but they were only at the very beginning, and her terrible track record bounced through her head like that mocking squirrel, leaping gaily from branch to branch, flashing its voluminous tail. She wanted to keep things light and easy, but light and easy wasn't easy for her. Cassy was like an emergency-room nurse when it came to romance—standing vigilant guard with a chart in hand, just waiting to clock that final breath.

Maybe she should just concentrate on the dog for now, the winding leash that kept him close?

The three of them had been together for seven days running. It hadn't taken nearly that long though—only four days, in fact—for Pete's kibble and leashes to turn to accidental brushings of hands and legs, and just a day longer for the ugly trainer to end up in Cassy's bed.

Still, it was much too soon for family portraits.

Cassy tried not to get ahead of herself; she didn't like to hope—not where other people's affections were concerned. She seemed bound to lose them every time. Better to keep it simple, she thought—just Rusty and me, for now. They'd be a pack of two, until she got it right. She could work her way up to loving Pete, and maybe Pete would stick around and love her back?

Early days still, she reminded herself.

Cassy glanced down at Rusty with a wide-open heart. He

was sniffing around the base of a silver streetlamp, ferreting out the places where other dogs had peed.

"Sundays aren't so bad," she said.

"Who said they were?" he asked, reaching for her hand again. There wasn't a jot of trouble on his face.

He'd moved beyond the trouble with the leash.

She squeezed his fingers in gratitude, wrapped long and easy around her own. All the lurid Sundays before felt like ancient history to her then—as far off as the lights on Second Avenue.

But she was getting ahead of herself.

Stick with the dog, she thought, remembering her plan.

"Isn't that your mother?" Pete asked—like a slap across the face.

"Where?" she asked, ducking her head quickly, like an ostrich, into navy wool.

"Up there," he said, pointing up a smallish hill.

Cassy shushed him, and swatted his finger down fast. She saw her mother and father up ahead, strolling on a path that would intersect with theirs soon enough.

"What the hell?" she mumbled, wriggling her hand free of Pete's.

He looked a little hurt, but she didn't have time for that now.

They were heading to her mother's place, in perfect time for Sunday dinner, but Cassy wasn't ready yet. She looked at Rusty and Pete with a jaundiced eye—her constant companions of seven days running.

What was I thinking? she wondered.

The dog was a given, she supposed—Cassy had to bring him; there was no telling what Rusty would do if she left him alone. But she regretted inviting Pete. She glanced at her mother on the path ahead: the pelts of her coat seemed to echo her conclusion. She wouldn't be surprised if poor Pete were skinned alive. She fixed on his store of orange poop bags, their plastic corners peeking brightly from his hip pocket.

A dog trainer, she thought.

Her mother would have something to say about that.

I should end it right now, she supposed, looking at his face and not even noticing his mottled skin.

"Aren't you going to say hello?" Pete asked.

"Are you crazy?" she replied.

Cassy had already explained how things worked with her mother: it had taken her two full days just to reach her that week, and all she wanted to do was apologize for the Sunday before, the dinner with Benjamin and Melora.

"Go throw her a bone," he said.

"She doesn't want a bone," she told him. "She wants the whole damn carcass."

"So throw her a carcass," he said, a little surprised. Pete didn't understand the problem at all.

Cassy checked her watch. "We've got fifteen minutes still," she said, like a petulant child at bedtime.

Her parents had walked nearly out of sight.

She heard the noises from Fifth Avenue filtering into the park—all the horns and brakes, the squealing tires. They'd have to leave their idyll soon enough, she supposed.

"You can't just ignore her," Pete said.

Cassy nodded, as if she agreed, but she knew that Pete was out of his depth. It took nearly everything she had to ignore her mother—the cool indifference that she'd made as plain as day—and still it wasn't enough.

Cassy wanted to start moving, but she knew she should stay still.

She looked to the end of the path in front of them.

She was tired of all her complicated equations: leaving before she got left; ignoring before she was ignored; denying that the twinkling apartment lights looked like stars, that she wanted to say hello to her mother, up ahead.

Rusty turned around and stared, his furry head cocked in wait, either loving her deeply or wanting another treat.

Maybe *both*, she thought in a flash of inspiration.

Maybe they came down to the same thing in the end. Hadn't the persistent puppy taught her that already: just keep staring until you get what you want?

"Okay," she sighed, caving in to Pete and all her onerous hopes.

She didn't have that much to lose.

Pete offered to take the leash from her hands.

"Are you kidding?" she said. "I'll need him for protection."

Cassy followed her parents down the path, quickening her pace and straightening her overcoat as she walked. She felt glad for the smart navy wool and her pointy-toed shoes.

Her mother would be happy with them, at least.

She saw that her parents were holding hands; she couldn't think of the last time she'd seen them doing that. She slipped her free hand into her coat pocket, but she knew it wouldn't keep her nearly as warm as Pete had. She turned around and motioned him to join them.

Everyone was walking toward Emma.

"Mom," she called, a little tentatively.

Her mother didn't turn around.

Nothing new in that, she thought, a pang of worry shooting through her. Still, the dog pranced forward; he had a thicker skin.

"Emma," she called, a little louder. "Emma."

THE ELEVATOR DOORS OPENED ABOUT FIFTEEN minutes later, framing an exquisite Shaker table on the opposite wall, a pale pink orchid off to one side. The other passengers stepped aside—her husband and daughter, the dog trainer with bad skin and a puppy in his arms. They leaned a little closer into the car's paneled walls, waiting for Emma to lead the way.

"It's housebroken," she said, turning to the trainer. "Right?"

The young man smiled back at her, a little sheepishly. She supposed Cassy must be dating him.

A dog trainer, she thought, not exactly thrilled.

Still, she tried to keep an open mind. There are worse things, she supposed—a puppy that's not housebroken, for starters.

She wished she hadn't asked.

Emma stepped out of the elevator and onto the terra-cotta floor, setting her shoes quietly down. The tiles were amber and old, salvaged from some far-off place and only recently installed in that vestibule. They had the landing to themselves. She made a slow pirouette, searching all around—up and down—her eyes narrowed.

"No second chance to make a first impression, Emmy." That's what her father always said.

Her other dinner guests would be arriving soon: Mr. and Mrs. Tanaguchi—he of the Nakashima table.

Emma was surprised to find a pane of glass leaning against

the back wall of the vestibule—nearly waist-high and eight or nine feet long. It was propped on its side, beneath a row of leather coat hooks. She might have missed it altogether, if she hadn't seen the frenzy of scratches on its canted surface, plainly legible beneath the overhead light.

"What the hell is it?" she mumbled, staring at the glass.

Then she recognized the beveled edges.

"Oh, no," she moaned, beginning to understand.

It was the glass top of her dining table. She was sure of it. "But where's the rest of it?" she mumbled—the beautiful ebonized base. "And what's it doing out here?"

A flash of panic coursed right through her.

Her eyes landed on two canvas bumpers—propped carefully between the glass and the plaster wall behind it.

Someone had thought to protect both surfaces.

"Benjamin," she said, running into the apartment.

She'd told them—Benjamin and the new girl, Tina—to switch out the dining table for the Nakashima in the basement, but she never imagined they'd do it that afternoon, with her guests arriving any minute. She and Bobby had only been out for forty-five minutes.

Emma's shoes clattered as she ran. She was well beyond caring.

"Benjamin," she called, louder that time.

This would never have happened, she thought, if she'd just stayed at home, fussing over her meal, instead of ordering in from the gourmet shop around the corner.

Emma ran past the living room and straight through the study.

She began to feel hot in her heavy fur coat, unbuttoning it as she went. She reached the dining room finally. They were both there—Benjamin and Tina—putting the finishing touches on her Nakashima table. They'd set it beautifully too, she had to admit it, trading the dark-rimmed plates for a creamy porcelain set. The white looked stunning against the burnished walnut top.

Emma's heart sank fast.

"The Tanaguchis," she cried, boiling over with heat. They'd be here any second. He'd see the table that she'd stolen out from under him. Emma shucked off her coat and dropped it on the floor. Her assistants looked on in quiet amazement. It was nothing like her to drop a coat.

Tina moved to pick it up, but Emma shook her head, warding her off.

"How did you get it up here?" she asked. The two of them couldn't have moved it themselves. It must weigh a thousand pounds.

Benjamin smiled, as if the question itself were a compliment.

If he were any closer, she might have slapped his face.

She never should have gone into the park with Bobby, no matter how sweetly he asked.

"We found some porters," Benjamin said. "Down in the basement."

"Working on Sunday?!" she asked.

Emma could scarcely believe her bad luck.

"Aren't there rules about that?" she said, in desperation.

The building's rules covered every eventuality. She couldn't imagine there wasn't something to prohibit their moving furniture on a Sunday afternoon—as if the violation itself might cause the table to float away, straight out the dining room window and back down to the basement where it belonged.

"They didn't mind at all," Tina said.

Emma gazed at the girl in her black sweater and nearly matching slacks. She sighed in exhaustion and despair.

Blacks are hard, she thought, almost sympathetic with the girl.

The worst thing, of course, as far as Emma was concerned, was that she'd asked Benjamin to coordinate the table move herself—during his presentation, not an hour before. She'd walked back to the dining room to verify that the old chairs would work with the Nakashima.

Emma shook her head: no one to blame but herself.

She should have been clearer. She should have told them to wait until *after* the Tanaguchis left.

"They promised to get the other one into the basement by six thirty," Benjamin said, sounding like a show-off.

Emma checked her urge to snap.

"We'd better check on that," he said to Tina, beginning to walk away.

"Hold on," Emma told him. She needed to think.

She had to come up with a solution—and fast! Otherwise, she'd be serving Tanaguchi dinner on a stolen table, his anniversary gift, no less. None of it boded well for her position at the UN.

Not unless they want a thieving spokesman, she thought.

Emma was losing her grip. She felt like chopping the table into pieces and using it for firewood.

"Maybe a tablecloth?" she wondered, picking up the chinchilla from the floor and running her hands across its silky finish, petting it almost.

"A tablecloth," she repeated softly.

It really was a gorgeous table.

There was no denying that, even as the walls tumbled down around her. A tablecloth wouldn't be any kind of solution; she knew that—not with the table's swooping edges. It would be like wrapping a pistol in string and brown paper. It wouldn't fool a soul.

"Maybe we should just move the old table back in?" she said.

Her assistants looked as if she were speaking in tongues.

"Go see if the old one's still there," she said to Benjamin—the doorbell ringing at that very moment, like a period at the end of her odd request.

"Never mind," she said.

It might not be the Tanaguchis, she thought—knowing full well that it was. They were the only guests yet to arrive.

"I'll get it," she said.

Emma walked to the door like a well-groomed Joan of Arc, heading off to battle in a camel-colored twin set. She waved the housekeeper off too; she'd get the door herself.

It was the Tanaguchis, of course, looking just as chic as she'd imagined, and just as tiny. Mrs. Tanaguchi looked as if she might fit into one of Emma's pockets. She ferried them into the living room like a runty pair of kittens frisking at her outsized feet. She introduced them to her husband and her daughter, the trainer with the puppy on a short leash.

"I'm sorry, Pete," she said, "I don't believe I know your surname."

She was at the height of grandeur on her way to the gallows.

Bobby knew that well enough. He flashed his wife a look of concern and quickly picked up the slack. "We've heard so much about you," he said, smiling at the new arrivals.

They beamed right back.

"Emma is so pleased for this opportunity to work with you at the UN," he said.

She knew her position would disappear once Tanaguchi saw what a double-dealer she was.

"And for such a good cause," Bobby continued, explaining what little he knew of the enterprise to Cassy and Pete—the Commission on Natural Disasters—drawing them into the conversational loop.

He asked Tanaguchi to elaborate.

Emma let her mind wander over a cavalcade of thieveries, the virtual encyclopedia of all her wrongdoings. She kept a mental list at the ready—always had, the better to lacerate herself. She toted crimes from her childhood and from two minutes before, the little maneuverings and big power plays, the ones she'd gotten away with, scot-free, she'd thought, and the ones she'd paid the price for too.

Her husband offered drinks all around.

Emma took a glass of wine.

Hang on a second, she thought.

Hadn't she learned this lesson already, while she was rotting in federal prison, no less? Hadn't she figured out that all those crimes ricocheted straight back to her in the end—every lousy caper she'd ever pulled, even the piddling ones that were scarcely worth her time?

Especially those, she thought.

They all came back to haunt her—the public mortifications and private shames. She pictured three hundred stars in a criminal sky, some burning brightly and lasting long, others flickering out fast, and every single one of them just another excuse to run herself down.

Emma had almost put it together, sitting in that nasty cell of hers.

Almost, she thought, but not quite—like looking at the picture on a puzzle-box top. She'd understood the broad strokes of it—the image that all those pieces would make—but she'd never assembled them for herself, one by one. It dawned on her then, like a brand-new day, sitting with her family and the Tanaguchis, an untrained puppy on her priceless living room rug.

Emma felt as if she were clicking the very last pieces into place.

It's the *secret* crimes, she thought—the hidden ones—that were most killing. They were the ones that lasted long after the others were forgotten.

She knew it then just as well as she knew her own name.

They were the ones she used against herself—slashing and flogging forever and a day. Emma knew how to torment herself much better than any lousy tabloid or tax auditor ever could.

Amateurs, she huffed, picturing those ordinary men from the IRS.

It was perfectly obvious to her then: it was the undiscovered crimes that retained the sharpest edges. They were the ones that made her father right about her all along.

She'd been going at this all wrong, she decided.

Emma pulled Tanaguchi aside, barely touching the sleeve of his tweedy blazer. "I'd like to show you something," she said.

Desperate times, she supposed—and all that.

Tanaguchi put his drink down—on a mother-of-pearl coaster, she noticed in gratitude—and followed her out of the room. She led him back to the dining room, and pointed straight at her Nakashima table, as if it were a corpse lying in the middle of the road, a hit-and-run victim she'd put there herself.

There, she thought—the nasty truth, the proof against her plain as day.

The table was laid with her Sunday best, the crystal and silver and creamy bone china. She hoped he'd see beyond the trappings.

"It's beautiful," Tanaguchi said, nodding his head at her.

"I stole it from you," she told him, pointing to the table still, that corpse a near relation to him.

"No, you didn't," he said.

"Of course I did," she replied.

Emma was determined to confess, and he wasn't going to stop her. No one was going to stop her. She pictured her brand-new position floating away—her UN gig like so much smoke up a redbrick chimney.

It might have been good for me too, she thought, bidding it a fond farewell.

"I rigged the whole thing," she told him. "At FitzCoopers," she added, as if some clarification were needed.

Her father must have had a saying about assuming responsibility, some football-coach perversion about wriggling out of it, but she couldn't think of what it was just then; she didn't want to either.

"I knew that," Tanaguchi said.

"You did?" she asked.

Wasn't this her moment for revealing facts unknown?

"The people at the auction house told me you wanted it from the beginning." That was wrong of them, Emma thought, reaching an index finger to the side of the table, running it along the curvy edge. "And I saw you talking to the boy who bid on it," he added.

Benjamin, she thought, nodding back.

She'd been worried about people seeing them together at the auction house, but she'd let her hubris get the better of her by then. She'd assumed she'd gotten away with everything.

"Believe it or not," Tanaguchi told her, a flash of pride running through his tiny frame. He stood a little taller, his chest puffed out slightly. "I was free to do as I chose," he said.

Emma didn't know what he was driving at.

"I could have kept bidding," he told her, "if I'd wanted to. You had no control over that."

The thought hadn't occurred to her.

"You could have kept bidding," she muttered, letting it sink in.

"Of course I could have," he said, a little pointedly. "We're all free to do exactly as we choose."

She heard the soft reproach in his voice.

"Still . . . ," she mumbled. But she didn't know what to say next.

"You weren't exactly gracious," he said—with considerable tact, she thought, under the circumstances. "But you made it up to me in the end," he told her, "taking me to SoHo to find another table, and agreeing to chair my committee."

Emma felt flustered.

This wasn't going anything like she'd expected.

She looked down at the gorgeous table with a sense of dread. She worried that it might be overdone, with so much silver glinting and all that cut glass.

She looked at Tanaguchi.

"I like mine better anyway," he told her, smiling back.

"I still want to apologize," she said. "Let me do that at least."

Tanaguchi nodded. "Apology accepted," he told her, extending his hand.

Emma took it with great relief, clasping it tight and shaking it hard. One less secret, she thought, halfway to forgiving herself.

GRACIE SAT IN A SHALLOW GULLY, A DARK RIBBON of wood curving all around her. She was no fan of Emma's new table: none of the edges were straight, for starters, and the chairs didn't line up either.

"My fingers leave marks," she whispered to her mother, lifting her thumb from the wooden top and studying the print she'd left behind.

"Don't touch it then," her mother replied, a little grouchy.

Gracie was sitting between her mother and Mr. Blackman, her two favorite people at the table, and even though she was right next to them, she practically had to turn around to see them—that's how deep the table's curve went: like she was sitting a row ahead of them at school.

She tried wriggling her chair a little farther back, but her mother pushed her forward again.

"Come on, sweetie," she said. "I don't want any spills."

Gracie had an easy enough solution for that. She laid her fork down onto the large white plate, twice as big as any plate at home, or any fork, for that matter.

It weighs about a million pounds, she thought—that fork fit for a giant.

Gracie hadn't liked Emma's food much either. It tasted funny, she thought, and there was too much sauce.

She knew better than to complain.

With her fork set down, and no worry of spills, Gracie tried inching her chair back again. Her mother squeezed her thigh beneath the table.

Don't! that touch said, clear enough.

She felt like a prisoner sitting there at the grown-up table, in such a fancy place. She pushed her chest right into the table's curve, as if to show her mother how foolish she was being, wanting her to sit so tight.

Her dress looked pretty against the deep brown wood.

They go together, she thought, staring down at the combination—the buttery yellow and dark, dark wood. She let her fingers brush against her taffeta skirt.

She got to wear her pretty dress, at least.

Things weren't so bad, she supposed. Gracie didn't like to be angry with her mother.

She sat back in her chair and began fiddling with the bracelet on her wrist, pulling the elastic away from her skin and twirling the candy hearts that were strung all around it, each of them printed with a sweet little wish—"Be Mine" in pink, "All Yours" in pale blue. Her grandfather had given it to her on Valentine's Day, just three days before. She loved that bracelet with all her heart, only took it off to bathe.

She hadn't eaten a single candy.

They were much too pretty for that.

Gracie lifted the bracelet to her cheek and looked to the mirror on the opposite wall. It wasn't quite the picture she'd been hoping for: the bracelet was practically invisible on her wrist, and her face so wide—much wider than a face ought to be.

She saw the man at the head of the table smiling at her, at her reflection anyway. Gracie looked back down into her lap.

She didn't like those mirrors at all, hanging all around the room.

Like a bathroom, she thought, only a million times worse. There were mirrors on every wall. She'd been tricked into looking at herself all night, sometimes when she least expected it: glancing up at her mother to ask her a question, or peeking at the pretty girl across the table.

Gracie liked preparing herself before she looked into mirrors.

She raised her eyes again; the man was smiling at her still—the older one at the head of the table.

Gracie turned in her seat to face him.

"Knock, knock," he said, looking straight at her still.

Gracie knew what she was supposed to say, but she felt too shy to say it. She looked back into her lap instead, plucking at the candy bracelet.

"Knock, knock," the man repeated, a few seconds later.

She felt a smile blooming on her lips; she couldn't help it.

"Who's there?" she said, still looking down—at her shiny yellow skirt and the bracelet on her wrist.

"Wanda," he said.

"Wanda who?" she asked, looking up at him. Gracie didn't know this one.

"Wanda be my Valentine?" he said.

She giggled and covered her mouth, pressing chubby fingers against her lips. She turned to her mother and saw her smiling too.

"I like your bracelet," Mr. Blackman said.

"She doesn't eat the candy," her mother replied. "They're all there still."

Gracie dropped her head again. She didn't like it when people talked about what she ate—not that that ever stopped them.

"They had bracelets like that when we were kids," Mr. Blackman said. "Remember?"

Gracie peeked up at the mirror again. She watched her mother nodding back.

"My grandfather gave it to me," she told him. "For Valentine's Day."

The holiday had been just as bad as Gracie imagined. She'd only gotten a handful of cards—a mere fraction of the number she'd handed out, and so many fewer than the other girls.

Her face lit up with shame.

Her handmade cards hadn't done a thing. But at least it was behind her now. Gracie had gotten through it.

"You keep your head up, Gracie"—that's what her grandfather always said.

But the little girl had deciphered already that head position had very little to do with it. Sometimes it was just about getting things over with.

She glanced up at the mirror, and found the man at the head of the table smiling at her again.

"Knock, knock," he said again.

Gracie swiveled to her mother, who nodded back.

"Who's there?" she said, a little more confidently that time.

"Banana," he told her.

"Banana who?" she asked. Gracie didn't know this one either.

"Banana," the man repeated.

"Banana WHO?!" Gracie said again, letting her voice grow louder that time, getting a little carried away. Doesn't he know how to play this game? she wondered.

Her mother shushed her.

"Banana who?" she repeated, nearly whispering.

"Orange," the man said.

Gracie squinted back at him. Maybe he really *didn't* know how to play. "Orange who?" she said, just in case.

"Orange you glad I didn't say banana?"

Gracie smiled at that, all open and wide. She looked around the table. Her neighbors were smiling too: her mother and Mr. Blackman, the pretty girl across the way.

"What's going on down there?" the lady asked—the one sitting at the other end of the table, her mother's new boss.

"Just a few knock-knock jokes," Mr. Blackman said.

"Are they funny, Gracie?" the lady asked.

She nodded her head in quick little strokes, then looked back down into her taffeta lap. She covered up her Valentine bracelet with her free hand. The lady made her a little nervous.

"I've got one for you," the lady said.

Gracie looked up at her shyly.

Everyone at the table did the same: the tall man at the head of the table and the pretty girl across the way; the tiny couple with the straight black hair; her mother and Mr. Blackman too. They looked at the lady like she was the star of the show.

Gracie admired her soft brown hair.

She sneaked another look back at the mirror. She knew her own hair would never be soft.

"Knock, knock," the lady said.

Everyone turned to Gracie then. It was her turn to be the star of the show.

"Who's there?" she replied, in her very best voice—hooking an imaginary hank of hair behind an ear.

"Vassar girl," the lady said, smiling in anticipation.

Gracie turned to her mother fast. She didn't know what that was.

"Vassar girl," her mother said, repeating it for her slowly.

Gracie screwed up her courage and said her line: "Vassar girl who?" she asked, but it made her nervous, not to understand.

"Vassar girl like you doing in a place like this?" the lady said, tossing her head back and laughing at her own joke.

Gracie didn't understand it still.

She looked around the table, surveying the faces of the people there, all groaning with pleasure and laughing along. She studied her mother, laughing and smiling along with the rest. It wasn't her mother's real laugh—not the one she used with her, but it wasn't quite fake either.

Gracie started laughing too.

She wasn't sure why exactly.

She pretended it was a funny joke.

Look at me, she thought, peeking up at the mirror and taking stock of her laughing face. She looked almost pretty like that—with rosy pink cheeks and bright white teeth, her yellow hair band tied perfectly straight.

Somehow she knew, though she couldn't have said how, that everyone was laughing just to be nice. Like when Mr.

Blackman gave her that coloring book that was too young for her by far, or when her friend Bessy admired the tiny pile of Valentines on her desk at school. It wasn't lying, she decided—pretending like that, not if it made your friends feel good.

Gracie laughed even louder then.

ACKNOWLEDGMENTS

Many thanks to Betsy Lerner, Jennifer Barth, and Jonathan Burnham for the excellent care they've given me and my book.

I'm grateful to my first readers, whose encouragement made it just a little easier to pass the manuscript along: Kathleen Galanes, Andrew Herwitz, Lori Finkel, Tracey Hecht, Mary Haverland, and Barbaralee Diamonstein-Spielvogel.

Finally, I owe a mountain of thanks to Michael Haverland and our inimitable Chiccio. I would never have found the goodness in Emma, much less myself, without them.